DEATH ON THE POINT

BLOOD BATH

Duane Wurst

Copyright © 2018 Duane Wurst
All rights reserved
Published by Duane Wurst

Without limiting the rights under copyright reserved above, no part of this publication may be reproduced, stored in or introduced into a retrieval system, or transmitted, in any form, or by any means (electronic, mechanical, photocopying, recording, or otherwise) without the prior written permission of both the copyright owner and the above publisher of this book.

This book is a work of fiction. Names, characters, places, brands, media, and incidents are either the product of the author's imagination or used fictitiously. The author acknowledges the trademark status and trademark owners of various products referenced in this work of fiction, which have been used without permission. The publication/use of these trademarks is not authorized, associated with, or sponsored by the trademark owners.

ISBN-13: 978-0-9883947-4-2

Text and cover design by Duane Wurst, Berne Studio
Cover images © 2018 Duane Wurst

Printed in the United States of America

Acknowledgments

First and foremost, my sincere thank you to my lovely wife Sharon for being my extra set of eyes on every draft and providing me with valuable input and suggestions to the completion of this novel. Without her understanding and support, this novel would have taken much longer to complete. Secondly, I'd like to thank my daughter Cyndi for her contributions towards its completion. And finally, I'd like to thank the readers of the first Colton Blackwell novel "Death on the Point." It was because of you, that this novel exists today.

To receive my newsletter, visit my website www.duanewurst.com. To keep up with my latest works, follow Duane Wurst on Facebook.

Thank you for your support,
Duane

Chapter 1

Michigan always has late October snow storms, but it makes for an uncomfortable afternoon football practice. The Lake Huron School football team, the Loons, were struggling with the winter conditions, and Coach Talbert was unrelenting.

"Hey Coach, can't we go into the gym and practice?" Aden, the team's captain and quarterback spoke on behalf of the team.

Coach Talbert replied, "How about two more laps around the field to warm up?"

"Guys, listen up! You are the UNDEFEATED LOONS, Lake Huron School's football team! Man up! If you can't play Michigan football during blustery, cold, and crappy conditions, you have no chance at winning on Friday and making it into districts. The season will be over. Will it satisfy you to end the season in October?"

"No, but if we get sick, we won't be any good on the field tomorrow night, sir," injected Aden.

"You're in good condition and won't get sick," Coach insisted. "Remember back in August? The first day you stepped on this field for practice was the hottest week of summer, and most of you couldn't run one lap without passing out. You were out of shape. Did I let you take it easy? No! I worked the hell out of you and now look at yourselves. You have proven you are the best team this school has produced."

Coach brushed snow off his playbook and continued. "Aden, run these five plays, and make sure everyone does their job. We want to surprise the Sebewaing Patriots, and these plays will help. Colton, you must work on holding the ball when your hands are cold and the ball is wet. Playing in the snow only makes the game more interesting. Now get to work and stop complaining."

The grumbling stopped as the team ran through the plays. The quick passes were hard to hold on to. Colton's fingers were freezing and when they hit the ball, he thought they would break off, but he never let go of the ball. He wanted to please Coach Talbert because he respected him and knew he would never put the team in harm's way. After forty minutes of grueling work, Coach told the men to hit the showers.

"Aden, you did a great job. We can win Friday and you know what that means." Coach said.

"Sure do, Coach. We'll be the District Champions. They claimed we would never beat Ubly in the playoffs and we did that last week. Now we'll overthrow the Sebewaing Patriots, too." Aden said.

Colton was listening to the conversation and added, "Damn right! We'll crush them, Coach."

The teens laughed as they walked into the locker room. Colton glanced toward the parking lot and smiled when he saw his yellow Jeep Wrangler parked in its usual place. A tragic misadventure resulted in the Jeep needing new tires, bodywork, and a few new parts. Tonight Colton will deliver his newspapers on The Point without having to borrow his mom's old Chevy S-10 pickup. There was nothing wrong with the S-10 except it wasn't his Jeep.

"Colton, I see you have your Jeep back," said Calvin Rowell, the extra large Loons Center.

"The owner of the body shop in Bad Axe said they would drop it off today. I'm so glad it's done."

"Me too... now I won't drive out of my way to take you home." laughed Calvin.

"If it caused you a problem, why didn't you say so before this," quipped Colton.

"I'm kidding, Colton. I was glad to give you a ride, considering all you've done for me and the team... it was an honor."

"Thanks. I appreciate your driving me around, too." said Colton. "You appear healed from that nasty Hampton game. Is Coach going to let you play tomorrow?"

"I hope so, I've been working out a lot and I feel stronger than ever. The doctor said I can do whatever I want. He said I need to be careful, because once injured, I'll be susceptible to future injuries. For the team, I'll take the risk," Calvin said as he took his practice uniform off and got ready for the shower.

Colton noticed how muscular Calvin was. No fat, just solid muscle. *It's no wonder he's feared by so many defensive linemen*, he thought.

There was a constant chatter in the locker room as the team changed into their street clothes. Colton told Aden that he was having another party after the game.

"You and Kathy are welcome to come. We only invited a few couples so it won't be a big party." he said.

"Is Seth and Linda coming?" asked Aden.

"Yes! He's my best friend. You don't have a problem with him, do you?"

"No. Seth is great. And Linda is hot. I was just asking, Colton. We'll be there. I can pick up a pizza," Aden offered.

"Thanks, but Lacie's dad is buying all the food and drinks. It's Her birthday Saturday and we'll serve cake and all that birthday stuff. She doesn't want us to bring her a gift though."

"With my finances, I wasn't planning on it. See you at school tomorrow," Aden said as he walked toward his beat-up Camaro.

Colton walked around his yellow Jeep and smiled. The body shop did a great job removing the signs of his last adventure. In fact, it looked like they even did a major cleaning of the interior. He couldn't remember when there wasn't a pile of old papers and empty coffee cups littering the floor.

Damn, I love my Jeep, he reflected. *All I have to do is keep her safe.*

***

The roads were snow covered and slippery. Colton drove the five miles home at less than forty miles per hour. The large white farm house looked warm and inviting as he pulled up to the garage, his and his dad's *man cave*. He wanted to pull the Jeep into the warm garage, but with an after game party planned for tomorrow night, the Jeep would create a mess on the floor.

Colton ran through the backdoor, into the kitchen. His mom, Cyndi, stood at the stove stirring what smelled like bean soup.

"Hi, Mom. I got the Jeep today. What's for dinner?" he asked.

"Bean soup, baked chicken with potatoes and carrots, and apple pie," she said. "Dinner is ready so wash up and let your brothers and sister know."

"I will Mom. Is Dad in Bay City tonight?"

"He has one more day of classes. I'm glad he's back working at the foundry, but now he works all day and studies all night," she complained.

"Mom, I understand how you feel, but Dad's happy. I can't remember when he was this excited about his job. I know he liked doing the paper route, but he's got a future in the foundry, and now I'm making more money delivering the Metro News than I did working forty hours a week at the dairy farm."

"Speaking of money," Cyndi said, "I deposited the store receipts and paid the newspaper bill. I wasn't sure if you needed any cash, so I kept out forty dollars. It's on your dresser. And please clean your room. It's as messy as Terry and Jason's."

"It's not that bad, Mom," Colton said.

"There's a problem with the Caseville newspaper racks, Colton," she said in a more serious tone.

"Are we missing a few Sunday papers?"

"Not just a few papers, you're missing a lot of papers."

"I left extra newspapers in the rack last Sunday, and they were all sold. What's the problem?" Colton asked.

"The problem is, each rack was short over forty dollars."

"Wow! Do you think someone stole them?" Colton asked.

"Well... they're not walking off by themselves."

"Mom, this looks like a job for Colton Blackwell, super detective. I'll try to solve the case this week."

"Just be careful. I don't want to see you get hurt."

"OK, Mom. I won't get hurt by the paper thief. Are there any more problems?"

"No, but if you don't call your siblings for dinner, everything will be cold," Cyndi said while setting the table.

Colton walked into the living room and soon Stephenie, Jason and Terry ran to the table, pushing, shoving, and arguing. Colton followed, after a quick trip to the bathroom.

Family time was one of Colton's favorite. Stephenie, a beautiful eleven-year-old fifth grader tried to ignore her ten-year-old brother Jason. He teased her because she got dressed for dinner. Terry, the youngest Blackwell sibling was Colton's nine-year-old best friend. They had a similar disposition and often played sports together.

"So Terry, are you trying out for basketball this year?" Colton asked his nine-year-old brother.

"No, I want to wrestle instead. It's more fun and I can make the wrestling moves like they do on TV," Terry said as he crushed a handful of crackers into his bowl of soup.

Jason laughed, "You're such a dope, Terry. Television style wrestling isn't what they do in school."

"Yes it is! Isn't it, Colton?"

"Jason's right. Wrestling in school is the same as college and Olympic wrestling. You work toward points, and you can't body slam and kick."

"And besides," said Jason, "On TV they know in advance who will win. It's not real."

"I don't care. I'm still trying out because I'm better at wrestling than I am at basketball."

"Jason, are you trying out for a winter sport?" Colton asked.

"I'm trying out for wrestling and archery. The coach said I should try out for both teams. Perhaps I can get good enough to go bow hunting with you and Dad."

"That's cool, Jason. We can set up targets and practice this weekend. I don't intend to hunt until the archery season in December, so we have time to work on our skills."

Colton could see Jason's eyes sparkle. Jason avoided doing things with his older brother, but he has become interested in spending more time with Colton, who is a football celebrity among the younger students. Jason's attitude toward Colton has changed. A few months ago he thought Colton was a "dork", but now he is just his famous older brother who used to be a dork.

"What about me," said Terry. "I want to go hunting with you guys too."

"You can practice with us, Terry, but I'm not old enough to take you hunting with us. Dad will have to go with you as your hunting mentor," said Colton.

"OK! I'll ask Dad when he gets home," Terry said, knowing his dad will take him hunting. Adam has a hard time saying no to Terry.

Colton turned to his mom and asked, "Why don't you go hunting with Dad?"

She put her fork down and smiled. "Deer hunting is a time when your dad can be with his friends. In my family the boys went with Dad on his famous hunting trips. God only knows what goes on in those hunting camps, but I swear they came back with little venison and bloodshot eyes. I'm sure they all had hangovers."

Stephenie laughed at her mom's comment. "I wouldn't want to kill a deer. They're too pretty, and besides, it gets cold in the woods and being with a bunch of guys would be gross," she said.

Colton appreciated his little sister's comments. He admired how mature she was for an eleven-year-old.

"Steph, there's nothing wrong with girls hunting. A lot of girls in high school hunt with their parents."

"Does your girlfriend, Lacie, hunt?" she asked.

"Well... no. She feels like you," he admitted.

After dinner Colton helped his mom with dishes and then walked up to his room. Every Thursday he picks up his newspapers at the storage shed in Pigeon by three in the morning. It is a routine he has become used to. When he first started, he got tired while driving and later at school. At least he isn't working a forty hour night shift like he did at the start of the school year. That job almost cost him his eligibility to play football and his life. Every morning he was late for school and his first hour teacher threatened that one more tardy would be the end of his football career.

Colton's dad convinced him he didn't have to work himself to death to help the family. Adam got laid of a year ago, but in September the foundry called him back as a foreman. Like Colton, Adam is very intelligent and has a photographic memory, but without an education past high school, he ended up with low paying jobs. After the foundry laid him off, he took a part-time job delivering the Metro Press newspapers to Bay Port, The Point, and Caseville. Now, thanks to his new job, Adam is getting the education he always wanted because the foundry pays for college classes to help him in his new position, and Colton has the job delivering newspapers.

Chapter 2

Colton worked on his laptop, checking his email and Facebook account. He didn't post many pictures and comments, but enjoyed reading all the stuff his friends posted. Sometimes he would add comments to the silly pictures and odd sayings. Lacie, his girlfriend, often posted pictures of the two of them. Her latest picture was of Colton and her after the homecoming dance. They both looked happy, but Colton looked uncomfortable in his blue suit. Seth, Colton's best friend, commented on how nice they looked, as did a dozen other friends. Colton, however, never worried about the way he looked. Even though he was almost six feet tall, two hundred pounds of solid muscle, with dark brown eyes and hair, he never considered himself good-looking. He was just Colton, the football player.

Lacie is beautiful. At five foot seven and only one hundred twenty pounds, she has a great figure. Her blond hair is long, and she has the most beautiful piercing blue eyes Colton has ever seen.

He checked his cell phone and noticed that Lacie left a message requesting a callback.

"Hi! I looked at the picture on Facebook. Seth is right, you are beautiful," he said.

"Well, I think you're great too," she said. "Did you get your Jeep back from the shop?"

"Sure did, and she looks almost as good as new."

"You must drive slow tonight. Did you see all the snow that fell this afternoon?"

"See it? Hell, I had to practice football in it. Coach wouldn't let us practice inside because he wanted to condition us to the bad weather we might face tomorrow," Colton said.

"Leave early so you're not late for first hour," she suggested.

"I can't. I have to wait until the newspapers get to the storage shed, but I shouldn't be late."

"Colton, the reason I wanted you to call back was because of something that happened during last hour in school. I was in the girls bathroom and Jenny Stillmore was cleaning her sweater. She had it off, and she was standing at the sink in her bra."

Colton laughed, "You've seen girls in their bras before, haven't you?"

"Stop it! Yes. That's not the point, Colton. She had bad bruises all over her arms, back, and stomach. Someone has been beating her!" Lacie sounded upset.

"I'm sorry. How could you tell it was from a beating?" he asked.

"I saw you after those farmhands beat you up in September, and I know what it looks like. They were marks from a fist, and her arms had the imprint of someone's hand holding her too tight," she said.

"What did you do?" Colton asked.

"I asked her who was beating her, and she got embarrassed. Then she said it was from an accident and not a beating. She tried to cover it up, but I knew she was lying," Lacie added.

"What happened then?"

"I told her that if she needed help to call me. I tried to make her understand I wanted to help, and she doesn't have to get beat up by anyone. But she wouldn't listen, and she walked out without saying a word."

"Well, Lacie, you tried. If she's being abused at least she knows you're willing to help. I don't see what more you can do," Colton said.

"Colton, look out the window. It's snowing harder again, and the news says the temperatures will stay below freezing all night. Like I said, drive slow and avoid hitting the deer. I love you and I'll see you in school. We can talk about Jenny then."

"Sounds like a plan. I will be careful and I love you too, Lacie. Bye."

Before speaking with Lacie, Colton looked forward to doing the paper route in the morning. Now he felt a twinge of dread. *Will it be slippery? Are the deer going to be out tonight? Why am I sitting here worrying about something I can't control?*

With that, he slid under the sheets, reached over and set the alarm clock for two in the morning and tried to sleep.

***

There have been gangs of killer deer reported in the woods near The Point and I, Detective Colton Blackwell, am on a mission to find the leader. If anyone can convince the big buck to surrender, it's me.

The snow is deep and the roads are icy, but I will find my deer. As I drive into the dense woods, I feel hundreds of eyes on me. I can't afford to hit a tree or have anything happen to my yellow Jeep, so I try to be as careful as possible. From the corner of my eye I spot them.

At least fifty gang members standing on the edge of the road.

"They have guns!" I screamed. "Damn, where did they get the guns?"

The leader, standing over seven feet tall, walks up to the side of my Jeep.

"Colton," he says, "You've got to get out of these woods, they belong to us now and we kill all trespassers."

"You can't do that," I scream, "You don't own these woods, and I am sworn to protect them from the likes of you."

The killer deer walks to the front of my Jeep and points his gun at me. I know what comes next, so I gun my engine and drive forward to scare him, but he doesn't move. I press down on the gas pedal. The Jeep lurches forward just as he pulls the trigger. The gangster slips and slides under the front of the Jeep.

I know it's serious, because I can hear the crunching of bones. I call 911 on my cell phone... requesting backup and get out to see if the criminal is dead. As I try to pull the body out from under my Jeep, I hear fifty guns being made ready to fire at me.

"You killed our leader, you scumbag human," one of the gang members yells. "Now you will die."

From behind me I hear ear splitting sirens. As the sirens grow louder, the deer fire their guns. I duck behind my Jeep. The deer's leg reaches up from under my Jeep and grabs me. It's the leader. He isn't dead. He's pulling me under the jeep with him. The sirens grow louder and I can feel the cold steel barrel of a gun pressing against my head.

"I'm dying, human, and so are you," the killer deer says, with a wicked laugh.

The siren is right next to my Jeep and I scream for help.

Colton sat up in bed and reached over to the nightstand to shut off the alarm. The realization he was having a dream was a relief. He didn't want his Jeep damaged and not being dead would be nice too.

It was two thirty, Friday morning, and Colton had three hours of newspaper deliveries ahead of him. He dressed, went down to the kitchen to make coffee, and prepared for his route. He turned on the Bad Axe radio station to listen to the forecast. At least three inches of snow was on the ground, the winds would gust to twenty miles per hour, and the temperature would not go above freezing. Lacie was right... it would be a challenge to finish by seven thirty, the time he needed to be in school. To stay warm, he changed into an old pair of sweatpants and a hooded sweatshirt.

The Jeep's interior was cold and didn't get warm until Colton pulled up to the storage shed in Pigeon. There were two other drivers parked next to the storage unit waiting for the newspapers. Getting out of the Jeep, Colton walked up to an old 1989 Plymouth Voyager. Joe Forest, the driver, rolled down the window. Smoke rolled out of the van and Joe grinned and flicked ashes out the window.

"Hey, kid, the papers are late. I called, and they said the driver was on his way, but the roads are slippery so he will be an hour late. Hope you ain't got anything to do, 'cause we're gonna have a wait," he said, and then coughed.

Colton stepped back from the smoke and said, "I guess we don't have a choice. If I fall asleep, please wake me when they get here."

Joe laughed and said, "Sure thing kid. Hope you have pleasant dreams."

Colton put his earphones in and listened to the latest Baldacci novel. Detective stories are his favorite novels, and Baldacci is his current favorite author. The novel, "Forgotten" features Army Special Agent, John Puller. John discovers his aunt has died in Paradise, Florida, and he suspects foul play. An investigation leads to action and adventure, and Colton loves adventure.

Forty minutes into the novel Joe honked his horn and pointed to the newspaper delivery truck that was pulling into the driveway.

"The truck is here," he yelled.

Colton turned his phone off, and loaded two hundred and fifty newspapers into the front seat of his Jeep. There were at least ten messages from the paper informing him which customers were leaving for the winter, the snowbirds flying south to their winter homes. Colton considered how lucky they were to be getting away from this snow and wind.

"Good luck," Colton yelled to the other two drivers as he drove out of the parking lot toward his first delivery near Bay Port.

During the hour that Colton waited for his papers, the roads got even more snow covered. After sliding a few times, he realized driving over forty miles per hour is dangerous. Driving faster could lead to him spending the night in a ditch; Something he didn't want to happen.

Colton had his headphone on and was listening to his audio book when he realized that he wouldn't be able to concentrate on his book and the deliveries tonight. Several times, as he approached a mailbox, he couldn't stop in time. Once, he almost slid into the mailbox.

He thought to himself, If I'm not careful, I'll wreck my Jeep before anyone sees how great she looks.

After having his Jeep almost totaled a few weeks ago, Colton slowed down and concentrated on his deliveries. It would take time to learn how to do his newspaper route in the snow. Even if there was less than three inches on the roadway, it forced him to drive slower.

He continued, avoiding the killer deer that shared the roadway. As he grew closer to the last few stops, he looked at his watch and realized that school was starting in a few minutes. He was five minutes from the high school, but he wasn't dressed for school. Wearing sweatpants and an old flannel shirt he looked like an old man hunting squirrels, instead of the football star he was.

Considering his options he tried to make it to school before the last bell rang. Even if he dressed down, at least he wouldn't be late again. Being late was something he hated. Since he got his job delivering newspapers, he was almost always on time. In the past he almost lost his eligibility for football because he was tardy too many times.

Colton delivered the last paper and sped toward Lake Huron High School.

As he slid into the parking lot, he could see that the last bus had already left. He parked and ran toward the side door and slid down the hallway toward his U.S. history classroom.

Mr. Dinger, the teacher, finished calling roll as Colton flew through the doorway.

"Am I late, Mr. Dinger?" he asked.

"You tell me."

"Yes, but I have a good reason again," Colton exclaimed.

"I'm sure you do. Perhaps another murder or gunfight?" Mr. Dinger asked.

"Not that serious, Sir. I'm late because of killer deer and slippery roads."

The other students laughed as Colton explained why he couldn't drive faster on his newspaper route, resulting in his being late for first hour.

"Colton, you've been on time for the last month so I will excuse you today. I'm just glad you didn't run over any of those deer. You know… that's my job. I've hit two of them so far this fall, and I'm sure there are more waiting to destroy my truck," Mr. Dinger said.

"Thank you, Sir."

Chapter 3

Colton moved over to his seat next to Connie Jackson. "Why were you late?" she asked.

"The roads were bad and my newspapers were late. At least I didn't run over a deer, slide into a deep ditch, or get into trouble with Mr. Dinger."

"So, you could say it's a good day, right?" she laughed and then saw Mr. Dinger looking at her. She smiled and opened her history book.

"Yes, it's a good day, Connie," Colton whispered. He thought about the coming events; the seventh hour pep assembly, the game tonight in Sebewaing, and the after game party in the family garage. Colton and his dad set the garage up as a work area and a man cave, furnishing it with items found along the side of the road. The garage featured overstuffed chairs and a huge flat screen TV.

The game in Sebewaing will be the district finals, and if the Loons win, they could become regional or even state champions. If they lose, they will end up as district runner-ups. That would be better than last year, but this year the Loons' team is the best team in many years, and Coach Talbert believes they could be State Champions.

Connie poked Colton in the arm with her ink pen.

"Ouch! What's that for?" he asked.

"You were sleeping again. I thought you solved that problem since you got into so much trouble with your last job," she said.

"I wasn't sleeping. I was thinking. And you need to stop poking people with your ink pen. I still have marks from the last time you poked me," Colton insisted.

Connie smiled, as the bell rang. "Sorry, but I like poking people. It's just my thing, I guess."

Colton walked to his locker while looking for Lacie. He hadn't talked to her since last night and was eager to tell her about his route. She disappeared, so he checked his phone to see if there was a message. None.

"Hey, Colton. I understand you got to school late again. What happened?"

Without turning around, Colton recognized the voice of his best friend, Seth

"It's all true. But my Jeep survived undamaged and Mr. Dinger let me off without a slip from the office," he said. "So, have you seen Lacie this morning? I always talk to her after first hour, but she isn't around and she never sent me a message."

"Wow! You have it bad for her, don't you? Can't be without her for a few minutes without knowing her every move. Seems a little over possessive," Seth said. "Perhaps you need a detective to follow her. I'm available, you know."

Seth looked at Colton from his feet to his messy hair and smiled. "Is there a reason you're dressed in your pajamas?"

Colton checked himself and remembered that he hadn't changed. Still wearing his old lounge pants and a worn out sweatshirt, he replied, "Yes, and when I think of it, you'll be the first one to know."

As they walked toward their class, Colton's phone buzzed. It was a message from Lacie. "See U in art."

"The mystery is solved, Seth. Perhaps something else will come up that requires your detective skills."

"Sure hope so. It's been boring since our last caper. And besides, all those spy toys are still in my car. We need to use them again, soon." Seth said as Colton turned into his classroom.

A few weeks ago, Colton and Seth spent quality time looking for drug dealers and killers. Seth used some of his dad's money to pick up security cameras and listening devices. It seemed like fun until they almost got themselves killed.

Second hour trigonometry, with Mr. Sellerman flew by. Colton kept his mind busy on the assigned problems and was surprised when the bell rang. Leaving the classroom he looked to see if Lacie was in the hallway. She wasn't. Art class was another hour away, so he would have to endure chemistry before he could see her.

Perhaps Seth is right, he considered. *Lacie is becoming an addiction. She's my drug of choice and I need a fix.*

Unable to concentrate on chemical formulas and scientific hypotheses, his mind stayed on Lacie.

Where has she been? What has she been doing all morning? Why do I feel like this?

He looked at the clock and realized there were still thirty minutes to go before art class. *Thirty minutes of pain. Thirty minutes of solitude. Thirty minutes without Lacie.*

Mrs. Quick, the chemistry teacher, walked up to Colton and put her arm over his shoulder. She whispered into his ear, "Colton, do you need to go to the nurse? You look like you're having problems."

"No, I'm fine. I was late to school and my mind is still catching up. I'll be OK... I have art class next hour and I can relax a little."

"OK, but you look like you should be in bed... dressed like you are," she said with a smile and a chuckle that Colton thought sounded like a put down.

Colton closed his book and got ready to run as soon as the bell rang. He started toward the door and heard Mrs. Quick say, "If you are standing, you're not excused."

Everyone sat down, just as the bell rang. Colton bolted out the door to look for Lacie. She wasn't at her locker so he started down the hall for the art room. He made his way into the art room and asked Jerry where she was.

"Like... how should I know. I just got here. Did you lose her or something?" he asked.

"No, Jerry. But I haven't seen her all morning, and she told me she would be here," Colton said. He was now over-anxious. It wasn't like Lacie to be late. All kinds of horror scenes ran through his mind as his imagination went wild.

The bell rang and Colton stared at the door. *Where the hell is she?* He thought.

***

Colton attempted to send a text message to Lacie, but Mr. Swansear, the teacher, kept watching him. Just as he was ready to try again, Mr. Swansear approached his table.

"Colton, is there a reason you are so stressed, and why are you dressed like you're ready for bed?" he asked, sounding concerned.

"Yes… and no," Colton replied. "I was late and didn't have time to change my clothes, and I'm worried about Lacie; she planned to be here, but she's missing."

As Mr. Swansear spoke, Lacie walked through the door and sat down beside Colton. She handed a note to the teacher and apologized for being late.

Swansear said, "That's fine, Lacie. I knew you were in the office, so I didn't mark you absent. Colton, now that Lacie is here, perhaps you both can get busy on your paintings. It looks just like it did two days ago. You know it's due next week, don't you?"

"Yes, Sir. I'll have it done," Colton said as he turned to Lacie.

"Where were you?" he asked. "I was worried sick all morning."

"I had to meet with my counselor, and I have good news, Colton," she said. "Why were you worried?"

Before Colton could answer Lacie added, "Gee, that's sweet; you were worried about me?"

Colton felt foolish. "Kind of dumb, isn't it? There were crazy thoughts going through my mind, and yes… I love you, and I was worried."

"Thank you. That's nice to hear, and I love you too. Do you want to hear my good news?" Lacie asked.

"Yes!"

"My mother works at the hospital in Pigeon and she got me a job as a student aid. I can work a few days each week to help decide if I want to go into the health field. I will also get paid, which is a good thing."

Colton could see that Lacie was stoked. The smile ran from ear to ear and she was excited. He knew this should be the time to encourage her, but he said, "I worried something bad happened to you."

"Colton, can't you be happy for me?"

"I'm sorry, I guess I'm selfish. I've had a rotten day, and I didn't know where you were, so I'm sorry. *It's not about me*; it's your good news, and I'm glad you got the job just like you were glad when I got my new job."

"That's better," she said. "Now let's get our paintings done, before Mr. Swansear has a cow."

Colton giggled at the thought of Mr. Swansear giving birth to a cow.

As they painted, they discussed Lacie's decision to consider a career in nursing. She talked before about wanting to be a nurse but now she indicated she might want to become more than a nurse.

Feeling guilty about thinking how this would affect him, he said, "Lacie, you would make a great nurse or doctor, and I'll support your decision."

"Well, I haven't decided. I've always wanted to be a nurse, and by working at the hospital, I'll be able to see what's involved. It's like when you worked for the diary farm and decided that you didn't want to be a dairy farm worker."

"Great idea. Perhaps I should get a job with the state police. Then I could see if I want to be a detective."

"And since when do you want to be a detective?" Lacie asked.

"Well... I solved a murder last month, and I know I am better than a few of the policemen I've met," he said.

"But, Colton, you're so smart. You should set your sights on something more than just a police officer."

"Lacie, you're being prejudiced. Police officers are smart. And some nurses are smart enough to be doctors."

Lacie smiled. "OK. I could be a doctor, or a nurse and you can be whatever you want. Just don't set your sights on being a paperboy for the rest of your life."

"That's cold," Colton said.

***

Having Lacie at his side, Colton let his mind return to the football game tonight. He walked to the storage countertop, next to the window, to check the weather. The smile racing across his face told Lacie the weather was good.

When he returned, she asked, "Well, what is it doing out there. Snow? Rain? Cold?"

"It's nice; the snow and ice are melting and there isn't a cloud in the sky. Yes, Lacie, it will be a great game tonight."

"I thought you wanted to play in the snow. Didn't you say it made for a more interesting game?"

"That was just talk. The snow would be a pain in the butt, and I hate winter," Colton said while considering how he would drive in the snow as he delivered his newspapers throughout the coming winter.

Lacie smiled and dabbed a little more paint on her picture. "Will we win tonight?"

"Yes! We will go to the Regional Championships, and we will be the state champions."

"Don't get overly confident and cocky! Everyone is talking about Sebewaing's winning streak."

"We are as good as they are, and we will beat them." Colton was trying to use the power of positive thinking. He saw Sebewaing play last year when they won the State Championship, and the buzz is they are even better this year. Colton wants to win, and he knows staying confident will help.

Mr. Swansear told the class to clean up and in a few minutes the bell rang. Colton and Lacie walked down the hall toward the cafeteria. Seth caught up to them and asked if he could join them for lunch. Colton said no, but then he laughed and said he was kidding. The three made their way to the line to get their trays when Lacie pointed out Jenny Stillmore and her boyfriend.

"She's the girl I told you about last night. I'm convinced someone is beating her," Lacie said.

"She looks good," declared Seth. "Really fine."

Jenny, a very attractive girl with long dark brown hair, turned many of her male classmate's heads. Her boyfriend stood at her side as they went through the lunch line. He's a senior and moved here from Cass City.

"Seth, aren't you still going with Linda Canberry?" asked Lacie.

"Yes. She told me I can look at other girls as long as I don't touch," he said.

Colton laughed and said, "Don't even try to talk your way out of that one, Seth. Lacie has all the comebacks. Trust me, I've tried."

The three teenagers sat together, eating and talking about what Lacie witnessed in the bathroom.

"I have a little knowledge about abusive relationships," said Lacie. "We talked about it in health class, but I didn't listen that well. I asked Jenny about the bruises and she got defensive and then angry with me. Jenny doesn't want to talk about her problems, but I would still like to help her."

"Well... no one wants to let other students know they have problems. We all are trying so hard to appear to be perfect," added Colton.

"I am perfect and everyone knows it," insisted Seth.

"Sure you are. That's why you wear expensive clothes and drive a new Charger around to show how perfect you are," Lacie said. "You're like the rest of us. Unsure about yourself, awkward in social situations, and afraid someone will learn your secrets."

She patted Seth's hand and added, "But we love you, and to us you are perfect the way you are."

"Thank you," Seth said. "Perhaps what Jenny needs is a friend who will listen to her. Someone she can trust."

Lacie thought for a moment and then said, "Perhaps."

Colton knew what her comment meant. She would meddle into Jenny's affairs.

"Be careful whose business you get your nose into, Lacie. I wouldn't want that beautiful nose hurt."

She smiled at him and picked up her tray. They cleaned their area and walked together to fifth hour study period.

Chapter 4

Ms Walker, the study hour teacher, was in a strange mood. She barked at the students for not having their worksheets done for the week, yelled at Colton because he didn't dress up, considering he is on the football team, and then she got upset with Seth because he said he had no homework to do.

"Everyone needs to bring work to do. If you don't have work to do, you need to bring in something else to do," she said.

"I did, I brought my laptop and I'll work on my game skills," Seth said.

That was not what she wanted him to say, so she sent Seth to the office.

Colton watched Ms Walker limping back to her desk and understood her foul mood and wondered if she had injured herself.

Seth returned from the office with a mountain of papers to sort. Miss Downer created work for him, which put a smile on Ms Walker's face.

Lacie saw Jenny Stillmore working on the algebra assignment and decided she would talk to her. She asked Ms Walker for permission to study algebra with Jenny, and Ms Walker approved.

"Jenny, do you understand the problems Mr. Sellerman gave us in algebra. I'm having trouble, and wonder if you can help me," Lacie said.

"Sure, Lacie, if I can. Algebra isn't my strongest subject, but I'm getting a respectable grade. So, I guess I'm doing OK," Jenny answered.

Wanting to take every opportunity to get Jenny to open up, Lacie used the algebra problems as a foothold to generate a conversation.

"I saw you with your boyfriend. He looks like a nice guy," she said.

Jenny's face became flushed, and she hesitated. "He's OK."

By her response, Lacie was prompted to ask if he's the one that's hurting her. Jenny's eyes filled with tears as she picked up her books as if to leave.

"Don't leave, I ask because I'm worried. I won't tell anybody, I want to be your friend."

Jenny smiled and said, "I've heard that one before."

After a minute of silence she added, "I love Luke, it's just that he gets upset so easy. I have to be careful. He gets angry, but then he feels bad about it. I think in time he can learn to control his anger."

"Well... if you ever need help, I'm here. I hope it works out for you because the two of you make a great looking couple," Lacie added, trying not to produce any waves.

"Thanks, Lacie. I don't have a lot of friends and most of Luke's friends are older bikers. They're a rough crowd."

Lacie considered inviting Jenny and Luke to the after game party, but decided she better not. She didn't think Colton would appreciate a group of bikers crashing his party.

"Jenny, we can talk later," Lacie said as she went back to Colton's table.

"That looked like it went well," Colton said. "Did she admit that someone is hitting her?"

"Yes and no," Lacie said. "Her boyfriend, Luke, has anger issues, but she loves him and that's the dilemma."

Seth glanced up from his stack of work and said, "How can you love someone who doesn't respect you?"

Colton shook his head. "I don't know. Some girls like tough guys. I think it's the *bad boy syndrome.*"

"That's a bunch of bunk," Lacie said with a note of sarcasm, "You're just making it up. But I guess everyone looks for something different in a lover. I mean, what attracts me to you? It's not money or good looks... or?"

"It's my mind; you love me for my mind," Colton interrupted.

"Everything; You never get angry, except in sports, and you are careful not to hurt the people you love, and that's a good thing," she said, touching his hand.

"Yes, and I love you because you're smart enough to know how great I am."

"Watch it. You don't want to make me angry, because I have a mean streak, as I'm sure you know," Lacie said with a teasing laugh.

The bell buzzed and Colton hugged Lacie and told her he would meet her after the assembly. They each headed to their sixth hour class.

***

After sixth hour all the Lake Huron High School students made their way into the gym. The band played the school song as the students filled the bleachers. The football team sat in the front row of folding chairs, and when everyone was in the gym, principal Zeller stood up and shouted into the microphone.

"Are we proud of our team?" he howled. The deafening response, *YES*, filled the gym.

Working the students into a frenzy, he continued asking the question. First asking the students, next the football team, then he handed the microphone over to Coach Talbert, who told the students how the team is working to win the districts. He introduced each player and after he called each name, the students screamed.

By the time the cheerleaders began their presentation, the noise in the gym was unbearable.

Colton was proud to be on the team. He turned to Aden and smiled. Aden bent over and yelled, "Feels good, doesn't it?"

Colton yelled back, "It'll feel better tonight after we win!"

The head cheerleader began another cheer and everyone jumped to their feet. The exuberant cheer ended as the bell rang and a mass of students headed for the gym doors.

Colton ran to catch up with Lacie. She turned as he called her name.

"I have to catch the bus, Colton."

"I know, but remember our plans to meet with Mrs. Hoffstarter on Saturday. If you can't go with me, I need to tell her."

"I wouldn't miss it, Colton. She's a special woman."

"Great. Please let me take you home so you don't have to ride the bus."

"No! You need to go home and rest. And throw away those ugly pajama bottoms." She said as she exited the school toward the long line of yellow busses. Colton watched as she got on the bus, turned, and waved. He waved back and turned toward the parking lot.

As Colton approached his Jeep, he watched Jenny and her boyfriend walking toward their car. From their body language he could tell they had been arguing. She had her head down, and he yelled something about being dumb. Colton couldn't make out all the conversation, but Lacie was right about their relationship. She is afraid of him, and he is *not* a nice guy.

Colton jumped into his Jeep but lingered to observe the couple as they sped off. Colton held a policy of avoiding conflicts between others. He'd seen too many fights start because someone couldn't keep their nose out of someone's business. It was better to avoid those situations, he had concluded.

But when should you become involved? He asked himself; *before or after the situation becomes violent.*

Not having time to worry about someone else, Colton started the Jeep and headed home. He had to do chores and get ready for the game tonight in Sebewaing. The buses were gone and a stream of student and teacher vehicles exited the parking lot at the same time.

As he passed Aden's old black Camaro, he honked and waved. Aden was self-absorbed and didn't hear him. *Or perhaps his music is too loud,* Colton considered.

Earlier in the season Aden and Colton learned they would receive offers from several universities. Since Colton is only a Junior, he will wait until next year for a formal scholarship offer. Aden, however, has already received scholarship offers from Central Michigan, Michigan State, and Northern Michigan. Since receiving the offers, his head has been in the clouds. Coach talked to him about his concentration and reminded Aden that a bad showing at the district and regional playoffs could alter the scholarship offers. The entire team hoped that Aden would concentrate on the game.

The WLEW radio weather forecast put a smile on Colton's face when he mentioned fifty degrees rising to sixty degrees this evening for this evening's forecast.

***

When Colton reached home, he saw Jason and Terry playing basketball in the driveway. His dad put the basket up several months ago as a way to help Jason improve his game. Terry loved basketball despite his statements to the contrary.

"Hey, you want to play with us?" Jason yelled as Colton stepped out of the Jeep.

"Can't now, but you two have improved," he said.

"Thanks, Coach said I might start the first game if I keep it up," Jason said.

Colton walked over to his brother and gave him a hi-five and a big hug.

"Well done. Are you trying out for the archery program?" Colton asked.

"Yes," Jason said, "Can you work with me after you get done winning the state football trophy?"

Colton laughed, "Sure, right after I bring the trophy home. I want you to remember that you are in line to win a few trophies too since you both have the *Blackwell thing* going for you."

"That's what Dad said," replied Terry. "But... what's a thing?"

"It's hard to explain," said Colton. "You know how Dad can throw a perfect pitch, catch every fly ball, and hit the longest home run? Well, that's the Blackwell thing. And you two got your share of it."

After a group hug, and a few baskets, Colton headed into the house where he greeted his mom with a hug.

"My word, aren't you in a good mood?" she said.

"It's great to see Jason and Terry getting along so well. I can't believe Jason wants to get involved in sports," Colton said.

"Well... it's all your fault. All he talks about is how great *you* are. He's proud of how you handle yourself on the field, and he's impressed with the way you solved that murder a few weeks ago," she said.

"Wow! Too much pressure, so I guess I need to screw up a few times so he doesn't get too proud of me," Colton laughed. "Will you and Dad be coming to the game in Sebewaing tonight?"

"Yes! Your dad is meeting me at the game. It's his last night at Delta College, so we're going to the game and then out to dinner in Bad Axe for a celebration."

"Great. What time can I expect to see you at our after game party tonight?"

"We'll be home late. Its parent's night out, and I want nothing bad happening in the garage, and please watch that old gas heater because I don't want a fire in the garage either."

"No problems. I'm done with problems, Mom. No police problems! No murder problems! Like I said, no more problems!"

"Excellent! Now I have to get dinner made for you kids. I'll have it ready by five. That will give you time to get ready for the game. If you want you can rest, and I'll call you when it's done," she offered.

"Great. I'll be upstairs," Colton said.

As he walked up the stairs, he heard his ten-year-old sister, Stephenie, talking. He peeked into her room and saw she was on the phone.

"Yes! I'm going to the game, too. My aunt is taking me and after the game we're going home with her. We get to sleep over tonight," she said.

Steph looked up. Seeing Colton in the doorway, she smiled and said, "Hi! I'm talking to my girlfriend Kayla about the game."

"I'll watch for you in the grandstands. Be sure to bring a blanket, in case it gets cold," he said.

"OK," she said as she returned to her conversation with Kayla. "That was my brother, Colton. He's the one that gets into trouble all the time."

Chapter 5

As the Lake Huron Loons' football team entered the school bus, they were smiling and laughing. The players appeared eager to confront the Sebewaing Patriots. Coach Talbert stood beside the bus door checking to make certain all his players were there. When the last player got on the bus, he blew his whistle for attention. The team grew hushed.

"Guys, this is exciting, but we have serious work to do before we can celebrate. Sit and think about what you have to accomplish tonight. I want to be district champions as much as you, and I know we can win tonight. Keep your mind on the jobs you must do and picture yourself doing them without mistakes." He then sat down in the front row with the assistant coaches, and the players did as He instructed.

Behind the team bus sat another two buses, each loaded with sixty students, including the cheerleaders. These students were not somber. They were yelling, screaming, and singing the school song. The Loons team members could hear the noise coming from the other buses as their bus pulled away from the curb.

To Colton it seemed like an hour passed before the bus reached Sebewaing. In actuality, it was a short thirty-minute ride. Stepping off the bus while carrying their gear, the team entered through the doors of the visitor's locker room. Colton found a locker and suited up. The tension had grown and the reality of the stakes for winning the game became real to each player. Coach Talbert had done a great job of directing the players excitement inward. Through silent meditation, the team members were becoming grounded.

"Men, gather around so we can talk. I will not give you any special last-minute instructions. No special plays or magic game plan changes. We have been through a lot this season and with every game we've played you have shown me what a great team you are. Tonight is just another game. I know the Patriots stand undefeated, just like us. I know that if we win, we will be the district champions, and if they win, they will. It's that simple," he said.

He picked up a coffee mug and took a long drink. He put his hand on Aden's shoulder. "Son, you have led this team better than any quarterback I have had the privilege of working with. I trust you will lead them to victory tonight. And Colton, I want you to run like the devil is after you. Another touchdown and you will have set a new school record. Men, get your butts out there, and show your school, your community, and yourselves how good you are."

With that, the team formed a group hug and headed out the doors toward the bright lights. As they entered the field, the band played the Loon's fight song, and the cheerleaders led them to the field. The stands, filled on both sides of the field, had hundreds of people standing at the sidelines. Colton could envision one hell of a game. The announcer introduced the team members to the screaming fans and then announced that the Loons would kick with the Patriots receiving.

Before running on the field, Coach asked the team to stop for a moment of silence and then a cheer. The team ran on the field and were ready for the kick. Chuck Smitherson's kick was long, and the Patriots called a fair catch, because the Loons were quick to run down-field.

These two teams were so well matched that it seemed like neither would make a touchdown. During the first half, neither the Loons nor the Patriots could get the ball past the fifty yard line. The score at halftime remained tied at zero.

In the locker room, Coach Talbert talked to Aden about changes in the strategy. "Aden, do you see any way we can get through their defense?"

"I wish I did. Our line is holding them back, but I don't have enough time to attempt a pass. It seems like they know where I am every second. Perhaps I should do more lateral passes, then Terrence can pass to Colton, while the Patriots' linemen cream me," Aden said. He knew the Patriots would tackle him before they realized that he no longer had the ball. It wasn't something he relished doing, but he would accept being knocked down a few more times for the team.

"Sounds like a plan. We'll keep trying to run, but mix it up to distract them. Remember, they seem to recognize your every movement. Their coach has trained them on that technique. Just like we taught our defense to follow the ball," said Coach.

"Men, you're playing great, and if we maintain our defense where it is now, I know we can score points. So... let's get out there and beat the crap out of those Patriots."

With a yell and a hug, the team rushed the doors, eager to get back into the game. As Colton stepped out, Coach pulled him aside.

"Colton, make that touchdown and break the school record tonight," he said.

"Yes, sir. I will!." Colton replied.

As the team ran onto the field, the band was marching toward the school. The third quarter was a repeat of the first two. A few yards gained, and then nothing. Both teams defense were holding their opponents offense. Aden tried lateral passes, but there wasn't time for Terrence to get off a good pass. The Patriots line rushed him.

Half way through the fourth quarter, one Patriot lineman twisted his ankle and had to leave the game. The replacement was a larger player, who was also a little slower. Aden tried the lateral pass again. Terrance saw that Colton was open and drilled a pass right into his hands. Colton was almost shocked but recovered and spun around. He was open, but the Patriots were moving on him. On the forty yard line, he gave it everything he had and worked his way through several Patriots who were trying their hardest to stop him. He saw an opening and like a cougar he was off.

When he reached the end-zone, he was so excited that he almost did a victory dance. But realized it wasn't the best choice. Instead he turned and hugged the two Loons who had followed him down the field, keeping the Patriots off his tail.

The Loon's cheerleaders were dancing, and the fans were screaming. Colton made the first and last touchdown of the game on a pass by Terrance. A combination that may become next year's dynamic duo as the two are Juniors and Terrance could be the next quarterback.

***

The bus ride back to Pigeon was noisy. The team, Coach Talbert, and even the bus driver were excited about the win. All they could talk about was how great of a pass Terrance had made.

"He was *Superman* under fire," someone said.

"No, he was the *Iron Man* in full armor," someone else commented.

Terrance was basking in the glory, and then coach said, "Don't forget who caught that great pass and ran 26 yards for the touchdown."

A cheer went out for Colton, who stood on the bus bench and bowed.

"I owe it all to the guys who cleared the path for me. Thanks guys," he said.

The bus pulled into the School parking lot and up to the sidewalk. There were over a hundred students and parents cheering for the team. Coach opened the bus doors, and said, "I told you we would beat Sebewaing and we did. Now I'm telling you we will become the next regional champions, and then we will become the state champions."

The crowd went wild and Coach and the team stormed out of the bus and into the locker room. They dropped their equipment off and started out for their rides home. Most of them were going somewhere to party.

When Colton stepped out of the school, Lacie and Seth were there to greet him. Linda walked up to Seth and said she was ready to go. The group would meet at Colton's home. They had another garage party planned. Even though only a few friends attended, Colton's parties always entertained.

Colton opened the door for Lacie and then got behind the wheel. Because there were many cars trying to get out of the school parking lot, Colton took his time.

"What do you have to do now to win the regional championship?" she asked.

"I'm not sure who we play, but next Friday we will beat them too."

"I am becoming a believer, Colton," Lacie said. "You beat the current State champions. I think you could be the next champions."

When Colton drove through Pigeon, he saw over twenty cars in the IGA parking lot, and around the party store. There were both students and adults trying to find out where the parties were. Colton didn't like that many of his fellow students would drink tonight. He wasn't opposed to alcohol, but underage drinking was illegal. He figured that when he was of age, he might drink beer or wine to celebrate, but getting drunk was not something he needed to do.

"I sure am glad you don't drink, Colton," said Lacie. "I can't see what is so great about getting drunk and puking your guts out."

Colton agreed and turned the corner, heading north, toward home. It was only a few miles, and he was at the large white farmhouse. At one time the farmer who owned the property around the house, lived there. Now, a large corporation farms the land and Colton's parents own the house and ten acres around it. Just enough land for a large garden, orchard, and a huge lawn.

The three car white garage was unattached and sat behind the house. Colton drove up to the far right door and parked. Seth and Linda were already in the garage, and Aden pulled in behind Colton.

He was with his girlfriend, Kathy, who was also Lacie's closest girlfriend.

Colton walked up to Aden's car and opened the door for Kathy. Aden jumped out of the black Camaro and yelled, "Thanks Colton, but I can get my girl's door."

"It's my pleasure, Kathy. Aden, I want you to get plenty of rest, because you will need all the energy you can muster up next weekend when we play to become regional champs."

"I'll need it? You're the one who will need more energy, since I have a new assistant quarterback. Terrance will take up the slack so I can take it easy."

As the two men joked with each other, Kathy turned to Lacie and said, "They act like little boys, don't they Lacie?"

"They sure do. Let's leave them here. It's warmer inside," Lacie said.

Seth and his girlfriend, Linda Canberry, connected Seth's iPhone to the stereo and sat on the couch listening to his collection of country music. Linda, a beautiful girl, made a great cheerleader. She had an infectious laugh and often became the life of the party. Tonight she was in a quiet mood.

Kathy noticed how subdued Linda was and sat down beside her. "Why so down, Linda?"

Linda laughed and said, "I'm wore out. I cheered so hard and screamed so loud that I feel like chilling tonight."

"I think we all feel that way, except the guys over there; they'll be replaying the game all night."

Seth said, "Then I won't tell them I have the video of the game in my pocket. I used my Sony HD recorder and shot the game for Coach Talbert. Since shooting the Hampton game, he's been having me record all the games. That last run was amazing, but if you don't want me to show them, I won't. I also have some nice shots of my favorite cheerleader."

"I'm too tired to even look at the video, Seth, but I want to see it before you go posting it on Facebook," Linda said.

Lacie told Seth that he could share the video with the guys. As he set up the big TV, several football players walked in. They didn't have dates and hoped the cheerleaders were there.

Linda told them the girls are late because they went home to change first. This made the guys smile.

A carload of girls arrived at ten o'clock. Seth put dance music on and they lowered the lights. The party was in full force and lasted until close to one in the morning.

As Colton and Seth were cleaning up, Colton asked, "Seth, can you help me do the route Sunday morning again?"

"There won't be any killers on the loose, will there? Last time I helped you I almost died."

"No, but we have another mystery to solve. Someone is stealing papers from my newspaper racks and I have to find out who it is. I'm losing almost one hundred dollars every week," Colton said.

***

Colton and Lacie offered two of their friends a ride because they lived close to her house. After dropping them off, Colton took Lacie to her family home.

"Do you think your mom is still up?" he asked.

"Yes. She rarely gets to sleep until after I get home. I guess it's a parent thing."

"I don't know if I could handle being a parent. I worry about my brothers and sister, and I'm just their brother. Imagine having three children depending on your every move; it's scary."

Lacie smiled and took Colton's hand. "You would be an excellent father, because you care."

Clutching her hand he replied, "Thanks... it's hard to separate caring from worrying. Like today when you were in the meetings and I didn't have a clue where you were. I had visions of something happening to you."

"That's natural; just don't let it turn into an obsession," Lacie added. "Colton, I don't think you're aware of this, but Linda told me she's breaking up with Seth."

"Wow! Did she say why?"

"No, but I believe Seth has another girlfriend. Linda said they haven't been on the best of terms."

Colton thought for a moment. "Strange, he hasn't said a thing about any of this. Should I ask him?"

"No. It would make it look like we were talking behind his back."

"You mean like we're doing now?"

"Yes," she said as she leaned toward him and gave him a light kiss.

Colton got out and walked around the Jeep to open Lacie's door. but she was already out of the Jeep, She took his hand as they walked up the sidewalk. He asked her about their plans to meet with Mrs. Hoffstarter, who was one of Colton's customers, and is now a close friend.

"Wouldn't miss it for anything," Lacie said. "What time will you be here?"

"She suggested lunch, so I'll pick you up at eleven o'clock."

At the door, Lacie gave Colton a passionate kiss and said good night.

"Lacie, I love you," Colton said with a sigh.

"Me too, Colton. I love you."

Colton smiled all the way home. He was happy about the game, and his feeling for Lacie. Winter was coming, Thanksgiving will be here in a few weeks and his world is good.

I hope nothing transpires to screw this up, he considered. *It seems like when things are going well... crap hits the fan, and everything goes wrong. Perhaps this time it will be different.*

Chapter 6

Colton replayed his winning touchdown throughout the night and woke up cheerful though a little achy from Friday's game. A long hot shower eased the aches and pains in his back and knees. After considering the days events, he wore an old pair of sweatpants and a tee-shirt. He would dress up later for the lunch date on The Point, but first he had some dirty jobs to do.

Colton eyed his mom making breakfast as he stepped into the kitchen.

"You look ready to work. Didn't you say you had to get dressed up for a date today," she asked.

"Lacie and I are having lunch with Mrs. Hoffstarter later, but I want to help dad with the cars this morning."

"It's so nice of you to visit Mrs. Hoffstarter. She's a wonderful woman. When your dad was delivering her paper, he would stop in twice a week. Just to say hi."

"I know. She told me how much she appreciated it. She acts young for a woman who's almost ninety years old," Colton said.

"Some people think young. My mom was one who thought she was old when she was in her forties. She dressed and acted like an old woman, and then she died young," Colton's mom said.

As the two talked, the rest of the family sat down for breakfast. Cyndi put the platter of pancakes on the table and then sat down herself.

Colton's dad, Adam, said, "Well Colton, that was a great touchdown you made last night. We are so proud of you."

"Thanks dad. I hear you're done with your college class now?"

"Yes, I took my final exam yesterday, and your mom and I celebrated. I'll be home more now. I still want to take more classes, but I can do them online," Adam said. "It was getting hard balancing work, school and family. Now I can spend more time with you guys and your lovely mom."

Cyndi smiled and got up for more coffee. "I missed you dear, but I know you loved school. I haven't seen you that happy in years."

Colton told his dad about visiting Mrs. Hoffstarter today and they discussed what a great lady she is. Terry and Jason talked about their basketball skills and Steph told everyone she wanted to become a doctor.

"Where did that come from?" Colton asked.

"Well, I saw a show and this beautiful woman doctor was saving people's lives in the emergency room. And my friend Jennifer said she would be a doctor, and I told her I would be a better doctor than she would be. So now I have to be a doctor."

"That's nice," her mother remarked. "What happened to your plan to become a lawyer?"

"Oh, Mom. That was last week."

Cyndi laughed and announced, "Enough talk! It's time you all start your Saturday chores. Steph, you can start with cleaning the upstairs bathroom. Remember, doctors have to keep everything clean, so the germs don't multiply."

"Awe, Mom," Steph said.

The Blackwell family had a tradition of doing chores every Saturday morning, and when the kids finish their jobs, they could play. Colton was at an age where he wasn't expected to do these chores, but he still helped his dad work on the cars and with the yard work. Together they went outside to work in the garage.

***

Colton pulled his Jeep into the garage and put lifts under the front so he could drain his oil. As he did, Adam checked the other fluids, while they talked about his dad's job, Colton's game, and the newspaper route.

"Dad, did Mom tell you about the problem I'm having with the newspaper racks in Caseville?" he asked.

"Yes, people stole papers when I was delivering, but not as many as you've had stolen. If it continues, you should stop putting papers into those racks. You can't keep people from stealing. They put money in, open the door, and take as many as they want. Only honesty keeps them from taking over one paper," Adam said.

"With Seth's help, I'll set a trap for the thieves. We're using the cameras Seth bought last month, so if I can catch their faces or, better yet, their license number, then I can turn them into the police. I hate it when someone takes what is mine."

"Just be careful. You are aware what happens when you try to solve mysteries," Adam said.

"Yes, I get my face beaten. You know Dad, I've been thinking about taking self-defense classes. I need to hit back as hard as I get hit," Colton said.

"Perhaps, but if you think you can defend yourself, then you will get into more fights. Sometimes it's the guy that walks away from a fight who wins."

"Dad, sometimes there is no place to walk."

"True."

When the two finished Colton's Jeep, they worked on Adam's car and Cyndi's S-10 pickup. By ten fifteen they finished with the vehicles and Colton told his dad he had to clean up.

"Colton, tell Trudy Hoffstarter I said hello. She's such a gem. In fact, ask her if she would like to come to our home for Thanksgiving. It would be great if she could."

"Great idea, Dad. I'll ask her and I will ask Lacie to come too."

Colton showered and changed into his good clothes. After picking up Lacie they headed for The Point where they drove past huge summer homes along the shores of Lake Huron. Colton pulled up to one of the largest homes, owned by Trudy Hoffstarter, a retired psychiatrist from Pontiac, Michigan. The two walked to the side deck and looked out at the beautiful beach scene.

"Come on in you two," said Trudy. She was about five feet-six inches and 130 pounds. Trudy was a beautiful woman with short gray hair and a rosy complexion. She didn't show her 89 years.

"Hi, Trudy," said Lacie. "I can't get over the view here; it's so peaceful."

"It's a very lonely place; that's why I appreciate your visits. You two keep me young."

"You are young, Trudy," Colton said. "Sometimes when we talk you seem more like one of our classmates than an...."

"An old woman?" she asked.

"No. I didn't say that, but I guess that's what I meant."

The three went into the huge room where twelve foot high windows formed a wall facing the water. In the distance Colton saw Charity Island and a few fishing boats. Just watching the water was relaxing.

"This is nice. I sure would love to live near the water. Not that I'm a big water person, It's just so calming," he said.

Trudy led Colton and Lacie to the table she had set next to the windows. There was soft music playing and Colton believed it might be a recording by Alfie Boe.

"Trudy, is this the *Storyteller* album?" he asked.

"How do you know Alfie Boe? I wouldn't expect anyone young to like his kind of music."

"My mom has one of his albums, and I enjoy listening to him."

"Yes, it's his album. Even though I like to think young, I still like my music slow and easy."

Lacie added, "And classic; I love the old standards. We sing a variety of music in choir."

As the three enjoyed the meal that Trudy prepared, Lacie approached a question she hoped her hostess could answer.

"Trudy, as a former psychiatrist, will you tell me why some girls stay with a guy that's abusing her."

"And what brings on this question?"

"I saw a girl in school with bruises and I believe her boyfriend is beating her. She's a lovely girl, but when I talk to her about it, she gets upset and says she loves him, and that I should keep out of her business," Lacie said.

"Perhaps you should," said Trudy. "There isn't anything you can do. If he is beating her, she is letting him. She can run from him, but she thinks it is normal, or she fears leaving. There are reasons girls stay with these hurtful men. But if she were to get help, she can break the cycle and learn to live without all the anger."

"So what do I do? Just look the other way?" Lacie asked.

"If you see him hit her, report it to the police. It is a crime to hit another person. If she will listen to you, give her phone numbers where she can get help." Trudy stood up and cleared the table. "No, don't look the other way. Don't put yourself in danger either. She needs professional help, and as her friend, you can help her with her low self-esteem. So offer your friendship, by letting her know you care."

Colton helped Trudy with the dishes. In the kitchen he thanked her for the advice. When they came back, Lacie was watching the geese walking on the lawn.

"Thank you, Trudy. You're such a good friend, and I love these visits," Lacie said.

Colton, remembering Thanksgiving, said, "That reminds me, Trudy and Lacie, would you two like to come to my family Thanksgiving dinner? Please don't say no."

Trudy and Lacie said "Yes!" at the same time. They laughed and Trudy said, "I would love to be a part of your family gathering. God knows, my family has no interest in me."

"Well, Trudy we do," said Lacie.

They visited a little while longer. After saying bye to Trudy, Colton took Lacie home so she can help her mother clean house. Since he was up most of the night reliving his touchdown, he wanted to get rest before doing his Sunday morning route. Lacie said if she wasn't able to stop by Sunday afternoon, she would meet him at school on Monday.

Chapter 7

Colton spent most of Saturday afternoon working in the yard with his dad. After dinner he went to his room to sleep because he must be up just after midnight to work all Sunday morning on his route.

The Sunday newspaper is huge this time of year. Area stores want to entice shoppers with early Christmas specials so they fill the paper with advertising. Colton increased his newspaper count and left more copies at each newspaper rack and store location.

Colton thought about the theft of his papers, *If I can't stop this loss, I must stop using the newspaper racks and only leave papers at the party stores and gas stations. I should make more money, not lose money to a thief.* Colton's plan is to use the hidden security cameras and listening devices that Seth owns. If he can catch the thief red-handed, he can report them to the police and perhaps get his money back, or at least stop the criminal from stealing more.

At 12:30 Sunday morning, Colton stood next to his Jeep, waiting for Seth. He considered calling him, but Seth wasn't late yet. Just when he pulled his cell phone out, Seth's Charger turned into the driveway and stopped next to the Jeep.

"Hope I'm not late, but I was hungry and had to make breakfast. Want a ham and egg sandwich? I made one for you, and I have plenty of hot coffee." he said.

"Perhaps later," said Colton, "Let's put the security gear in the Jeep and hit the road. We can eat while we wait for the papers in Pigeon."

Death On The Point - BLOOD BATH

The two put the spy equipment behind the front seats and Seth put his bag of snacks and coffee thermos up-front, between his feet.

"Ready to go?" asked Colton.

"Ready, captain; let's hit the road. I can't wait to find out who the criminal is that's stealing your precious newspapers."

"It's not a joke, Seth. I'm losing a hundred bucks a week, and that's money I need for my college savings. Unlike you; I don't have a rich family to help me out."

"Hey! I'm not making fun of the situation, Colton, I'm just eager to get back to our detective work."

Seth and Colton had been friends since kindergarten, and over the years they've had many adventures. Last month they almost got killed looking for a murderer in Detroit. They both enjoyed the thrill that came with trying to solve a mystery, and this is a mystery. Not as thrilling as murder, but still a crime needing a solution.

When they arrived at the Pigeon storage locker, they could see that both the other delivery drivers still waited for the delivery truck. Colton got out to talk with Rob and Joey.

"When do you think the truck will be here?" Colton asked.

Rob said he called earlier, and the trucks left about an hour ago. "They should be here any minute unless the driver stopped for a late night snack."

Joey laughed, coughed, and had another drag on his cigarette. "I wouldn't put it past them. As long as they are being paid they'll do anything to waste time."

"Colton," yelled Seth, "Is that the truck we're waiting for?"

A large white van pulled up to the gate, and a woman punched numbers into the keypad lock. The gate beeps as it slid open.

"Yep, that's them," Colton yelled back.

The delivery truck drove up to the waiting drivers and stopped. As soon as Colton knew where his stacks of papers were, He and Seth loaded the Jeep. It amazed Colton how fast he could load his papers, with Seth's help.

"I need to have you here every Sunday, Seth. It took half the time to load these papers with your help. Now we need to deliver them in half the time and we'll be in great shape," Colon said.

"Loading the papers is one thing, but delivering them is your job. Last time I helped you put the papers in those tubes, I almost lost my arm."

"OK, you can relax and I'll deliver them." Colton remembered when Seth helped him a few months ago. It was raining, so he let Seth get the wet arm. A few times Seth's hand was in the paper tube when Colton drove away. Seth yelled, and Colton had to stop. It took longer to have Seth do the deliveries.

***

Colton and Seth talked nonstop about football, girls, their past adventures and the mission this morning. Time flew by and they were at the first newspaper rack. Colton told Seth to set up the cameras so they can see who opens the rack and also what vehicle they are driving. As Colton loaded the papers into the rack, Seth checked his equipment.

"I think I have it, Colton. We'll be able to see who opens the rack and I have a broad view of the parking lot. If someone tries to steal papers here, we'll get a picture of them."

"Will it be recording them?" asked Colton.

"It's set up as a motion detector. Any movement will start the recording. I have it going to my laptop using a wireless connection," Seth said.

"Sounds good. I want to catch the thief tonight. I already told Deputy Ned Wooddell what we are doing. He's on duty tonight."

"Any idea who is stealing your newspapers?"

"No! It makes no sense at all. They can't sell the papers. The only thing I can think of is that some kids are playing a trick on me," Colton said. "Everyone knows this is my route, so they might want to screw with me, but I don't know who would do that."

"Perhaps the guys from Hampton? They're out of jail now, and they would love to get even for what we did to them last month."

"No, they got out of jail last week and this has been going on for over a month. It started out with a few papers, and now each rack is losing about thirty papers."

As they continued delivering newspapers along The Point, one spy camera caught a man in his pajamas buying a paper and two deer walking by the rack.

By four in the morning every rack had a motion-activated camera. It would take another two hours to finish the home deliveries along the Lake Huron shoreline and within the City of Caseville.

Colton stopped to adjust papers, so he could reach them. Seth looked at his laptop. "Look, Colton!" He exclaimed. "That woman is taking a bunch of papers, and we got her red handed. She's your thief."

Colton leaned over and saw the video as an elderly woman held the rack open with a stick. She had her trunk open and took stacks of papers out of the rack.

"Why the hell would an old woman be stealing my papers. I don't know her, so she can't be trying to get even with me. Why is she doing this?"

"Call Deputy Ned, let him know we have a thief on the hook," said Seth.

Colton called Ned and told him that the rack at the end of The Point was being robbed. Ned said he was about ten minutes from Caseville and would meet them behind the Village Grocery Store. There was a rack there and the thief might strike that one next.

"Don't be stupid, Colton. This time you have to wait for me to get there. Is that understood?"

"Yes, sir. Nothing stupid."

Colton and Seth drove to the store and parked just out of sight of the rack. Using the camera they kept watching for the black car that the thief was driving.

Seth yelled, "There she is, Colton!"

Together they watched as the old woman back up to the rack and get out. She again propped the door of the rack open and loaded her trunk with papers.

"Where the hell is Ned?" asked Colton. "She will get away before he gets here."

"We can always catch her at the next rack," said Seth.

"No, I want to catch her now. She's already messed up my morning and I don't want to drive half way across town to catch her doing what she's doing right now."

Colton called Ned, but his line was busy. He then got out of the car and walked toward the old woman.

"Ned said not to do anything stupid," said Seth, as he followed Colton across the parking lot.

"I guess I don't follow orders well," replied Colton.

Colton was a few yards from the woman when he yelled, "Stop! Those are my papers!"

The old woman, looked at the two teenagers running toward her and screamed.

"Don't hit me. Help! Leave me alone." She closed the newspaper rack door and slammed her car trunk shut. As she ran toward her car Colton grabbed the door and held it.

"You're not getting away with my newspapers. Get out and face the music, lady," he yelled.

The old woman had to be at least eighty. She had gray hair, was heavy set and wore a long calico dress.

Colton wanted to keep her from getting into the front seat of her car. He stood between her and the door. She called him many names, some that Colton had never heard an adult use. Then she hit him on the side of the head with her cane, not once but three times. Colton didn't want to harm her, because she had to be someone's grandmother, even though she was *nuts*.

"Get out of my way you damn hoodlum," she yelled.

Seth was standing back, laughing at Colton. "Hey, Colton. The State Police are here."

Colton turned toward the parking lot entrance and saw the blue patrol car approach. It pulled up next to the old woman's car and Trooper Steve Lithowski, opened his door.

The old woman hit Colton with her cane one more time and reached out with the cane and hit Seth on the side of the face, then she yelled, "Help! These hoodlums are trying to steal my car and rape me."

"She's lying, Trooper Steve," yelled Seth, holding the side of his face. "She was stealing Colton's newspapers, and we caught her red-handed. Then she hit us with her cane."

"That's a lie," the woman cried. "I'm an old woman. I wouldn't hit anyone."

Trooper Steve laughed as he approached Colton. "So kid, you can't stay out of trouble for more than a few weeks, can you?"

"Trouble follows me, Sir. I think it's a curse," laughed Colton.

Deputy Ned's patrol car pulled up and stopped next to the trooper's car. Ned got out and the old woman cried.

"Oh, thank God, Ned. You're here to save me from these hoodlums. They tried to rob me and I became frightened of what else they might do," she said.

Ned told the woman to sit in the front seat of his car, so he could talk to the *hoodlums.*

"Trooper Steve," Ned said as he walked up to him. "Thank you for responding to the call." He turned to Colton and Seth. "I asked Steve to help. I was on my way from Bad Axe and I knew I would be late. So, Colton, this is how you avoid doing something stupid?"

"She was getting away, and I couldn't reach you," Colton said. "We have a video recording of her stealing the newspapers, and you saw her hit me."

Trooper Steve barked at Seth, "What's with you and that damn video recorder? Why do you always make a damn recording?"

"Yes, sir. You wouldn't believe us without proof, would you?" Seth said.

Colton added, "I asked Seth to help me setup the recorder. We wanted to catch whoever was stealing my newspapers. The recorder worked for us in the past, and it looks like we trapped another crook."

Seth showed Deputy Ned and Trooper Steve the video of the woman stealing the newspapers. As they studied the two videos, Trooper Steve asked why the old woman would take the papers.

"If I knew, I would tell you," said Colton. "I've never seen her before so it can't be some kind of grudge. Maybe she's just a nut case."

Seth added, "Perhaps she has pet birds and needs lots of papers for their cages."

"Stay here and wait; I'll talk to her," Ned said as he opened his car door and sat down next to the old woman.

Trooper Steve said he had to get over to Sebewaing. He warned Colton about getting into more trouble. As the police car drove away, Colton walked back to his Jeep and drove it up next to the woman's car. Seth walked up to his window and said, "She isn't happy. Deputy Ned had me give him my laptop, and he showed her the evidence. She's crying on his shoulder now."

Colton shook his head and said, "He better not feel sorry for her. She's already cost me a lot of money. I don't care who's grandma she is, she's a damn thief!"

He watched as Ned talked on his car phone. Ned then got out of the patrol car and walked up to Colton's Jeep.

"I will take Mrs. Wilding to Bad Axe. The newspapers in her car's trunk are evidence, so I'm having them impounded along with her car. I also need the video recordings you made of her stealing the papers. Does the video show her hitting the two of you with her cane?"

"Yes, it was all caught on the tape. Will the District Attorney press charges, or will he let her off with a warning?"

"I can't say for sure, Colton. But she said she will pay you back for your papers. She admitted that she has been stealing them for the last few months."

"Why?" Colton asked.

"That, she wouldn't say. Perhaps she'll tell the prosecutor when he talks to her in Bad Axe."

Seth copied the videos to a USB drive and gave it to Deputy Ned.

"If you need anything else, here's my cell number," Seth said.

"Colton, do you and Seth want to press charges against Mrs. Wilding for hitting you with her cane?" Ned asked. "I would be a witness and you have video evidence, if you decide to."

Colton looked at Seth who was shaking his head. "No! As long as she pays me for the papers she's stolen I will OK. Besides, she didn't hurt us."

"OK. Well, boys, another mystery solved. But next time don't take matters in your own hands."

"Understood, Sir." Colton said.

A second patrol car drove into the parking lot and Deputy Ned handed the officer the keys to the old woman's car. As the scene cleared, Colton and Seth sat watching.

"That was fun," said Seth. "Any more crimes we can solve?"

"Not today, I'm too tired. We still have papers to deliver, so let's get done before we look for more trouble."

Chapter 8

Colton and Seth completed the route by eight o'clock, Sunday morning. After loading the spy equipment into Seth's car, Colton asked if he would like to come in for breakfast.

"I would, but I'm picking up Linda in an hour, and we're going to Bay City for lunch and shopping for Christmas," he said, opening the car door.

"Well, enjoy spending your money," Colton said.

"I will. And thank you for the exciting evening. We should do more detective work. Perhaps we could put an ad in the paper or telephone directory. Have spy cameras, will travel?"

"I'll consider the idea," replied Colton with a chuckle.

"I'm serious, Colton. We should go into the spy business. I'm sure my dad would help us. He's always pushing me to earn money."

"Perhaps," Colton said. "I'll think about it, but now I have my brothers to deal with."

Colton's brothers were standing on the porch watching him and Seth talk. As Seth drove off, Terry and Jason ran out to greet Colton.

"Want to shoot hoops?" yelled Jason.

Colton gave them a big hug and said, "No. If you come in, I'll tell you how we caught an old woman stealing my papers. It was awesome, and the police took her to Bad Axe and may put her in jail."

"Wow, why would anyone want to steal your dumb papers?" asked Jason.

"I don't know, and she wouldn't tell us."

Jason looked at Terry and said, "I think I would rather shoot hoops. How about you?"

"Hoops! Terry said, "Old women aren't fun like basketball."

Colton agreed and went into the house. His mom was in the kitchen and yelled, "Breakfast?"

"Yes, please. Whatever you're making is fine."

Colton's dad, Adam, walked in from the living room.

"So, did you catch the thief?" he asked.

"Yes. It was an elderly woman from Caseville. Lacie's uncle Ned helped us catch her. I can show you the video we took of her breaking into the newspaper rack. I put it on my memory card," Colton said.

"Sure, I'll get the laptop and we can watch it over breakfast," he said.

After his morning nap, Colton was ready to face the day. He shot hoops with his brothers for an hour, helped his dad clean up the orchard, and then he called Lacie to let her know about the old woman thief.

"Any idea what her name is?" asked Lacie.

"Ned said she was Mrs. Wilding, from Caseville. I can't recall ever seeing her around."

"What will happen to her?"

Colton said, "I'm not sure. Ned said Mrs. Wilding admitted to stealing my newspapers from the rack, so I imagine she will face the prosecutor, or perhaps even the Judge, on Monday."

"Call and tell me what happens," Lacie added. "I can't stop over today because we're having company and Mom needs my help. Sometimes I worry about what she'll do when I leave home. It seems like she depends on me more than ever."

"She'll adjust, or you can live at home forever, and be her personal maid."

"That will not happen," Lacie said. "I've got too many plans, and they don't include being a personal maid to anyone."

"Hope I'm in those plans."

"Some of them," she replied.

"Well, let's plan on meeting at school tomorrow. Unless you have other plans," Colton said.

"That's a date," Lacie said. "See you at school, Colton."

"OK. Bye, Lacie."

***

Colton arrived early to school Monday morning. He dressed up, wearing a white shirt, black dress pants, and a new tie. Even though he wasn't required to dress up today, he wanted to prove that he can dress better than he did Friday when everyone teased him for wearing what looked like his pajamas.

To Colton's surprise, most of the football team wore dress clothes. Even Coach Talbert wore his suit instead of his usual Loons uniform; a polo shirt and warm up pants.

Aden, in a crisp black dress shirt with a white silk tie, walked up to Colton and said, "Wow, don't you look nice. What happened to your pajamas? Did you forget them today?"

"Smart ass, I wanted dress up in case they have an impromptu assembly to celebrate our winning the districts," Colton said.

"I think it was on all of our minds," said Aden, as he pointed at two more team members wearing dress shirts and ties.

"Besides, Aden, I only wear my best pajamas when we should get dressed up, like last Friday's pep rally."

Aden's girlfriend, Kathy, caught his attention. She put her arms around him and snuggled up.

"Hey, let's find a quiet place to talk," she said.

Aden and Kathy leaned against a classroom door to get out of the hallway traffic. Colton could hear kissing sounds, but he didn't want to know for sure, so he walked toward his first hour class.

At the end of third hour an announcement came over the intercom. "There will be an assembly in the gymnasium during last hour."

Death On The Point - BLOOD BATH

Everyone understood what the assembly was for. It was the only subject the students talked about. The Lake Huron Loons are the district champions, and they are only two more wins from being the Regional Champions.

The Loons had been regional football champions in the distant past, but Coach Talbert knows the Loon's have the talent and determination needed to go all the way to the State Finals this year.

Before Colton realized it, the announcement came for all students to go to the gym for the assembly.

As Colton walked toward the gym, he felt his cell phone vibrating. For privacy he slid into the boy's locker room to answer it.

"Colton, this is the Huron County Prosecutor, Mark Bagley," said a man with a deep voice.

"Yes sir," replied Colton. "How can I help you?" The last time Colton had dealt with the prosecutor, He dropped the case, and the criminals were let off with a warning. Colton thought he would tell him he dropped the charges against the old lady.

"I need you and Seth in Bad Axe tomorrow morning at ten o'clock. Mrs. Wilding pleaded guilty to the charge of theft, under $1000.00, and she would like to apologize to you and Seth. She will also pay for the papers she stole. I understand she hit you with her cane, so she will also plead guilty to assault."

Colton replied, "Yes, we'll be there. But, Deputy Ned said you wouldn't charge her for hitting me if I didn't press charges."

"Well, Colton, Ned told me he saw her hit you with the cane, and when I asked her, she confessed."

Feeling guilty, Colton asked, "Will she go to jail for hitting me?"

The Prosecutor did not answer Colton's question. He told him they would discuss the matter at the meeting, and not to worry about it.

Colton put his cell phone in his pocket and pushed the locker room door open. He stopped because he heard two students yelling at each other in the hallway. Colton didn't eavesdrop on conversations, but he could tell by their voices who they were.

Jenny Stillmore yelled, "Luke, I am going to the pep assembly, with or without you."

"No! I said we're getting out of here early, and you don't get a say. Understood?"

"Ow! You don't have to hit me every time you want something. Ow! Stop it Luke."

"I'll stop when you stop acting like a child. We don't need this school spirit crap. We're adults and can do what we want."

Colton could hear Jenny crying. "Why do you always hurt me, Luke?"

"You know I'm sorry, honey, but I want to spend time outside of school with you. I love you, Jenny."

The two walked past the locker room, but didn't see Colton standing behind the door. When they left, he ran into the gym where Coach Talbert introduced the team members and questioned where Colton was.

"Here I am, Coach." Colton yelled.

As Colton took his place in the team line, the students stood and chanted, "Colton, Colton, Colton…"

***

After the assembly, Colton told Seth and Lacie that he needed to talk to them. He asked Seth to drive Lacie home, and he agreed.

"I have practice in fifteen minutes, but I want to tell you what I saw before the assembly. Jenny and her boyfriend, Luke, were fighting in the hallway. I overheard them and he hit her at least once."

"I told you he was the one abusing her," Lacie said.

"We should go beat him up and see how he likes it," Seth suggested.

"No! Hitting him won't fix the problem," said Lacie. "The last time I talked to her I gave her information about the safe house in Bad Axe, and the Hotline. If she wants help, she knows how to get it."

"Lacie is right, Seth. We have to get her away from that creep, but she has to make the ultimate decision." Colton said. "Jenny has to accept blame because she is allowing this to happen to her."

"That's what Trudy said," Lacie added.

"You mean the old woman who lives on The Point?" asked Seth.

"Yes. She is a psychiatrist, and she helped Lacie and I better understand abusive relationships," said Colton.

"We'll just have to hope she asks for our help. Then, and only then, can we help get her away from that creep," Lacie said.

As they walked out the back door of the school, Colton told Seth about the meeting in Bad Axe.

"Will this be like last month, when they let those Hampton guys go free after they beat us up?" he asked.

"According to the district attorney, the old woman pleaded guilty to the charges against her and she will pay me for the newspapers she stole."

"Good. I hope they throw her in jail for a few years to teach her a lesson," said Seth. "You know… old people shouldn't steal stuff; it isn't right."

Laughing, Colton said, "What about young people? It's not right for anyone to steal from me."

"It looks worse when an old person breaks the law. They know better."

Lacie stopped at Seth's Charger and watched the two guys joking. She added, "I thought you had something to tell me, Colton."

Colton turned toward Lacie and told her what the district attorney said. She urged him not to get upset if he lets her off without going to jail.

"She must have a family. Just think about how much she suffered from humiliation already. To send an old woman to jail would just be too much." she said.

"You're right, but if she didn't want to go to jail she shouldn't have stolen my papers. If a teenager had stolen something, what would happen to them?"

"Their parents would have paid the bill, and the kid would have gotten off with a slap on their wrists," said Lacie. "You know it happens all the time."

"Yes, but that doesn't make it right," said Colton."If they were poor though, they would end up in jail or on probation."

Looking across the flat fields of dried corn, Lacie thought about the inequality between the rich and poor kids. Her family was not poor, but many things like vacations, snowmobiles, and fancy cars were out of their reach.

"You're right, Colton. Everyone should be treated the same," she said.

"Wow, that's a first. I'm right?"

Lacie laughed and put her hand on Colton's arm. "Yes, that's a first."

"Are we done? If not, give me the keys and I'll drive myself home."

"We're done," said Colton. "Seth, I'll see you in Bad Axe at ten."

Colton opened the door for Lacie, blew her a kiss, and started back to the school locker room. He could see that most of the team was already on the field, so he hurried to get dressed.

Chapter 9

As Colton ran onto the field, he heard Coach Talbert call for the men to circle him. He told them the practice would be a simple exercise to help them stay in shape.

"Men, Saturday afternoon we will play against a team we have never played. Like our school, Pewamo-Westphalia High School is in farm country, between Grand Rapids and Lansing. Trust me, the team comprises big farm boys. After we practice, we'll watch a video of their last game. They have our speed, ambition, and came close to winning the state playoffs last year. This year they want a state championship for their retiring coach. You must break their coaches heart by not letting them ruin our dream. We have two games to play in the regional competition. The first win takes us one step closer to the regional trophy Saturday afternoon. And then we will win the next game and become the Regional Champs," Coach said as the team cheered.

Aden yelled, "We will bring the trophy home for you, Coach."

"That's the spirit! Now, let's practice. Remember, I don't want injuries; so we're just working on our skills." Coach warned, "Don't kill each other."

It was an easy practice, and the Loons were in a great mood. The video proved the Pirates were an impressive team. Coach pointed out several of the Pirates' star players. The quarterback was not as fast as Aden, but he could throw better than most college players.

"If the quarterback gets his sight on a receiver, he will make the throw. We have to keep him too busy to see any receivers," Coach said.

Aden pointed out that in this video it looked like the Pirates threw passes more than they ran the ball.

Coach agreed, but added, "Like us, they change with the game. If need be, they can run. And when they run, they run hard and fast."

Colton injected, "Then we will run harder and faster."

"Yes! I want you in top shape for Saturday's big game. We'll do workouts and lift weights every afternoon, except Friday. Friday's a half day at school, and I want you to rest. Saturday at 9:00 am the bus will leave school. We'll stop for a light Lunch in Caro, and then we'll head for Reese High School to face the Pewamo-Westphalia Pirates."

Coach added, "I have tickets for your families, and more are available in the office at a student discount. Let's make sure there is a big crowd cheering for us. Trust me... it helps. Tell your friends we need them. They can ride the buses if they need a ride."

Aden asked if Colton was having an after game party.

"No, we won't get home early enough, so Lacie and I plan on watching a movie or something."

"Sounds like a smart move, but I want to party down after we win the game," Aden said.

"Well good luck finding a party. Lacie and I want to get home and enjoy the victory by ourselves. Perhaps we can have a party Sunday afternoon."

"Let me know so I can tell Kathy. We both enjoy going to your parties." Aden said, as he started out the locker room door.

"OK! I'll let you know, Aden," said Colton.

Colton didn't follow Aden into the parking lot. He turned and walked into Coach Talbert's office.

"Coach, I need to ask you about something that happened in school today."

As Colton described what he witnessed before the assembly, he saw Coach's concern.

"Are they aware you were there?" he asked.

"No. Coach, I need to know how I can help Jenny. No one deserves abusive treatment, but I don't know what to do."

"I'll report what you saw to the school office tomorrow and they can look into the situation. Please, Colton, don't get involved. You can't do anything to help her. She has to take action herself, and if you ask her, she would say he did nothing wrong."

"That's what she told Lacie.. Lacie gave her some numbers to call in Bad Axe, but I'm sure Jenny hasn't called for their help," said Colton.

Placing his hand on Colton's shoulder, Coach Talbert smiled and said, "I've seen this before, Colton. In fact my wife's sister had an abusive relationship with her husband, and there was no way we could convince her to get help. She ended up in the hospital with head injuries, and he landed in jail. You know, she blames herself for what happened. That's the twisted truth about abuse. It's hard to understand the reasons Jenny stays in an abusive relationship. She may feel trapped. He could be the nicest man she has ever been with, and after he hits her, he makes her feel like it was all her fault. But remember, she is the only one who can seek help. If we see him hurt her, we can call the police, but I hope she doesn't end up in the hospital like my sister-in-law, injured and blaming herself."

"Well, thanks for the help. I won't do anything stupid. but I hope someone stops him before she gets hurt."

"Like I said, I'll tell the office. They know how to deal with this kind of problem."

***

Colton pulled into his driveway and noticed that both his mom and dad were home. He parked the Jeep and ran into the back door.

"Mom... Dad... I'm home," he yelled.

"In the kitchen, Colton," his mom said, "Your brothers and sister are upstairs, tell them dinner is ready, and wash your hands."

Colton ran up the stairs and told his siblings to get ready for dinner. He then changed out of his school clothes and into an old pair of jeans and his favorite Loons tee shirt. Checking his phone, he saw that Lacie had texted him while he drove home. He read the text, "Got job - working two hours Sunday afternoon - Sorry."

So much for the party, Colton thought as he ran down the stairs.

"Grab a plate and help yourself, Colton. It's buffet style tonight," said Colton's mom.

Colton looked over the offerings on the kitchen counter. Hamburgers, potato salad, green beans with bacon, baked beans, roast beef, and a tossed salad. He filled his plate and took a place at the large kitchen table.

"Why so much food, Mom?" he asked.

"It's everything left over from the last two days," she replied. "You know the routine. Nothing new until we use up the leftovers."

Terry said, "It tastes just as good as it did yesterday, Mom."

"Better." said Jason.

"Well... thank you boys; I glad you like my food," Cyndi said, grinning with pride.

"So, Colton," Adam said, "I hear you have to be in Bad Axe for Mrs. Wilding's court date."

"Yes, but how did you hear about it? I got the call today."

"I have my sources."

"Is your source Detective Wooddell?"

"Yes! Ned Wooddell," Colton's dad said with a chuckle. "He called today and asked if I planned to be there with you."

"Do you want to go?" Colton asked.

"Only if you feel you need me. It would require my taking time off, but that is doable."

"I appreciate the offer, but I can handle it. This fall I've gotten a lot of experience dealing the authorities in Bad Axe, and this case will be a piece of cake." Colton said.

"Cake? Are we having cake, too?" asked Terry, looking around the kitchen.

"No, Terry. That's just an expression," said Adam. "Your mom has cookies in the jar, so if you need something sweet grab one after you clean your plate."

"Sorry, Adam," Cyndi said. "I ate the last one this afternoon. If you want dessert, I have pumpkin pie and ice cream."

"Mom, you're the greatest," said Stephenie. "I want to grow up to be a good cooker like you."

"Great. You can start by clearing the table and washing the dishes."

"That's not fair, Mom."

"All part of the job, Steph. Good cooks clean up after themselves."

"I vote we appoint a bus boy to help Stephenie with the dishes," said Adam.

Jason and Terry both said, "Not me."

Adam appointed both while he and Colton took their dessert into the den to talk. There was a heated argument about who would do what job. Cyndi settled the matter, and the three worked without further comments.

***

Colton and his dad had a long discussion about Colton's plan to become a detective. Adam questioned why he wanted to go into law enforcement, and Colton explained that he discovered it excited him, because he loved the puzzle aspect of figuring out who did what and then building a case of evidence.

Even though he wasn't tired, he knew the route would require him to be alert, so he excused himself and went to his room. Because it is hunting season, there will be more deer on The Point. It's strange, he considered, how deer seem to be aware that there is no hunting on residential property. Colton is obsessive about his Jeep and doesn't want to hit a deer while doing the newspaper route. Since he started the route, there have been several close calls, but no deer/Jeep impacts. It took almost an hour for him to drift off into a deep sleep.

When his alarm clock woke him, he remembered dreaming about football, but he wasn't sure if his team won or lost. With only a few days until the big regional competition, Colton's mind kept returning to football. He realized that all he can do is play to the best of his ability, but he wanted to win with all of his heart.

After a quick trip to the bathroom for a shower, he dressed in his school clothes, just in case the route took longer than usual. *If I'm dressed for school and I am late, at least I won't have to go to school looking like the freak in pajamas again,* he thought.

The newspapers were already at the storage shed and he started his deliveries early. There were hundreds of deer, but Colton made sure he wasn't close to hitting any. As he turned onto the main road at The Point, he noticed two dead deer in the street, along with broken glass and assorted car body parts. Someone wasn't watching for deer because from the evidence it was quite a crash.

He stopped for a moment to study the scene. Walking around with his flashlight, he determined that the vehicle was a newer Lexus. The drivers' side headlamp, quarter panel and hood was severely damaged. There were no fluid leaks, so the vehicle was drivable, however the steering was probably difficult as it appeared that the drivers' front wheel could have been damaged. The two deer were dead and mangled.

For the safety of other drivers, Colton put gloves on and pulled the deer carcass to the side of the road. He then moved the larger auto parts to the side.

As he got into the Jeep, he wondered if he would see the damaged Lexus. It took a moment to find where his audiobook had left off, but once he found the spot, he was back in action.

Driving down the main street of The Point, he was careful to check his list of customers who had a stop order placed on their account.

Many families, from Detroit and the Metro area, only use their homes on The Point for Summer vacations. During the fall and winter their home is closed up; minimal heat and no water. They may return for a Christmas party, but often they spend the entire winter in places like Florida, Texas, or Arizona.

Colton thought for a moment about how nice it would be to have enough money to own two homes. One for summer, and another for winter. Then he noticed a rental moving van in the driveway of one of his customers. He checked his list and saw that the Livingston family had left for Florida last week. That's odd, he thought. I wonder why they would be moving stuff now. They usually leave all the furniture in their summer cottage.

Using caution, Colton drove past the driveway and stopped a few doors down from the Livingston's house. He got out of the Jeep and moved secretly around, staying behind the trees and shrubs. When he reached the driveway, he listened. There were several men talking. One man said, "Check the bedroom again, and let's move this big television out. Come on men, we don't have all night. Get a move on."

Colton slid back behind a pine tree when he heard the door open. He watched two men carry a huge flat screen television out. As they loaded it into the truck, one man stopped. "Did you hear that?" he asked.

"Hear what?" replied the second man.

"Nothing, I guess. Come on, I'm getting edgy. We've taken too long here, we need to move out." he said.

Colton wanted to call the police, but realized that the light from his cell phone would draw attention to him. And if these weren't criminals, but were instead the family picking up things for their trip to Florida, he would be in trouble with the police, again.

He moved a little closer, but he couldn't see the van's license number. He decided to stay out of the police radar tonight. Not that Colton got into trouble, it was that trouble seemed to follow him. Since Colton would like to become a police detective, he considered his actions in a new light.

Colton returned to his route and finished up his store and rack deliveries in Caseville. As he drove out of the Clark Gas Station parking lot, he saw a youngster standing at the side of the road, waving his hands. Colton wanted to just wave and drive on, but he knew this kid.

Colton rolled down the passenger window and yelled, "Hey Tony, what's up?"

"Colton, I need your help," said Tony in broken English.

About a month ago, Colton got beat up and sent to the hospital trying to help Tony, an illegal immigrant who worked with him at a large dairy farm. He was not in the mood for a beating again, but he was curious, so he asked, "What do you need me to do this time, Tony?"

"Señor, Colton. I fear the man who was hurting my family is out of jail again. He will hurt my family and even my family in Mexico," Tony said. Tears were filling his big brown eyes and Colton's heart was touched.

"I thought Bill Smittwell would go to jail forever. What happened?"

"Papa wouldn't tell the police what he did, because Smittwell told us our family in Mexico will be killed by the drug gangs if Papa talks to the Judge. We come from a bad area of Mexico. There are much drugs and gangs and they kidnap people and sell them to Americans for slaves."

"Do the police know why your dad wouldn't testify?"

"No. Papa is terrified of the police. He still thinks they might send us away from America."

"How can I reach you if I get information that could be helpful?" Colton asked.

"I have a phone," Tony said, pulling the small cell phone out of his pocket. "It is cheap, but it works good."

Tony and Colton exchanged numbers and Colton promised that

he would do whatever he could to help his family.

"Thank you. Thank you so much. I knew you would help, Colton. You are a good man."

"I don't know about that, but I know that no one should be able to threaten you and treat your family like slaves."

As he finished his route, he realized that he would reach school on time. Relief flooded his mind. As he drove, he considered the men who were moving items from his customer's home. *What if they were stealing, and I let them go free? Should I have called the police? How bad will I feel if my customer discovers I did nothing to help them?* Then he considered the young illegal immigrant, Tony Lopez's plight. *And, why am I so eager to help Tony, when I'm afraid to report a possible theft?*

He pulled into the school parking lot, parked next to Aden's Camaro, and headed toward the school entrance. Colton stopped for a moment and called Lacie's Uncle, Deputy Ned Wooddell. He gave Ned the address of the suspected robbery and described the van.

Ned thanked him for the information and said he would look into the matter.

"It's the least I can do, Ned. I'm just sorry I wasn't able to get a plate number from the van."

Chapter 10

Colton stopped at his locker and looked for Lacie. She stood next to her locker and waved for him to come to her. He grinned and walked down the hall, stopping in front of her; his face was a few inches from hers.

"Well?" she asked.

"Do I get a kiss?" he asked.

She smiled and kissed him on the forehead. "Like that?" she asked.

"No. Like this," he said as he kissed her lips.

"Oh. Yes! That's nice, Colton. So, how was your paper route this morning?" she asked.

Colton leaned back against the wall of lockers and said, "Interesting. I think I might have witnessed a robbery, and I talked to Tony Lopez, the illegal immigrant kid I helped last month. Tony says he needs my help again because someone kidnapped his grandmother in Mexico as a way to force his dad to drop charges against the creep who tried to molest his sister. I'm not sure how I can help him. As for the robbery, I'm uncertain that's what I witnessed, so I didn't call the police. I wanted to prove I don't always have to get involved."

"But if you saw a robbery, you should have called the police," responded Lacie with a puzzled look on her face. "Why would you think it was correct to avoid reporting a robbery to the police?"

"Because every time I call them when I'm on my route, it seems like I'm the one who gets criticized. I get in trouble and have to explain to everyone what I did and prove to them I didn't do what they think

I did. Earlier this morning I reported the robbery to your Uncle Ned. He said he would look into it and thanked me for keeping my eyes open."

Colton had convinced himself that he took the right action by not calling the police to report the robbery, but now Lacie was questioning his actions. "You think I should have tried to stop them? You know, I would have waited an hour for the police to arrive. By the time the police arrived, the crooks would have be gone and I would have to convince the police I wasn't drunk or on drugs. Lacie… I can't win!"

"Awe, I think you need a hug, Colton," she said as she put her arms around his shoulders. "Everything will be OK. I'm just glad you called Uncle Ned."

"I also needed to talk to the police about Tony Lopez. His family is being blackmailed. Bill Smittwell, the guy who was keeping all the immigrants in his farmhouse, is out of jail and he's back to his old tricks."

"Hey, lovebirds, take it outside," chided Seth, as he approached the couple. "You know you're not supposed to be touching each other in the hallways. I think it's a school rule."

"You're just jealous, Seth," said Lacie, as she pulled her arms away from Colton. "I have to make my way down the hall for my first hour class. So now you boys can play by yourselves. Have fun in Bad Axe."

"Bye, Lacie," said Colton. "I'll text you when I find out what's happening with the old lady."

"That reminds me, Seth. We have to go to the office to get a permission slip to leave our second hour class."

The two walked down the halls toward the school office. As they walked, it seemed like everyone wanted to give Colton a high-five, or congratulate him. It's nice being a star football player, he thought.

The first bell rang, just as Colton and Seth walked into the office. Miss Downer, the school secretary, handed the two a permission slip to leave early. "I'm sure this is what you boys want," she said. "Now, get to class or you'll need a late pass too."

***

When Colton entered Mr. Sellerman's classroom, he handed him the permit to leave early.

"I hope you're not in trouble with the Bad Axe police again, Colton."

"No, Sir. I have to be at a hearing for an old woman we caught stealing newspapers from my paper rack in Caseville."

Mr. Sellerman laughed, "You are pressing charges on an old lady for stealing a newspaper?"

"Not *a* newspaper, Sir. Hundreds of Sunday newspapers. Each worth two dollars," Colton added. He already felt guilty about charging the old woman, but he didn't like being ridiculed by Mr. Sellerman.

"Oh, I'm sorry. That makes more sense. When the time comes, you can just leave, or do you want me to remind you?"

"I'll remember, but thank you for the offer," Colton said. He turned and walked to his desk. A few students wanted to know what his conversation was about, but Mr. Sellerman asked them to stop talking as he took attendance.

Fifteen minutes before the end of the class, Colton got up and walked to the door. Mr. Sellerman smiled and excused him.

Colton dropped his books at his locker and watched Seth walking down the hall toward him. "Are you ready to go too?" Seth asked.

"I am now, but will you drive to Bad Axe? There isn't enough gas in my Jeep and I would rather fill up in Pigeon after school. We have an account there."

"I can drive, but I must drive slow, since I don't want to get a ticket driving to the courthouse to talk with a Judge. That would be a huge mistake, wouldn't it?"

Colton laughed as they exited the building. It seemed strange leaving the school without everyone else clamoring for the exit.

"Seth, I have something important to ask. I want no jokes or puns for an answer because it's serious."

"Crap. Are you breaking up with me?" Seth asked.

"What part of *no joking* didn't you understand?"

Seth pulled out of the parking lot and headed east toward Bad Axe. "OK. I'm listening. So let me have it with that *serious* question."

Colton took a deep breath and said. "You're always talking about how we should go into business and become detectives so we can find more mysteries to solve. How serious are you?"

"Is this a joke, Colton?"

"No! You are aware I've been talking about becoming a police officer after I leave high school. Well, I was wondering what your plans are. What do you want to do with the rest of your life?"

"I don't want to be a police officer. That is out of the picture, but like I told you last week, I'm working on becoming a security expert. Computer security and home and business protection is a big business now, and I would also enjoy being a detective or investigator. Solving a mystery is fun too."

Seth turned toward Colton as he waited for his response. "Well, aren't you going to say something?"

Colton stared ahead in deep meditation. "Yes... I like your ideas and I don't want to be a policeman either. I know that's what I said I wanted, but I hate following orders."

"Are you crazy? You always walk the straight and narrow. You're the poster boy for good behavior."

"And I hate it," Colton said with a big grin filling his face. He looked at Seth and added. "Let's start a business. *C & S Investigations* or perhaps *C & S Security*."

"Oh sure. And why would the C come before the S?"

"Because it does in the alphabet."

As they drove through Elkton, they were both considering their options. Colton considered the ramifications of going into business. Seth would make a great partner, and if they work hard, they may make enough money before graduation to attend college without borrowing money or asking their parents for help. Colton always admired how some teenagers made a fortune before they left school. Perhaps He and Seth would be as successful as the students he read about on the internet.

Seth broke the silence when he stopped for the light at Pinnebog Road. He checked both directions and drove through "So, we will start a business?" he asked.

"I'm game if you are," Colton replied.

"Hot damn... I'm in. Now what?"

"We need to register the name in the courthouse and set up a business plan. I'm not sure if we should incorporate, form a partnership, or set up an L.L.C. Once we set up the business, all we'll need are customers," Colton said.

Seth stopped at M-53 and turned south toward downtown Bad Axe. "My dad's business is an L.L.C. and he seems to like that arrangement. Instead of C & S Investigations, we should call our business *C & S Security*. I'll agree to that name, if you agree that we are 50-50 in this venture."

Colton didn't need time to think. He said, "Deal."

They pulled up to the courthouse and found a parking spot on Main Street. Seth asked, "Will the meeting go past the two hour parking limit?"

Colton laughed. "The police never check the cars parked along this street," he said.

***

Being in business thrilled Colton. The prospect had been on his mind for the past several months. When Seth brought up the idea in the past, he almost said yes, but he needed time to consider all the ramifications. Now he can concentrate on the new business, instead of the prospect of having one. He was sure this new venture would fit well with his newspaper delivery job, and he wasn't worried about it interfering with his school work. He has a 4.0 grade point average and couldn't see how that would change. Seth may have to work a little harder. Colton wasn't sure how good his grades were, but he believed they were below his.

They entered the courthouse from the south and as they walked down the long hallway, Seth pointed out Sheriff McNabb at the far end of the hallway, talking with District Attorney, Mark Bagley. The boys knew the Sheriff from past run-ins.

The middle-aged, gray-haired County Sheriff walked up to them and shook their hands. "Well boys, I hear you're still hunting criminals. You two are just what we need in this county... more citizen involvement. Colton, I want to talk with you and Seth after your meeting with Mr. Bagley."

He turned to the District Attorney and said, "Mark, call me when you and the boys finish with the Judge, and if possible, I'd appreciate you sitting in on our meeting."

"Will do, Sir. I'd be happy to meet with the three of you." He turned to Seth and Colton, "This way boys; the Judge is waiting for us."

Mr. Bagley opened the door of the District Courtroom. There were several people sitting in the back of the room on the benches, and Mrs. Wilding was behind a table with a younger man, who appeared to be her attorney. She was smiling and whispering to him. When she noticed Seth and Colton, her smile disappeared and she looked down, perhaps in shame.

Mr. Bagley directed Colton and Seth to sit with him at the prosecutor's table, a few feet from Mrs. Wilding and her lawyer. He whispered, "Don't worry about anything. We have a made a deal with Mrs. Wilding and her attorney, and this is just a formality. District Judge Anderson will ask a few questions, and then he'll sentence her."

The room was silent when the Judge entered from behind the bench. "All rise," the bailiff announced.

Just as Colton and Seth stood, the Judge said, "Please be seated."

Colton smiled at Seth.

After introductions of the plaintiff, defendant, and Colton and Seth the Judge spoke about the charges against Mrs. Wilding. There was one charge of theft under $1000.00, and two assault and battery charges involving the plaintiffs Colton Blackwell and Seth Seamoore. He then announced that today he would sentence the defendant. He asked, "Are there any objections? Mrs. Wilding, do you plead guilty to one charge of theft under $1000.00 and a single charge of assault involving the plaintiffs Colton Blackwell, and Seth Seamoore? Do you understand the charges being brought against you?"

At her lawyers urging, Mrs. Wilding stood. She looked toward Seth and Colton and then back toward Judge Anderson. Colton noticed tears were running down her face. His heart was aching for her, and he wished she had never stolen his newspapers and hit him and Seth with her cane, but he couldn't change history.

Mrs. Wilding said. "Yes, Your Honor, I understand the charges."

"Mrs. Wilding, are you pleading guilty to these charges?" Judge Anderson asked.

"Yes, Sir. I plead guilty to the charges."

She looked like she wanted to say more ... perhaps explain why, or ask for forgiveness, but her lawyer took her hand and asked her to sit back down.

The judge looked toward Colton and Seth as if to speak to them. He said, "These charges that Mrs. Wilding has plead guilty to are very serious. I accept her plea, and would now like to consider her sentence. We often allow several weeks between a verdict and sentencing of a defendant. But Mr. Jackson, Mrs. Wilding's attorney, said his client would like to finish this matter today. Mr. Bagley, do you have any objection?"

"No, Your Honor. I have no objections."

"Mr. Jackson, I understand your client will make a statement to the court?"

"Yes, Sir."

"Then I would like the defendant to step forward and take the witness chair."

The elderly woman, walked forward and stepped up and into the chair. She put her cane down and looked at the Judge with pleading eyes.

Mrs. Wilding's attorney stood and walked toward the judge's bench and his client. "Your Honor, my client would like to apologize to the court and the boys she assaulted."

He turned to the old woman and said, "Having pledged to tell the truth; Mrs. Wilding, please tell the court how you came to be here today."

"Your honor, last year I lost my husband after fifty years of marriage. He was my world. I married when I was eighteen and my entire life was wrapped around his. He took care of me, like my Dad took care of my mom, and my grandfather, his wife. My skills revolved around housework and taking care of our children. When Edgar died, I didn't know how to pay the bills, fix things around the house, or anything. I found that *our* so called *friends*, were *his* friends. He would arrange a get-together with his friends and I tagged along and visited with the wives. I tried to ask my family for help, but they thought I was being a silly old woman. They offered to help me with this or that, when they were around, but they weren't around often. Someone suggested I join the Senior Citizen Club, and that's when it all started with the newspapers," she said, looking toward Colton.

"I bought a newspaper every Sunday and clipped out the coupons. One day at the Senior Center, I brought in my coupon collection and asked if anyone would like some. I was the *bell of the ball.* All the ladies wanted my coupons. It made me feel important, and I wanted that feeling to continue. You know what I mean?"

"But I only had a few coupons to give away, and I had to wait until the next Sunday's paper. That's when I stole more newspapers. I figured that the big newspaper company wouldn't mind if I took a few extras. Soon I was taking almost all of them. It was like an addiction;

I couldn't stop myself, so I took all the newspapers home, cut out the coupons and give them to my new friends. They loved me, 'cause I was the coupon lady."

Mr. Jackson interrupted. "How long did this go on, Mrs. Wilding?"

"I was taking papers for about a month before these boys caught me last Sunday. Lord, they scared the dickens out of me. I knew I was doing wrong, but when I saw them I didn't know what to do. I tried to act like they were in the wrong when the police showed up, but Ned, the deputy, made me tell the truth, and I'm glad I did. Now I'll be able to get help. I understand that I have a problem, and I need to get help. The nice doctor told me I have to learn to love myself for who I am. My husband is dead and I have to live on."

She wiped tears from her eyes and opened her purse. "I want to pay for the papers I took, and I want these two boys to know I am sorry I hit them with my cane. I need to pay my debt to the community because I know I was wrong."

"Your honor," Mr. Jackson said, "I ask for leniency in your sentencing of my client. What Mrs. Wilding did was criminal, but we are not dealing with a hardened criminal. She is a lonely woman searching for her place in the community after her husband's death."

He turned to the district attorney's table and handed the check to Colton. "Colton, accept our apology and this payment for your troubles."

Colton took the check and showed it to Seth. The amount surprised him. "Your Honor," Colton said. "This is too much. There were less than a five hundred dollars worth of papers missing and Mrs. Wilding gave me a check for three thousand dollars."

"Colton, that is the amount she wanted you to have. Is that correct, Mrs. Wilding?"

She nodded and smiled. "I wanted to give you more, but my lawyer said no."

Colton sat down, saying thank you.

Mr. Jackson walked back to the table and sat down. The Judge looked toward the prosecuting attorney and said, "Mr. Bagley, have you prepared a statement?"

"Yes, Your Honor. The prosecution agrees that Mrs. Wilding has suffered enough and we ask the court for leniency."

District Judge Anderson looked toward Mrs. Wilding and asked her to stand. "Considering the circumstances of your actions, I will not sentence you to the standard 30 days in jail. Instead, I am sentencing you to six months of probation and $500.00 court costs. I also order you to continue with counseling. You are excised, Mrs. Wilding."

"Thank you, Your Honor," replied Mrs. Wilding.

After thanking her lawyer and Mr. Bagley, Mrs. Wilding hugged Colton and Seth and again apologized for hitting them.

After she walked away with her lawyer, the prosecuting attorney reminded the two teens that Sheriff McNabb would be in his office for their meeting. Seth turned to Colton and whispered, "Any idea what this is about?"

"Not a clue," replied Colton. "I guess we'll find out soon, though."

Chapter 11

In the hallway, Seth tapped Colton on the shoulder, "I need to hit the men's room."

"Same here."

They told Mr. Bagley and went down the hall and turned right. Standing at the urinal, Seth asked, "Do you plan on telling them about our new business venture?"

"Only if they ask," responded Colton as he zipped his jeans. "They'll know soon, but I'd rather it be later. I have a few things to tell the Sheriff though. I promised Lacie I would talk to the police about a potential robbery I witnessed on The Point, and then there's Tony, the Latino boy who's still having trouble."

"You mean the illegal kid you helped a few months ago? What's wrong with him, now?"

"More of the same crap as before. He said drug dealers kidnapped his grandmother in Mexico."

Mr. Bagley and Sheriff McNabb were standing in the hallway waiting for Colton and Seth.

"Come on boys, I haven't got all day," grumbled the Sheriff. "I have some important matters to discuss with the two of you."

Colton and Seth took a seat in front of Mr. Bagley's desk. The Sheriff sat in Mr. Bagley's chair making him stand next to the bookcase.

"Colton, I understand that You and Seth are thinking about starting a detective business. Tell me about it because I have ideas to help the two of you."

Colton almost fell off the chair while Seth chuckled.

"What's so funny, Seth?" asked the sheriff.

"We didn't plan on telling anyone until later," Seth said. "So Colton, I guess this is later?"

"I guess. Sheriff, I believe you've been talking to Lacie's uncle Ned."

"Yes, and I even called your dad and talked to him. I want to talk the two of you into working with my men. Colton, you have a nose for trouble, and we need someone like you to keep their eyes open and report back to us. Now, tell me about your plans, and don't waste words."

Colton took a deep breath and said, "I had considered becoming a police detective, but after talking to Seth I agreed to start a security business. We'll offer a home, business, and Cybersecurity solutions in the area, and as we grow, like I expect we will, we can expand into the Metro area."

"Sounds like a plan, but you need an education to accomplish that. If you plan on being a private eye, you need to know he law to find your way around it. I want the two of you to sign up for the class I teach at the Tech Center, here in Bad Axe. It's an accredited program and will count both toward high school and college credit."

Seth looked at Colton, "That's a great idea, Colton. There are students going to the Tech Center from our school, and we'd learn the tricks of the trade."

"Tricks? Boy, I don't teach tricks. It's science, math, psychology, and the law. These classes help you deal with people and their rights."

Seth looked embarrassed and replied, "Sorry, I didn't mean to be disrespectful. I'm not sure your course will fit into our plans for graduation because we need specific class credits."

"That's the beauty of this program. You'll get credit for your math and English requirements, and specific credits for several colleges. It's a two-year program, but if you let me get you into next semester's class, I know you can make up the first semester. Trust me, I'll get you through the program," the Sheriff said.

Mr. Bagley added, "This would be a good choice should you want to go into law. Colton, with your ability, you would make a great lawyer."

Colton looked at Seth who was beaming with excitement. "What do you think?" he asked.

"I love the idea, and if it helps us succeed in our business, what more could we want?"

"OK. I guess we're in. Now we have to talk to the school to make all kinds of changes to our schedule," suggested Colton.

"I already took care of that," said Sheriff McNabb. Sign this paperwork."

The Sheriff handed a sheet of paper to both Seth and Colton. "Sign here, and you are in the program. You will start in January at the start of the second semester. You must pass the exam to get credit for the first semester which you've missed, but I'll help you pass that exam."

Colton looked at Seth, and then he turned to the Sheriff and said, "Thank you Sir. We'll take the paper with us. I don't want to sign anything without talking to my parents. Seth," he added, turning his head toward his friend, "don't you agree?"

"Yea, my dad will want to be a part of this decision."

"If you must, but don't waste too much time. It's important that we get this going as soon as possible," insisted the Sheriff.

Colton and Seth agreed to have their decision soon. After thanking the Sheriff they headed outside. There was a light snow covering the parking lot, and it took a minute for Seth to find his car.

Seth started his Charger and let the car idle. "Well, are we going to do this, or not?" He asked.

Colton was in deep thought. He turned to Seth and mumbled, "You can, but I'm not."

"Why?"

"Do you want to be under the spotlight of the Sheriff? Do you want to have them knowing our business before we even tell our friends?" Colton didn't give Seth time to answer. He turned to the window and said, "I want to do this on our own. We're smart enough to learn what we need to know without someone telling us. If we make mistakes, so be it. Damn it Seth, I don't want to be that man's *boy*."

Seth burst out laughing, "Damn right. We can do it without him."

"Colton, I like this new side of you. Being decisive looks good on you. So let's go back into the County Building and register our new business."

"Deal! There are two items I need to take care of. I forgot to ask the Sheriff about the robbery I reported on the Point and I still need to find out what the police know about Tony's grandmother. As soon as we're done, we have to get back to school."

The two returned to the County Building, to begin their new Security Agency. Beaming with pride they requested the business papers. While Seth waited for copies to take home for their parents signatures, Colton went into the Sheriff's office. The Sheriff wasn't there, but Deputy Ned was. After telling him what they decided, Ned handed Colton the information he wanted about the robbery on The Point and Tony's grandmother.

"Tell no one who gave you this, Colton, and I promise I won't share your business with the Sheriff, either/"

Seth walked in to the office as Colton said, "Great, Ned. I know that Seth and I will make mistakes, but I hope we can count on you for advice."

Colton and Seth walked out the County Building. Seth laughed as they approached the car. He tapped Colton on the shoulder and said, "I thought you didn't want the police to be in our business."

"Ned is almost family, and he's agreed to keep our business to himself, from now on."

"Good. It was a little unsettling when the Sheriff knew everything about our plans. Are you going to mention that to your girlfriend?"

Seth asked.

"That will take diplomacy, but I'm sure I can make her understand that she has to be careful what she says. When we have clients, there is a code of ethics we need to follow, like a Lawyer or Doctor."

"Well, Doc., we better get back to school. You have practice tonight and I have paperwork to complete so we can form the corporation."

***

Colton and Seth walked into the school fifteen minutes before the ball rang for the sixth hour. They handed Ms Walker the hall pass and sat at the table where Lacie and Jenny Stillmore were talking.

"Well, Lacie, I have to get back to my table. Seth, Colton, I hope you had a good day in court today."

Colton smiled as he sat down. "The judge convicted the thief, but she didn't have to go to jail."

"Good," said Lacie, "I didn't want that old lady to spend time behind bars. It isn't right."

Jenny laughed and turned to walk back to her table where several girls were studying. She turned her head back and said, "Lacie, please remember what I said about not telling anyone."

Colton took Lacie's hand and asked, "What was she talking about?"

"I can't say. I promised to keep her secret."

Seth laughed. He looked into Colton's eyes and asked, "Well, what do you have to say about secrets?"

"Later, Seth."

"No! Now, Colton." Seth insisted as he turned toward Lacie. "We learned the Sheriff and everyone in his department already knew Colton was thinking of becoming a policeman and that I was going into security. Any idea who told them that?"

Lacie's face turned several shades of red as she considered the question. "Well," she stammered. "I guess I'm not good at keeping secrets. But then... well... Colton never told me to keep it a secret. And besides.. ah... I'm sorry, guys."

Colton chuckled, "You're forgiven, but from now on we need to know you will respect our privacy. I mean, how can we run a security business if we can't keep secrets?"

"Fine," said Seth, "Now, Lacie, tell us what Jenny told you. All the juicy details."

"No!"

"Good!" Colton said as the bell rang for the seventh hour. "Lacie, I can see you're exercising your willpower. I'm very proud of you and I'll call tonight after practice so you can tell me what she said in private."

Chapter 12

Coach Talbert let the team off easy. After running a few plays they watched a video of the Pewamo-Westphalia Pirates, the team they will face Saturday. It surprised the Loons to see how powerful the Pirates were. Coach talked about their size and speed, and a few weeks ago they saw several short videos, but watching the Pirates in action again was an eye opener and a reminder of how hard it will be to beat them.

"Don't worry about how good *they* are," Talbert said, "Just remember how good *you* are when you're at the top of your game. We will be the regional champions if we play our best game, which I trust you will."

As Colton drove home it snowed and by the time he arrived, there was a good quarter inch on the roads. He was glad he didn't have to do his route tonight. As he opened the back door of the house, he heard a video game upstairs, the television in the family room, and soft rock music coming from the kitchen. It was a welcoming sound that defied the stillness of the falling snow outside.

"How are the roads?" his dad asked as Colton hung up his coat.

"Snow covered, but not too bad. I'm just glad I can stay home tonight."

The family talked weather, sports and news around the table, and after dinner Colton excused himself to work in his room.

Colton emailed Seth a list of his newspaper customers on The Point and an idea for a flyer they could mail to each.

Colton took out the information Deputy Ned Wooddell gave him earlier. The file was on Bill Smittwell, the Bad Axe man who claims to have kidnapped Tony's grandmother. There was no information in the file regarding the grandmother, so Colton called Tony.

Tony gave him his grandmothers telephone number and address. He said his father had tried to call many times and could not reach her. Mr. Smittwell warned his father that if he testified against him in court, his friends would kill the old woman in Mexico.

"Are you going to help us?" Tony asked.

"Yes. I'll make calls and see what I can find out," Colton replied. He wasn't sure what he could do to help, but he felt obligated to help the boy.

Colton dialed the number Tony gave him and received a recording advising that the number was no longer in service. He considered the situation and searched on the internet. It only took a few minutes to locate the number for the Police Chief of the small town where she lived.

Colton sat down and prepared himself for the call. Attempting to speak in Spanish he reached the Police Chief and told him about the situation with Tony's father and grandmother. The Policeman knew the elderly woman and the Lopez family.

"I have been trying to reach Mr. Lopez about his mother," the Chief stated. "We had to take her to the hospital a few weeks ago, and since there are no family members here she's being taken care of by the church. She's OK, but she cannot live alone, so we closed her home up and moved her into a home for the elderly."

Colton asked why she didn't call her son, and the Chief explained that she had a stroke and is suffering from a mild form of dementia. "I don't think she remembers he is in America. She keeps asking for him, but she talks about him like he never left home. She is being taken care of, but it is a sad situation."

Colton told the Police Chief that he would inform Mr. Lopez of the situation. He also told him about what had happened to the Lopez family here in Michigan.

"Ben Smittwell is a terrible man," the Police Chief said. "He better not come around here or I will put him in jail for a long time. I put many of his cohorts in jail already. They prey on the poor and promise them riches in America. Then they take all their money and often they don't even take them to America. There are many bodies between Mexico and America. Lost souls left to die along the dusty road. We feared Mr. Lopez and his family were among the dead. I hope you can help put that evil man behind bars."

It was a little after six when Colton finished talking with the Mexican Police Chief. He called Tony and gave him the information he had uncovered. Tony was very excited and said he would tell his father.

Colton was proud of what he had accomplished and went downstairs for a quick snack. He told his dad about his telephone calls. Colton was ready to go back to work in his room when his phone rang. It was Tony. He was almost hysterical.

"Help! Papa called Mr. Smittwell and told him he would tell the judge what he did, and now Mr. Smittwell is on his way over here. He said he will kill my father."

"Tony, you have to call the police for help. I can't stop Mr. Smittwell."

"No! Father says he will lose his green card if he gets into trouble. Please help, Colton."

Colton agreed to go over to Tony's but he said he would have to call the police if there is a fight. "The police will help, Tony. They want to put Mr. Smittwell behind bars. They don't want to harm your father."

Colton told his dad he had to go help Tony. His father asked if he needed his help. Not wanting to involve his dad he said no, but he did need help. As he walked toward the Jeep, he called Seth for backup.

***

The snow was still falling as Colton left to pick up Seth who was standing in the snow, waiting for Colton to arrive.

Holding two baseball bats, Seth jumped into the passenger seat of Colton's Jeep.

"Did I suggest somehow that we would play baseball tonight?" Colton asked sarcastically.

"No, but you said Mr. Smittwell was a mean dude and since I don't own a gun for protection, this is my next best choice."

"Let's hope we don't need them," Colton said. He drove back to the main road and turned toward Bad Axe. Tony and his family were living east of Bad Axe in a small rented farmhouse. Mr. Lopez was working for the farmer who owned the house, and both Tony and his young sister have been attending school in Bad Axe ever since their father got a visa to stay in Michigan. He and his family came into the country illegally, and Mr. Smittwell was charged with trafficking illegal immigrants. He only received a fine and got no jail time. There was evidence he molested Tony's sister, but his father refused to testify. Mr. Smittwell told him the Mexican thugs would kill his mother if he talked to the police.

The roads were becoming slippery with over two inches of snow on them. Luckily there was no wind, otherwise visibility would have been zero. As Colton approached the farmhouse, he noticed a red pickup truck parked in the driveway and Mr. Smittwell was pounding his fists on the front door,

"Get your ass out here Lopez. I called home and your mother will be dead before the night is over if you don't come with me," he yelled in Spanish.

"No, I will not go with you. I know my mother is safe and I will put you in jail for what you did to my little girl," Mr. Lopez yelled back.

Seth and Colton got out of the truck and started toward the house.

"Colton, can you tell what they are saying?" asked Seth.

"Yes! Mr. Smittwell, we found Tony's grandmother and we know where she is. There's a Mexican Police Chief who wants us to send you to him so he can put you in a nice jail," Colton teased.

"Colton, I should have gotten rid of you when I first met you. You've been nothing but a pain in my ass," Smittwell said as he started toward the boys. Colton held his ground and grabbed a bat.

"Do you like baseball, sir? I have a great swing and your face looks like a good target," Colton said.

Mr. Smittwell reached in his coat pocket and pulled out a handgun. "You can swing that bat all you want. It will only take one bullet to bring you down, boy."

Mr. Lopez was standing behind Mr. Smittwell with a fry pan. He took aim and hit the man in the back of his head.

"That must hurt," laughed Seth.

It may have hurt, but it didn't phase the large man. He reached out and grabbed Mr. Lopez's arm. Pointing the gun at his head while he dragged the man to his red truck. "Boys, don't follow us. I'm taking him with me and you'll never see him again."

"No," screamed Tony as he ran out of the house. By the time he reached the truck, Mr. Smittwell was already driving away. Come on, Tony, yelled Colton as he and Seth ran toward the Jeep. The three boys jumped into the Jeep and Colton followed the truck.

"Seth, call 911 and tell them what's happening."

"OK! But don't let them get away," Seth replied.

Colton was driving a little over forty five miles per hour. He couldn't overtake the red pickup but he was right on his tail.

"Colton, I have State Trooper Steve Lithowski on the phone. He's right behind us and wants you to pull over so he can talk to you," Seth said.

"Put it on speakerphone, Seth. Sir," Colton said to the Trooper, "Bill Smittwell has Mr. Lopez held in his truck at gunpoint. I'm following him and I won't stop until he does. You can plan on arresting him then, but be careful, he has a gun and said he will kill him."

"Colton," the state trooper yelled. "I've had enough of your foolish antics. Stop or I'll run you off the road."

Tony picked up the phone and yelled, "You are an idiot, señor. Please help my father. Mr. Smittwell is a terrible man and Colton is a good man. He's just trying to help."

Smittwell ran the light at the Pinnebog Road as he turned north. Colton followed him, trying not to spin out of control on the snow-covered road. When Smittwell turned left on Richardson Road, the state trooper tried to pass Colton, but he couldn't, because another truck was driving east. Colton pulled up close enough to the red pickup to hit his bumper when the passenger door flew open and Mr. Lopez jumped out, onto the side of the road. Colton slammed his brakes, Trooper Steve avoided hitting the Jeep by swerving around it. The Patrol car swerved past Colton, and ran into the side of the Bill Smittwell's truck, forcing it into the ditch.

Mr. Lopez jumped into the back seat of the Jeep as Colton and Seth watched the police car and pickup fly over the ditch. The police car stopped, but the pickup flew over a ridge and disappeared. Seth moaned, "It looks like Smittwell is getting away. Where did he go?"

"I don't know, Seth, but we better see if Trooper Steve got hurt. Are you injured Mr. Lopez?"

Tony's father said he was fine and glad he wasn't killed. Tony kept hugging his father and thanking Colton for saving him.

"You're welcome, Tony. You two stay in the Jeep, We're going out to help the Trooper," Colton said, as he opened the Jeep door.

The two ran to the patrol car. Trooper Steve was talking on the car phone. "Send a wrecker and make it fast. I don't know what happened to the other vehicle and driver, but I'll check it out now."

"Colton, you are in so much trouble. Why didn't you stop? That's resisting arrest and causing an accident. Get back to your vehicle and stay there. I will see if the other driver is OK."

Colton knew it would be useless to explain the facts to Trooper Steve. He's always had a grudge against him and Seth, even though they saved his life several weeks ago.

The trooper was standing on the ridge, pointing his flashlight.

"Colton. Seth. Come here and see what your foolishness caused."

Seth and Colton walked up the ridge and saw Mr. Smittwell sitting in his pickup truck, surrounded by a pool of manure. The red truck was sinking and the liquid manure was almost up to the window. He yelled, in a shrill voice, "Get me out of here. I don't want to drown in this crap."

The trooper looked at Colton and smiled. "Son, you caused this, you can go down there and help him out."

"Sir, you caused this. I was following him because he kidnapped Mr. Lopez at gunpoint. We told you that on the radio but you wouldn't listen. You never listen," Colton said.

Seth added, "Yes, and besides, it's your job, not ours. You're the State Trooper. We are just two high school students, trying to help. You save his sorry ass."

"Likely story," Steve said.

Colton whispered into Seth's ear and then called out to Mr. Smittwell, "Hey Bill, if you tell this officer why you kidnapped Mr. Lopez, I'll help save you. Otherwise you can drown in manure."

"You can't do that. I have my rights," cried Bill. As the liquid manure ran into the truck cab, he panicked and said, "OK! I kidnapped him. I didn't want him to testify against me. Help me, there are witnesses here. Don't let me die like this."

Seth walked back to the jeep and returned with a heavy rope that Colton keeps behind the back seat. "Here's the rope, Colton."

Colton took the rope and tossed it toward Mr. Smittwell. The end of the rope landed at the edge of the window and Bill grabbed hold of it.

Trooper Steve, Colton and Seth pulled on the rope. "Tony, we need you and your dad's help."

The group tugged on the rope until Smittwell was at the edge of the pond. When Trooper Steve saw the gun in Smittwell's hand, he walked forward and stepped on his hand. Smittwell cried out in pain as Steve bent down and took the gun. "Well, Mr Smittwell, it looks like these boys might have been telling the truth about you."

As Colton heard more sirens approaching, a voice behind him said, "Colton, do you need any help here?" It was Deputy Ned, followed by several men from the Emergency Fire and Rescue department.

Steve walked Mr. Smittwell to the road and yelled orders for the men to pull his patrol car out of the shallow ditch. "And don't dent my car. Deputy Ned, you will have to take the prisoner back to County Jail."

"But, Steve, he's covered in manure."

"Yes! Better your patrol car, than mine."

Grumbling, Ned led Smittwell into the road. After finding a large plastic bag he placed the prisoner into the back seat of his patrol car. "And if you touch anything, I will tell them not to let you shower until after your court appearance tomorrow."

While they pulled his car out of the ditch, Trooper Steve held his laptop and interviewed Colton, Seth, and Tony and his dad. When his car was out, he had them sit with him until he knew he had all the information he needed.

Trooper Steve said, "I'll take Mr. Lopez and his son back to Bad Axe. I have more questions for them, but the two of you can head back to Pigeon. Colton, I hear you and Seth are starting some kind of detective company. Please be careful; there is a lot you don't know, and I'd hate to see you behind bars for doing what you thought was a good deed."

Seth laughed, "We'll be careful, Sir."

Chapter 13

It was almost ten when Colton reached Seth's house. "Well, here we are," he said. "It looks like we're on a roll, doesn't it?"

Seth laughed, "Yes, but we're starting this business to make money, not just to help people."

"You're right." Colton replied. "We need to get down to the business of making money. I completed the corporation paperwork online and applied for all the licenses we need. We both need to sign the legal papers tomorrow. Since we're not eighteen yet, our parents will have to cosign the forms. I also sent you a list of the summer residents on the Point and a flyer we can mail. If you order the flyers tonight and send them the address list, they will print and mail them in one day. We can convince some of my newspaper customers to sign up for our security service."

Seth smiled, "Good going, Colton. I talked to dad, and he is our first customer. I'll order the security equipment we need, so if we play our cards right, we might make a profit in the first week of doing business."

"Send me a copy of the equipment and supply order so I can have Mom record the expense. Just order what we need, I trust your knowledge for purchases like that."

"Now I have to get my homework done, and you need to get home. At least it has stopped snowing, and it feels like it will warm up," Seth said.

"It should be nice and warm for the big game, Saturday."

"And you have to win. I want to be in business with a winner, not a loser. Understood?"

"Understood." Colton said, as Seth walked past his Jeep window. "Seth, I am glad we're in business together. I feel like this works into both of our dreams. And thank you for helping with Tony's dilemma."

"I enjoyed the adventure, and it's good knowing we put another bad person in jail."

"It sure is," mused Colton as he rolled up his window and backed out of the driveway.

Colton spent the evening thinking about football, then business and as he fell asleep, he was thinking about Lacie, hoping she will support him in his new business plans.

***

I drove around the office building until I found a safe parking space. There is no way I will park my new 1950 Jeep MC just anywhere. Detroit is a tough city with a reputation for rampant car theft.

My office is on the third floor of what was, in its heyday, a modern office building. Today it is a shabby, low rent building. Some contend that even rats would refuse to live here, but when you are a struggling private detective, you take what you can afford. A third-floor rat hole.

I took the stairs as the elevator hasn't worked for months. When I reached the door to my office, I stopped to admire the beautiful etched window of the heavy wood door. I ran my fingers across my name, Private Detective Colton Blackwell. There was extra fancy gold leaf trim running around the window.

When I entered the office, my beautiful secretary, Lacie, smiled at me. "I see you're still in love with that door," she said with a grin.

"You know it, Kid. When I move up to better digs, I'm taking that door with me, and you'll be there too."

"Nice to know, but please pick an office building with a working elevator. I had to take my heels off halfway up the stairs."

As we bantered, the door flew open and a tall, beautiful brunette stood in the doorway with a terrified look on her face.

"Help me," *she screamed.* "My boyfriend is trying to kill me. He may have followed me here."

I ran into the hallway, pushed the woman into my office, and locked the door.

As I calm her down, Lacie offered her a cup of coffee. She declined, but was thankful.

"Tell me all about this boyfriend of yours," I suggested.

She told of the abuse she's been suffering and how she has been trying to get away from him. Somehow, he found out about her plans, and this morning he told her she was a dead bitch walking. "I can't live this way," *she cried.*

I put my arm around her as we stood in front of the large office window. The city was coming to life as the sun broke through the clouds.

I heard a gunshot. I turned and saw the figure of a man outside the door. The glass of my beautiful office door shattered into a million pieces. I turned back to the woman and watched as she fell backwards into the glass window. It shattered and the last thing I saw was the bright red of her five inch heels. Lacie ran toward me, and we watched as the brunette floated down toward the street. My new Jeep stopped her fall. Blood covered the hood. I grabbed my revolver and ran into the hallway. He disappeared. I returned to comfort Lacie. We could hear the sirens blaring in the street and I knew what we would do the rest of the day.

As the sirens grew louder, Colton reached out and turned off his alarm clock.

For a moment he considered his dream. *Was it a warning? Is Jenny in danger? Is Lacie in danger because she's trying to help Jenny get away from her boyfriend? And why was my new Jeep trashed? Why indeed?*

It took a few minutes for Colton to realize that he did not have to deliver newspapers this morning. He wiped the sleep from his eyes and headed for the bathroom. As he did his morning business, he considered what he needed to do to get the Security business up and running.

***

Colton planned to talk to his parents about his business plans during breakfast. He had informed them of his intentions a few days earlier, but now it was official. By the time he ate breakfast and got ready for school, Colton had secured the garage for his business office, hired his mother as the office manager and bookkeeper, and appointed his two brothers the official janitorial team. His sister didn't want a job.

Excitement filled the school as everyone talked about Saturday afternoon's regional championship game at Pewamo-Westphalia. Apprehension was also present, their opponents are a fantastic team. Every year, the Pirates are in the running for State Champions. This year they are undefeated in their conference games, with the best record in the league. The Loon's have been great at defeating unbeatable teams, but a Loons win on Saturday would be a huge upset.

Lacie was waiting for Colton at his locker. She smiled and said, "I'm now dating a private eye?"

"No... you are now dating a businessman specializing in security."

"Does that mean from now on you won't involve yourself in detective work?" she asked, looking straight into his eyes.

"No… it doesn't mean that either. If, during our security business, I should come across a mystery, I will investigate until I solve the mystery," he said.

"That means you are my private eye," Lacie said as she kissed him on the lips.

"Hey! No kissing in the hallways!"

"You're jealous, Seth," Lacie said, laughing.

"Jealous of you? No way! Colton and I are just friends and business partners."

Colton put his hand on Seth's shoulder and said, "She's made a joke, Seth. She knows you and Linda Canberry are a hot couple."

Seth became somber. He lifted his puppy dog eyes and whispered. "We used to be a hot couple."

"I thought so," laughed Lacie. Linda seemed depressed the last couple of days, and all she talks about is how her world is ending. God, Seth, what did you do to that poor girl?"

"I got caught going out with Beth Sutterman. You've seen her, the cute redhead. We went to Saginaw for a shopping trip and hit it off well. I have more fun with Beth than I ever had with Linda. For now, Linda and I are still doing things together, but we're not dating. I will break that off if Beth and I get serious."

The bell rang. Colton kissed Lacie and told Seth he wanted to meet up during fifth hour study period.

"What's the meeting about?" Seth asked.

"It's a business planning meeting. Bring your brainstorming cap."

"See you then,"

As Colton turned to enter Mr. Dinger's History class, he noticed Jenny Stillmore standing with her boyfriend, Luke Hadderton. It appeared they had been arguing again. Colton couldn't help but notice that Jenny dressed just like the girl in his dream. She even had bright red shoes.

Sure hope that's the only thing from my dream that is real, he mused. *I would hate to have my Jeep crushed.*

He walked into the classroom, and Connie Jackson poked him with her finger.

"Why the long face?" she asked

"Oh... I was thinking about my Jeep and how tragic life can be. You know, Connie, no one should have to fear the actions of another person. It isn't right."

"Well, aren't we *deep* this morning? I like you better when you're late to class... much more fun."

"Yes and thank you for not poking me with your damn pen."

***

During art class, Colton and Lacie sat with Jerry Cultrain and Beth Sutterman. Jerry was in black jeans and a black leather jacket with a hand-painted Star Wars scene on the back.

"Jerry, I never thought you were a *Star Wars* freak. You're just, more 1960's. You know?"

"Colton, my man. I'm into art. All kinds of art," replied Jerry with a smirk on his face. "I'm also into making money, and at $150.00 each, I sold four jackets. It's all about the ART!"

Colton laughed so loud that Mr. Swansear, the teacher walked over to investigate. "Jerry, I love the jacket. How many of this model have you sold?"

"Four, sir. But I hear Colton is also in business these days. Isn't that right, Colton?"

Mr. Swansear sat down next to Colton and smiled. "Let me guess. You will become a private investigator and run a security business out of your garage?"

"Damn, Sir. That's remarkable. I take it you have physic abilities?" asked Colton. He wondered how Mr. Swansear learned about his business plans.

"No, my brother-in-law took a job with your partner, Seth. My brother-in-law, Jim Owens, is an electrical contractor, and he subcontracts with other businesses. He wants to set up his own business, because he doesn't like to be the employee, but I can't see him managing a big business, either. Give him a job, and he gets it done!"

Colton wasn't aware Seth had hired an employee, but it didn't surprise him. "Well, Seth knows the job, and it's his decision who he hires."

During the hour Colton and Jerry talked business, while Beth and Lacie exchanged information about, Seth, Beth's new boyfriend. Colton showed Jerry the website he was setting up and asked for Jerry's design advice.

"Colton, why don't you let me create the site. I'll use a Word Press Template I can customize. It's important that your website looks as good as the professionals. You know, the big guys. I'll search the biggest security firms and set them as our competitors. If you look better than the best security company on the web, then people will trust you. If your site looks like cheap crap, then that's how you appear to customers. And your business will crap out."

"Thanks, Jerry. How much will this cost me?"

"Ah, yes… money. Nothing, if you will let me build my website on your server account. It appears you have an unlimited account that you're paying for. I can put my site on yours and it won't cost you anything more. But I'll get a better site with lots of bells and whistles. I want to sell my tee shirts and jackets online."

"Deal. But will you help us keep the site up and running? I'm OK at adding information and pictures, but it looks like you're the best around," Colton said.

"Well, thanks for the ego boost, boss. I'll help, and if it gets to be a lot of work, I may need payment, but that shouldn't happen for a while, not until we're both rich."

Colton gave Jerry the security passwords for his website and together they organized the information they wanted online.

When the bell rang, Lacie took Colton's arm and whispered, "Beth is a nice girl. I can see why Seth likes her. She's down to earth. Did you know she even raises her own cows and chickens?"

"Seth has all the luck," Colton laughed.

Chapter 14

Colton and Lacie sat with Seth and Beth during lunch. Lacie wouldn't allow the two men to talk about business. She wanted the conversation to revolve around the girls and their plans for the weekend. Colton and Lacie were talking about a victory party in the garage after the game on Saturday.

Beth had never been to one of their parties, but she had heard about them. In her words, "Some students think your parties are boring because alcohol isn't allowed."

Colton asked, "Do you drink?"

"No! I don't drink, smoke, or take drugs," replied Beth. "I'm not making a comment on your parties, I'm repeating what I heard around school."

Seth laughed, "Trust me Beth. We know what some students think. There have been a few times when we had to ask guys to leave because they thought they could smoke or bring beer to the party. We are not against the use of alcohol. It's just illegal for us to use, and we don't want to get into trouble. Besides, I've seen too many students get caught up in *escaping life by getting high*. They get to where they aren't living anymore. I know what depression is, but I would hate to always feel like my life sucks. I also know you can't run away from yourself. You must figure out how to live with your problems, or you get help."

"For me, just working on the farm helps. Being outdoors, riding my horse, feeding the chickens. It gives me time to think about how good I have it and how petty my problems are, and I pray a lot."

Seth smiled. "My little farm girl. You have your feet on the ground."

"Trust me, sometimes they're in the mud too."

The bell rang and Seth and Colton volunteered to clear the table. They caught up to the girls and walked them back to the lockers.

During fifth hour study period, Seth and Colton worked on their business plans. Seth told him he had ordered the business flyers, and they would reach the customers today.

"I sent them to everyone in Pigeon. We printed color advertisements and mailed them to over a thousand homes for less than three hundred dollars."

"Did you put the address and phone number I gave you on the flyer?" Colton said. He feared Seth may have forgotten.

"Yes, I did. Why would I spend that kind of money on a flyer that didn't have the contact information?"

"I'm sorry; I should know better than question your abilities. You're a good business partner and I think we'll make a great team."

During seventh hour gym class, Colton exercised on the weight machines, and when he finished his routine, he got ready for football practice. It was a beautiful, warm and dry afternoon so the team was looking forward to working outside. They weren't disappointed. Coach Talbert had the team run and then do strength training in the weight room. On the field, Aden worked on his throwing arm while Colton and Terrance Dundee worked on catching passes.

Driving home, Colton smiled and sang along with the radio. *Life is good*, he thought. *I love it when a plan comes together.*

Both Terry and Jason were practicing basketball in the driveway so Colton joined them for a game of HORSE. After losing, he went into the house to see if his mom needed any help with dinner.

After dinner Colton and his mom went over the business plans. Cyndi had already set up a bookkeeping system on the computer in the garage office.

"Colton, I see you installed an internet phone in the office. That was a great idea. Now you can advertise your business and I can take calls from customers. I want to get a new business style phone that will send calls to my cell phone, so I don't have to always sit in the office."

"Mom, you're the greatest. Just order what you need." Pulling out a new checkbook Colton continued, "I set up the checking account, and they gave me some starter checks. Can you order more? I also need you to go into the bank and sign papers, so you can sign our checks. Seth is doing that tomorrow afternoon."

Since Colton would get up early to do his Thursday route, he went to his room before nine o'clock, and after sending a few messages to Lacie and Seth, he fell asleep.

Throughout the night, Colton dreamt of football, basketball and deer hunting. It was getting close to the fifteenth of November and he would love to go hunting with his dad. A few of his friends have already been out bow hunting, but Colton decided to wait until December, when he will have time to take his brother, Jason, into the woods for two days of hunting. Terry wants to go too, but Colton's dad told him he would have to wait another year.

***

When the alarm rang, Colton was wide awake and ready to get busy. He checked the weather. No snow, rain or fog. He showered and dressed in his school clothes instead of his work clothes. *I'm a business person now. I need to look good at all times;* he thought.

The newspapers were already at the storage shed and both Rob and Joe, the other delivery drivers, had their papers loaded and were ready to leave.

Joe jumped out of his old van and walked over to Colton; a trail of smoke following him. "Colton, the word on the street is your starting another business. If you're giving up your route, let me know because I would love to take over your cushy route on The Point."

"Yes, I'm starting a business with my friend, Seth, but I have no plans to stop delivering the newspapers. It doesn't take that much time and like you say, *it's the best route; nice and cushy.*"

Colton laughed as he loaded his Jeep. "If I quit, I'll let you know, Joe."

"Thanks, Kid." Joe said. "I appreciate that. My route is OK, but I have to drive all over hell to get it done. Your route on The Point is half the distance, with twice the drops. You know, *more money, fewer miles.*"

Colton finished loading his newspapers, checked for changes to the route, and put on his headphones. Having finished his last audio book, he picked something a little lighter. Instead of another Baldacci detective novel, Lacie suggested they both listen to the Stephanie Plum novels by Janet Evanovich.

They watched the movie, *One For The Money,* a few weeks ago, and Colton discovered there are over twenty five novels recorded. Tonight it's *Two for the Dough*, and Stephanie, a bounty hunter, is trying to bring Kenny Mancuso in for the reward. Colton liked that it would be a series he could share with Lacie, but he hoped the stories will have enough adventure for his tastes.

Colton laughed through most of the route. The novel's characters and action were funny especially Stephanie's coworker, Lula… a large black woman who was a former prostitute, or as she would say, *a hoe.*

As he listened and delivered his papers, Colton watched for the van he saw last week. He decided that if he sees another robbery, he will call the police. The Sheriff's Department said they are unsure there was a robbery, because the owners haven't returned from Florida to check the house.

Colton finished the route earlier than usual, but instead of heading to school, he stopped at the gas station in Pigeon and picked up a large coffee. He parked in the school lot and finished a few more chapters of his audiobook. He walked into the school with his coffee when he saw students getting off the buses.

Seth was standing at his locker talking to Beth. Colton checked his phone and found a message from Lacie. *At the dentist with Mom. See you in art class. Love.*

"Colton, you're dressed up a day early. It's not Friday yet."

"Aden?" Colton turned to face the voice behind him. "It's my new look; I'm trying not to look like I just got out of bed."

Beth and Seth, laughed. "Like you did the other day? Whatever made you want to wear your PJs to school, anyway? Beth asked."

"I didn't want to; I had to. I was late and didn't have time to go home after I delivered my newspapers."

Seth put his hand on Colton's shoulder, "Partner, when are you going to give up that newspaper route. You know, you have a real job now."

"Don't *dis* my job, Seth. It pays well and I'll continue doing it until I decide otherwise."

"No problem," Seth replied. He was a little shocked to hear Colton's decision, but knew it wouldn't help to point out how his job might interfere with their new business because he could be stubborn.

"I'm not stubborn, Seth. I like doing the route. It gives me a few hours to think about stuff and listen to my audiobooks. If it interferes with our business, I'll deal with it then."

The bell rang, and they all headed to class. There was excitement in the air and everyone was asking Colton if he was ready for the big game. He realized that he hadn't thought about football since yesterday's practice.

As the day progressed, Colton found his mind jumping from football to the new business. During art class, he caught Lacie up on the progress of their business and informed her he had started the new audiobook.

"Don't you love it? I finished the second book last week, but I'll wait for you to catch up before I start the third," Lacie said.

"It seems strange. I guess I haven't adjusted to the concept of sharing a book. I listen to my mystery novel and then go on to a new one. It'll be different having to discuss the book with someone else."

"You don't *have to*," Lacie insisted. "I thought it would be fun to share."

"Lacie, I want to share.."

"Good, because I do too."

Colton smiled to himself. He learned that having someone to love requires a lot of sharing.

***

Colton lifted weights in gym class during seventh hour. He was on his last set when Aden sat down next to him and asked, "Do you think we have a chance Saturday? I mean, they are so damn good."

"Aden, don't do that. You're as good as they come, and if you question yourself, you could make us lose," Colton warned.

"There are huge butterflies in my gut and I'm afraid we might lose."

"Don't be afraid," Colton insisted. "We'll do our best, and if we lose... tough. As long as we do our best no one gives a shit. Is that understood?"

"Got it! Thanks for the pep talk, and you should watch your language," Aden said with a laugh.

Colton understood Aden's feelings. He had been thinking all day about how difficult it will be to defeat the Pirates. *I better take my advice*, he thought.

After practice, Colton went straight home where his brothers were practicing with their bows. He went into the garage and took out his new compound bow.

"Wow, that's nice," exclaimed Jason. I wish I had one like that.

"Well, I'll tell you what," Colton said. "Run up to the house and ask Mom if she has the package I ordered last week."

Jason ran in the back door and in a few moments he returned

dragging a large box behind him.

"This gift is for both of you, so open it together," Colton instructed.

The two boys tore at the box. Jason pulled out a used compound bow and started his happy dance. "Wow! Is this mine?" he asked.

"No, give that to Terry. It might be too big, but he can grow into it."

Jason reached into the box and pulled out a brand new compound bow. He was so happy, he cried. "This is what I've wanted all my life, Colton."

He ran up to his big brother and gave him a huge hug. Terry also got into the hug and the three of them stood in front of the garage, laughing and checking out the new archery bows.

The boys practiced for an hour and then ran into the house for dinner. Colton's mom took him aside and said, "I was watching from the window and I want you to know how proud of you I am. That was so nice of you, Colton."

"Mom, it's great being a big brother. I hope I can set a good example for them, like you and dad did for me when I was their age."

After dinner, Colton talked to Lacie about the game Saturday afternoon. She said Seth and his new girlfriend, Beth, asked her to drive with them.

"That's a great plan, Lacie. After the game why don't you have Seth drive to my house?" Colton suggested. "I'm not sure when I will get there, but I shouldn't be too late. Oh… I wanted to let you know I like the Stephanie Plum novel. The mysteries I've been listening to are dramatic and lack any comedy. In fact, I'm looking forward to finishing the Stephanie Plum novel tonight."

"Great! I'll see you in school tomorrow and remember to dress up for the assembly."

"Will do, I'll see you in the morning."

Chapter 15

Throughout the night Colton kept fumbling the ball and getting tackled. They were only dreams, but when he woke, he became disgusted. As he thought about it, he realized that he was trying to prepare himself for the possibility the Loons might lose.

The newspapers were again on time and he listened to the audiobook "Two for the Dough" while making his deliveries. Colton's mood improved as he listened to the silly antics of Stephanie and Lula. Stephanie's grandmother was becoming a new favorite character. A gutsy old woman who loved to hang around funeral homes to meet widowed men. She made Colton think about Mrs. Hoffstarter and all the troubled characters she met during her years working as a psychiatrist.

Colton finished the last chapter of the novel as he drove into the school parking lot. He wore a white shirt with a black jacket and tie, which he put on before leaving the Jeep.

Today the students get dismissed at 11:00 am. Before they leave, the band will walk through the halls playing the school song, followed by the football team.

As Colton walked toward his locker, happy faces and good luck pats on the back greeted him. There was a can-do mood in the school. Even though Colton had doubts about winning tonight, he could see that his fellow students had no questions about how good their team was. It is true, *school spirit is contagious.*

Aden was standing next to his locker talking to his girlfriend, Kathy Dorsher.

Kathy yelled to Colton, "Are you ready to win tomorrow?"

"Yes! After regionals, we're off to the State Championship. Isn't that right Aden?"

"Damn straight, Colton. We're ready to show everyone how good our team is," Aden said.

All the students who heard him cheered, and Colton could tell it would be a wild and crazy morning at school.

Lacie walked up to Colton and hugged him. She turned to Aden and wished him good luck.

"Luck is just part of the formula, Lacie; only our skill counts."

"Well, good skills to you," she said with a huge grin.

Colton led Lacie to her locker. "Are you ready for today? I'm sure it will be crazy. You can feel the excitement in the halls. I hope we can do a good job tonight, because so many people are rooting for us, and I'd hate to disappoint everyone."

She held his hand and said, "You won't disappoint anyone. Even if you lose, you guys have won our hearts as the greatest Loons team."

***

The bell rang, and the hallways emptied. Colton gave Lacie a quick kiss. "See you after school," he added. "Remember, we're having lunch with Mrs. Hoffstarter."

Jerry interrupted Colton and Lacie to show them the new business website he created. Colton loved it and said, "You did a great job, Jerry. Did you have time to do your site too?"

"It's almost done. I set up a storefront so I can sell online. I need more products to sell and I need a credit card account. Did you get one for your business, yet?"

"Working on it, but not yet," replied Colton. "Lacie, look at my website. Jerry worked magic, again."

Lacie checked the site out and agreed with Colton.

Colton asked Jerry to stop by the business office in his garage.

"We should be back around two, so we can meet then. Seth will also be there; we want to go over the progress we've made so far." Jerry agreed.

After third hour, Colton went down to the locker room with the football team and lined up behind Coach Talbert and the high school pep band until there was an announcement telling the students to line up along the halls and watch for the team.

The band played the school fight song as they paraded down the halls followed by the cheerleaders and then the students. They lead the students out of the building to the busses.

Seth and Beth wished Colton good luck, and Lacie hugged him. "I'm so proud of you, Colton," she told him.

Seth told Colton he would be at the meeting later, and he and Beth left for lunch.

Colton took Lacie's hand and together they walked to his Jeep.

Chapter 16

Colton and Lacie arrived at Mrs. Hoffstarter's home on The Point. He helped Lacie out of the Jeep and walked with her to the side door.

Mrs. Hoffstarter greeted her two guests at the door with a smile and hearty welcome.

"Well, come on in. I want you to meet Al Doyle, my new next door neighbor."

Mr. Doyle was a larger man. He stood almost six feet and must have weighed two-hundred-fifteen pounds. With short gray hair, Colton guessed he was in his late fifties or early sixties.

"Trudy has told me all about you two. I've known this young lady for almost forty years. You could say she saved my life when I was a police detective in Detroit."

"Now Al, you know you did that yourself," laughed Trudy. "I grew up in Greektown and knew Al's parents. After a rough time on the job, the department wanted him to get a psychological release before he could return to work, and he didn't want to accept help from the police doctors, so he asked me if I would work with him and sign his release to return to work."

Al injected, "We were always friends, but we have been closer friends ever since I left the police force. Trudy called me when she heard her next door neighbor, Mrs. Torengia, listed her home with a realtor. Having your grandchildren arrested for murder and drug dealing is costly and she needed extra cash, which I had."

Colton laughed, "I might have had something to do with their arrest."

"Oh, I heard all about that. Anyway, I am now Trudy's neighbor and I'm glad to meet the two of you. Trudy deserves to have such caring friends."

"We're also pleased to meet you, Mr. Doyle," said Lacie.

"Please, call me Doyle or Al." Doyle added, "Now, let me get cooking. I will prepare lunch for the four of us. I hope you like cheeseburgers."

Lacie and Colton laughed. "We sure do," said Colton. "You know we have a festival to honor the cheeseburger."

"I sure do. In fact I attended the crazy parade last summer," Doyle said as he set his ingredients on the kitchen island.

Lacie and Trudy walked to the large windows overlooking Lake Huron while Colton sat at the kitchen table so he could watch Doyle prepare lunch.

Doyle told Colton about the three restaurants he had operated after he left the Detroit Police force. Colton had read a newspaper article about the restaurants; *Doyle's Downtown*, *Doyle's Birmingham*, and *Doyle's Troy*.

Doyle admired how intelligent and grounded Colton was, and Colton couldn't believe an ex-police detective could cook.

"Where did you learn to cook?" asked Colton.

"My mom owned a small Greek restaurant in Greektown. She felt that all of her children should know how to cook. Besides, we were cheap labor. Since we lived above the restaurant, it was a part of our lives. Cooking became second nature. When I left the Detroit Police, I received a legal settlement, and I used that money to start my business. I got lucky. It was a success, and I sold them last year for a very nice profit."

"Congratulations. I hope you enjoy your new home and I would love to sign you up for newspaper service, and my company also specializes in security systems for the home and business." Colton advised.

Doyle burst into a hearty laugh. "Smart and ambitious, a great combination, Colton."

"Thanks. I better find Lacie."

"Colton, I'm right here," Lacie said from behind him. "I was listening to the two of you."

Colton stood and offered Lacie a chair, just as Trudy walked into the room and asked, "Doyle, do you have drinks ready for our guests?"

Doyle reached into the huge refrigerator and pulled out a pitcher of iced tea. "I sure do. Colton, would you grab some tall glasses and ice? I have to run these Greek burgers to the patio. The grill is hot and ready."

Colton poured four glasses of tea and walked to the patio to watch the burgers with Doyle..

Trudy smiled, "Lacie, I think your boyfriend likes Al."

"Policemen and detectives impress Colton. He dreams about being a detective, yet he doesn't want to be a policeman. It may be one reason he started the security company."

"Are you still planning a career in nursing?" asked Trudy.

"I'm not sure what I will do. Colton wants me to shoot for the moon, but I don't know what field I want to practice in. I could be an RN or perhaps something more challenging… like becoming a doctor."

"Oh, how wonderful! Yes, Lacie, go for the moon," laughed Trudy. "You will make a wonderful doctor."

Trudy put her arms out, and the two hugged.

Lacie laughed and hugged her friend back, adding, "Trudy, I appreciate your faith in me, but don't tell Colton I'm considering becoming a Doctor."

***

Colton and Doyle returned from the grill with a platter of burgers and potato wedges.

"Lacie, look at these burgers. This man knows how to cook, and he has fantastic stories about crime in Detroit," Colton reported. "I'm impressed, Sir."

"Well, you haven't tasted my Greek burgers yet," Doyle replied.

The four diners gathered around the kitchen table as Doyle finished preparing the meal. He placed the burgers on warmed homemade buns, sprinkled feta cheese on the meat, added sliced onions and a slice of tomato. On top of this, he poured a mixture he called Tzatziki Sauce, a Cucumber/Yogurt Sauce with sliced onions. He drizzled olive oil over the potatoes and added garlic and grated cheese. On the side was a small Greek salad.

After taking a bite of the burger, Lacie exclaimed, "Oh my God, Doyle! Enter this hamburger in Caseville's Cheeseburger contest next summer. This is fantastic."

Everyone agreed with Lacie. A lively conversation continued during and after lunch. The topic centered on Doyle's adventures as a detective and the abuse of Jenny Stillmore. He advised Colton and Lacie to be very careful in trying to help

"Don't get involved," he said. "You reported the abuse, you tried to get her help, and she knows you care. If you continue to interfere, you will only get hurt. Trust me, domestic violence is a delicate matter. There are reasons Jenny continues this relationship, and you cannot change her. She must make the change.

As Colton and Lacie prepared to return home, Doyle offered Colton his card, and said, "Please, if you ever need help, call me. I have many connections and would be glad to assist you. Also, I am interested in your security service. Have your partner call to set up an appointment."

Colton agreed and thanked Doyle for the great meal. He then reminded Mrs. Hoffstarter that they would pick her up for Thanksgiving dinner next Thursday. Colton asked Doyle if he would like to join them for dinner, but he declined.

"I would love to join you, but I am helping to prepare Thanksgiving dinner at the Church Outreach Hall. It's my opportunity to give back to the community. You know, there are many people who need our kindness."

Lacie replied, "What a wonderful gesture. Perhaps we can get together some other time. Come on Colton, you have a business meeting this afternoon."

As Colton and Lacie drove through The Point, Colton tried counting the deer along the drive. "It's too bad I can't hunt these deer. Instinct tells them they are safe here.

"Even though I understand the thrill of hunting, I hate to see these beautiful animals killed. Let's talk about something else."

"Something like our future?" asked Colton.

"That would be nice." replied Lacie.

***

After dropping Lacie off at her home, Colton returned home and did a few chores in the yard. At two o'clock he went into his security companies new office. As he went over the bookkeeping reports prepared by his mom, Seth walked in with Jerry Cultrain and Jim Owens. Jim was the art teacher's brother-in-law. Colton had never met Jim, but he appeared professional.

Jerry walked around the garage, admiring the electronics and decor. "This place is rad", he said.

"Yes, and it makes for a nice office, too," laughed Seth.

Colton asked everyone to sit around the desk and he handed each a copy of the printout his mom prepared. It included a list of new clients, and potential customers. Next to each name, notes showed what had to be done at each home or business.

"This will be our goal for this week. If we can get these new customers set up, we will generate a profit before Thanksgiving. That's less than two weeks to complete these tasks," Colton advised.

Seth told the group that Jim has been doing a great job installing the security equipment. "Do you think you'll be able to do these installs?" he asked.

Jim laughed, "No problem, boss. As long as you provide enough equipment, I can complete the jobs. I'll let you know when and if I need more help."

"Great," said Seth. "Now Jerry, how is the website coming?"

"It's done, and online. I finished it a few days ago. We must get business cards done, and signs posted to increase traffic. We should put yard signs on each of our new client's front yard."

Colton projected the website onto the large screen television set so everyone could see it. It was impressive and had the look of a large corporate site.

"Wow, Jerry. You outdid yourself," admired Seth. "Do you want to continue as our computer guy? We could use your expertise, and you can also run your site from here. The pay will be what we can afford until we are making 'big bucks.'"

"Sounds great," replied Jerry. "I have to get going, though. I promised my Dad I would help with his chickens. We have over twenty to clean and freeze."

"Have fun," laughed Jim. "I like chicken, but I wouldn't like to kill that many."

"I'm used to it. Dad's a butcher in Bad Axe and he runs a small business from our place. He smokes great beef and turkey jerky and his smoked fish is out of this world. I'll bring some next week. I think you'll enjoy it."

After the meeting, Seth and Colton talked about Saturday's game. Colton reminded Seth to take care of Lacie.

"I'm counting on you," he said.

Seth could sense that Colton expected some kind of trouble at the game. He promised to take care and suggested that nothing bad would happen.

"I know," agreed Colton. "It's just that I've been having some strange dreams about death. And they all revolve around Lacie and Jenny. It's very unnerving."

"Hey, don't go there. Dreams are dreams... not some kind of window into the future. But if it helps, I will be extra careful to keep our girls safe." Seth assured.

Chapter 17

Colton had a good night's sleep and was ready for game day. Instead of having breakfast at home, He met the team at the high school kitchen for breakfast.

After a great meal, Coach Talbert and members of the Athletic Boosters talked about the upcoming game and the role of sports in the community. The program lifted the team's spirits, but Colton felt even more pressure to win. He told Aden how he felt and Aden said he also felt the pressure, but suggested that it was normal in a situation like this.

"We've never been this close to becoming regional champs, as a team. I'm just surprised that we haven't felt more pressure with our other competitions," Aden told Colton.

"You're right. All we can do is our best. I hope it's enough."

Coach Talbert told the team members to gather their belongings and head to the bus. "I want to thank everyone. We have a long drive ahead of us. Since the game starts at one o'clock, we must be on our way," he said. Everyone shook hands and Aden thanked the Boosters for the great pre-game celebration.

As the team enjoyed their breakfast, Seth, Beth, and Lacie were eating at Main Street Cafe, in Pigeon.

"I'll get the bill," Seth insisted.

Lacie wanted to leave a tip, but Seth insisted that he would cover it.

As Seth went to pay the bill, Beth said, "He's generous with his money, but he doesn't show off about how much money his family has.

Sometimes when we go out, he acts like he's spending his last dime."

"Yes, he's well grounded, just like Colton. I'm sure it's why they're such good friends," Lacie said as she put on her coat and scarf.

Lacie laughed, "Oh... look, Beth. He's buying a bag of cookies and doughnuts. Isn't that sweet?"

"Too sweet," Beth said. "He's not helping me watch my weight; is he?"

Seth helped Beth with her coat and the trio walked out to the parking lot. Lacie insisted on sitting in the back seat, but Beth asked her to sit behind Seth so she could talk to her.

The Loon's school buses pulled into the parking lot of the Pewamo-Westphalia High School fifteen minutes before Seth. Lacie suggested he park close to the gate to the football field, but Seth said he wanted to park in the back lot.

"I don't want a ton of people walking by my car. Too tempting for someone to deface my baby." he said.

Seth dropped the girls off at the gate before driving across the lot to his parking space. He opened the back of his Charger and pulled out his professional video camera and tripod. Coach Talbert asked him to record tonight's game again.

When he returned to the gate, the three of them found a seat in the upper bleachers where Seth could get a good view of the entire field. There were two other people setting up video cameras near him. Three photographers, including two television stations, had their cameras on the sidelines of the football field.

Both teams were on the field doing warm up exercises, fans were filling the bleachers, the bands from both schools were taking their places, and school personnel were making sure everything was ready for the big game.

As Seth adjusted his camera, Beth and Lacie watched the teams practicing. Beth enjoyed sports and was on the girls softball team last year.

"You should go out for a sport, Lacie. It's fun, and it helps me keep my weight down," Beth said.

"I've never worried about my weight," Lacie replied.

"You're lucky," Beth said. "Everyone in my family is overweight. It's part genes and part farm eating. Dad always wants a huge breakfast and dinner, which is great if you're working hard on the farm. But with today's farm equipment, the work is not as physical as it was for our ancestors. If I don't watch what I eat, I could be heavy. When I was in grade school, I was the *fat girl*. But with sports and by watching what I eat, I'm keeping my weight steady."

"You look great. Just don't let yourself become too skinny. I hate to see that. Have you noticed how Tracy is just skin and bones?"

"Sure have. A friend of hers told me she still thinks she's fat. Now, that's an extreme weight problem." Beth said.

"Weight problem?" asked Seth as he sat down next to Beth. "Do I look too fat? Be honest!"

"No! It's not always about you," said Lacie. "We were just talking."

Seth adjusted his jeans and tried to pull his stomach in tighter. Beth laughed. "Are you kidding? What do you weigh? One-hundred-fifty?"

"I knew it. You think I'm fat!"

Beth looked at Lacie and smiled. "You know, boys can have an eating disorder too." She looked back at Seth and said. "Trust me, Seth. You do not have a weight problem. You look great, just like you are, and you shouldn't lose anything... including me."

They hugged and Seth gave her a kiss. "Thanks, and you look great, too."

"You two are making me feel like a third wheel. I'm going down to get something to drink. You need anything?"

Beth stood and offered to go with Lacie. "All this talk is making me thirsty, too."

Seth said, "If I drink too much now, I'll be in the men's room when I should record the game. I'll get something after the first quarter."

***

Colton finished adjusting his football gear, and sat on the locker room bench, next to Aden. The two men sat without speaking. After the rest of the team finished suiting up, they sat on either side of the two teammates.

There was no talking. Just the sound of breathing and an occasional cough. Coach Talbert walked into the room and stood in front of his men.

"We made it this far, didn't we? People told me there wasn't a chance in hell we would make it to districts this year. Last year we had a good team and lost many seniors, but this year we have a great team. We beat opponents considered better than us. We climbed the ladder until we won the districts. Now we can go beyond districts and become regional champions, and who knows, perhaps state champs."

Coach turned toward the exit and pointed at the door. "When we run onto that field, I want each one of you to remember how hard we've fought, how proud our community is of us, and how proud I am of you. Even more important is how proud you should be of your accomplishments."

"Are you ready to become regional champions?" he asked.

"Yes!"

"Then let's get our butts out there and win another game."

With that, the team burst through the doors; running toward the bright lights of the football field, patting each other's backs, and shouting, "Let's win another game for Coach Talbert!"

Lacie was watching for Colton, and when she saw the locker room door burst open, she nudged Beth. "Here they come. Coach Talbert must have given them a great pep talk because they're fired up."

The team ran onto the field facing the Pewamo-Westphalia High School Pirates, who were also fired up. Screaming fans filled both sides of the bleachers.

Colton tried to find Lacie but gave up when he heard a young girl begin the National Anthem. Watching the American Flag wave in the breeze, he felt excitement and pride.

The announcer advised that the Loons would receive and Colton ran toward the end of the field... ready to win another game.

It was a high kick. Colton judged that he would be open, so he ran with the ball. He caught it on the thirty yard line and was off. His team was with him, blocking as he ran down the center of the field. He wasn't stopped until he reached the ten yard line.

The team huddled and lined up. Two hand-offs went nowhere. Aden tried a pass without success. The Loons couldn't move beyond the twelve yard line, and the Pirates were eager to take over possession of the ball.

For the entire first two quarters, the two teams couldn't run or pass. Colton said it was like there was a brick wall between them.

During the halftime program, Beth and Lacie walked down the bleachers to the restroom. They came back with potato chips and drinks for themselves and Seth, who was guarding his equipment.

"What happens if neither team gets a point?" Beth asked.

"Don't worry, there will be a winner. You can't tie for regional champion," Seth advised.

In the locker room, Coach and Aden were working on plays and strategy. Colton complained that there are always two men shadowing him. "Every time I try to complete a pass, they're there. Can't we stop them somehow?" he asked.

Coach Talbert devised a plan of action, and the team was ready for the second half. "Let's win this game!" Aden yelled, as the Loons ran out the door.

Lacie had been watching for Colton's return and when she saw the team bolt through the doors, she nudged Beth with her elbow. "They're back," she said.

"Seth, the teams are returning," Beth yelled.

"Got them. Now, let's hope they are better than the first half."

The Loons kicked and the Pewamo-Westphalia Pirates called a fair catch on the twenty yard line. From there they worked their way to a first down by running hard against the Loons line.

Coach Talbert yelled at the linemen. "Tighten up that line." They tried, but the larger Pewamo-Westphalia lineman were staying low and plowing through the line. Then it happened. After running hard on the ground, the Pirates completed a surprise pass, for a touchdown.

The Loons regrouped again and Coach Talbert set another game plan in motion.. The rest of the second half of the game in a dead heat with the Pirates. Neither team could run or pass. The Pirates won by one touchdown. The only touchdown of the game.

After congratulations, and presentation of the trophy, the Loons headed to the locker room. There was no laughing or cat calls.

Coach Talbert tried to lift their spirits by talking about how good they played, and how hard they worked to get here. Colton and his teammates knew they disappointed the Coach and the community, and it will take time to heal from their defeat.

***

Seth packed his camera equipment and carried the case down to the foot of the bleachers where Beth and Lacie were waiting.

"I need a pit stop before we head home," he said. "It'll be a long drive, and I'm sure you wouldn't want me to take a leak on the side of the road."

Beth said she also needed to go, Lacie wanted to head to the car. Seth suggested she wait for them, but she insisted that she would walk ahead. "I need some alone time to let the loss sink in," she said. "Can you imagine how devastated Colton will be when we get home."

"Yes. But I promised Colton I'd look out for you. Please wait here for us."

Lacie agreed to go with Beth, for the sake of keeping Seth happy.

The drive back to Pigeon was long and quiet. Seth played soft music on his car stereo and he and Beth kept talking about the songs. Lacie had her headphones on and she tried to listen to an audio book. It wasn't working because she kept losing track of the storyline. Her mind was on the game and how upset Colton would be.

Seth made one pit stop in Frankenmuth and then the trio headed for Caro.

Beth turned to speak with Lacie. "If you don't mind, Seth and I want to stop at the Walmart in Caro. I need to buy a few things."

"That's fine," Lacie responded. She again put her headphones back in and continued to listen to her book.

When Seth reached the Walmart parking lot, he parked as far from other cars as possible. He found a secluded spot.

"I know, it's a long walk, but my car will be safer here." he explained.

Lacie walked with the two into Walmart, but explained that she wanted to use the bathroom. "I'll meet you at the car," she suggested.

Seth wasn't happy. He wanted Lacie to go with them, but she insisted.

"No, I'll wait outside. The weather is nice and no one will bother me here."

"Here, take a key to my car. If you get cold, you can run the engine. We won't be long."

Lacie used the bathroom, stood by the front doorway for several minutes, and walked to Seth's Charger. Before she reached the car, she saw Jenny Stillmore and her abusive boyfriend, Luke Hadderton. They parked a few cars away from Seth's car.

Luke was yelling at Jenny as she rummaged through her purse looking for the car keys. "You're so damn stupid, Jenny. Here, give me your purse. I'll find the keys myself."

"I can find them." Jenny insisted. "Just stop yelling at me. You're making me nervous."

Luke reached over, grabbed the purse from her hands and slapped Jenny across the face with the back of his hand.

"Stupid bitch! I'll make you more than nervous if you don't stop whining."

Lacie walked up to the couple and yelled, "Luke, leave her alone. What kind of monster are you, anyway?"

Luke pulled the keys from Jenny's purse and grinned when he saw Lacie. "I thought the stupid Charger looked familiar. Where is that dumbass Seth and his airhead girl friend?"

"They're coming," Lacie answered. She looked at Jenny and said, "You want us to give you a ride home, so you don't have to take any more of Luke's crap?"

As Jenny answered, Luke turned and swung Jenny's purse into Lacie's face. Jenny tried to stop him, but he was out of control.

"You stupid bitch," he said to Lacie.

Lacie ran to Seth's car. Just before she reached the back door, he kicked at her leg and caused her to fall backward. "Jenny will drive with me, and when I'm done, they'll carry you home in a body bag."

Terror filled Lacie's eyes as she tried to protect her face from his foot.

"Don't hurt her," screamed Jenny.

Luke kicked her several times in her stomach and then once in the back of the head. Jenny was crying as Luke dragged her back to his car, opened the door, and pushed her in the passenger seat. "Shut up or you'll get the same treatment when we get home."

Lacie lost consciousness as Luke squealed his tires and sped away.

Seth's Charger was sitting by itself when He and Beth approached it. "Where did Lacie go?" asked Seth. He looked around and then walked to the passenger side. "Oh God!" He yelled. "Call 911!."

Beth ran around the car and saw Lacie. Her face was bloody, and she appeared to be dead. Beth fumbled for her phone and then dialed. "We need help. Someone hurt our friend. She looks like she might be dead," Beth said, crying. "We're in the Caro Walmart parking lot. We're next to a red Dodge Charger at the south end of the lot. Please hurry."

"Tell them she's alive. It looks like someone mugged her." Seth insisted. "Come on Lacie. Wake up. Oh God! Colton will kill me, Beth. He will kill me for this… I promised to take care of her. Shit, look what I did. Damn … Damn it all."

"It's not your fault and Colton won't get mad at you," Beth said, holding her hand over the phone. "No, it wasn't an accident. It appears someone beat our friend up. She's alive but injured. Yes, I understand. We won't move her. Please hurry and send an ambulance and the police. Hurry…."

***

The ambulance arrived, followed by a State Police car. Two E.M.S. paramedics, a woman and man, ran from the ambulance to help Lacie. They pushed Beth and Seth aside and tended to her.

Trooper Laurie Claybern approached Seth and Beth and asked, "What happened Seth?"

"While Beth and I were in the Walmart someone attacked Lacie. We saw nothing happen, but when we got here, she was on the pavement, unconscious."

The trooper turned to her partner, a young officer who Seth had never seen before. "Jimmy, take photographs of the scene, before they move Lacie. And then check to see if Walmart uses a surveillance camera to cover this part of the lot."

"Yes, Ma'am," he said. He walked to the patrol car and returned with a digital camera.

"Well, I guess we will wait until we can talk to Lacie," said Trooper Laurie. "Have you notified anyone in Lacie's family about the attack?"

"Not yet. I have Lacie's mom's number, but I would prefer you call her. I wouldn't know what to say," said Seth.

Seth gave the trooper the phone number. "Well, I guess I better call Colton," he said. "This will be the hardest call I've ever made."

Beth put her arm over his shoulder and said, "Don't worry. Everything will be fine. Just tell him what happened."

Seth opened the door on his car and sat behind the wheel. He dialed Colton's number and waited, while it rang. The call went to voicemail, and Seth said, "Colton, someone mugged Lacie outside the Caro Walmart, and they're taking her to Hospital. Trooper Laurie is here, and she is calling Lacie's mom. I'm sorry, and I'll keep you updated."

Trooper Laurie just finished her call to Lacie's mom when Trooper Jimmy yelled, "Laurie, the young girl has regained consciousness. Do you want to speak with her before they move her to the hospital?"

"Yes," she said as she stepped around the Charger.

"Lacie, do you know who did this?" she asked.

In a strained voice, Lacie said, "It was Luke Hadderton. He was with Jenny Stillmore, and he got mad at me for interrupting a fight he was having with Her."

"What kind of car was he driving?"

"I think it was a Chevy Impala... four years old, black, with white racing stripes on the hood."

"Thank you Lacie. I'll see you in the hospital later."

Chapter 18

As the school bus pulled into the Loon's parking lot, Colton reached for his phone, remembering he turned it off. Coach Talbert asked the team to turn their electronics off, and the players were in deep thought for the entire trip. To say the team was disappointed would be an understatement. They were crushed.

Colton turned the phone on and saw a message from Seth. He thought it was strange that there wasn't a message from Lacie. As he walked to his Jeep, he read the message. He ran the remaining distance and threw his duffel bag in the back, jumped behind the wheel and sped off.

Nightmares raced through his mind as he drove to Caro. Realizing he was speeding, he slowed down, and tried to keep to the limit. It wouldn't help Lacie if he was in an accident, or arrested for breaking the speed limit.

Colton wanted to call Seth; he wanted to know what had happened, and why his best friend let it happen. He wanted to talk to Seth, but he couldn't. His anger was boiling up, and he knew he wouldn't be able to yell at Seth and drive.

The thirty-minute drive, took Colton twenty five minutes. He pulled into the hospital parking lot and saw Seth's Charger; next to Seth's car was Lacie's mother's car and a state police patrol car. He sat for a moment, took a deep breath and opened the Jeep's door.

His walk to the hospital doors, turned into a sprint. The doors flew open, and he rushed into the waiting room. Seth and Beth were sitting together alone. Seth looked up and saw Colton rushing toward him.

"What did you do? Why did you let her get hurt? Damn it Seth, I trusted you to take care of her..."

Beth interrupted him, "It wasn't Seth's fault, relax and sit down."

"Keep out of this, Beth. My best friend just screwed up, big time. I'm so disappointed with you, Seth. I'm so God damn angry, I want to..."

"Colton!" Lacie screamed as she stepped through the emergency room doors, into the waiting room. "Stop it! Stop blaming Seth. He didn't want me to go to the car without him and I wouldn't listen. If you want to be angry at someone, pick me for being independent, or yourself for not trusting your best friend."

Colton walked toward Lacie, but she turned her head away. "Don't be all nice with me. I'm OK, but I don't want to be with you; I don't like this side of you."

Lacie took her mom's arm and asked, "Can we go home?"

Colton slumped into a chair with his face in his hands. Lacie looked at his sad condition and added, "I'll call you when I get home, and I still love you. I'm sorry you lost the big game tonight."

"I love you too, and I'm sorry I lost it. I shouldn't let my anger..."

Colton turned to Seth and Beth. "Seth, can you forgive me for being such an ass? Tonight was not my proudest moment."

Seth laughed. "I knew it would piss you off, and I still feel guilty. I keep asking why I let her go to the car without us?"

"Because Lacie is a strong independent woman, and you are not her protector. We women love it when you care about us, but we don't expect you to rule our lives and lead us around like cows," Beth said.

Colton listened as the nurse gave Lacie instructions. "The doctor thinks you may have a slight concussion. If you get dizzy or have blurred vision, you must go to the Pigeon Emergency room for treatment. Lacie's mom thanked the nurse and helped Lacie walk out to the parking lot.

Beth took Seth's hand and said, "I will use the restroom before we take off. I'll be out in a minute."

Seth and Colton walked outside together, to wait for her. Standing next to Seth's car they went over the events of the evening.

"We've got to stop Luke before he kills someone," Colton said. "Did Trooper Laurie say she would let us know if they catch him?"

"No, but she gave me her cell number," Seth said. He pulled a card from his shirt pocket and handed it to Colton. "Why don't you call her now?"

Colton dialed the number on the card. "Hello, Trooper Laurie? This is Colton Blackwell. Lacie will be OK, but I was wondering if they caught Luke, the guy who hit her."

As Colton listened to the Trooper, Seth could tell by his expression it was not good news. Colton ended the call and said, "The police talked to Luke and Jenny and they swear they didn't hurt Lacie. Jenny backed Luke's story. She said they left Walmart without seeing her. Since there are no other witnesses and nothing appeared on the security camera, the police investigation is finished. Trooper Laurie thinks Lacie fell, hit her head, and imagined Luke hitting her. The doctor agrees."

Shocked and angry, Seth said, "That's crap. If Lacie said Luke hit her, he did! Lacie doesn't tell lies."

Colton laughed. "I agree. It looks like we have a new case to solve! Somehow we need to get Jenny away from that creep and convince her to tell the truth. We know he's abusing her, we have to find a way help her."

***

Beth returned from the restroom, and asked, "Seth, it's been a long day, and I have to do chores early tomorrow, so can we get going, now?"

"My gal, the farmer," Seth said to Colton.

"Well, this farm girl is tired, so let's get going. Colton, I hope you and Seth have made up. I always admired you for your calmness, but tonight I saw a side of you I didn't like."

Colton lowered his head. "I'm sorry, and I apologize to both of you. There is no excuse I can offer, and I was wrong to accuse Seth. You can trust me; it won't happen again."

Seth put his arms out for a hug, and Colton responded in kind. Beth soon was hugging the two men. With tears in her eyes, She laughed, "Enough already, guys. I need to go home!"

Colton's phone rang. "My phone won't stop ringing tonight. I'll either have to turn it off, or use the hands free phone hookup I got for the jeep. Spending the night in a ditch is not my idea of a fun night."

"Good idea. I use mine all the time because the ditches around here are like the grand canyon."

On the drive home, Colton talked to his mom, dad, Aden, Coach Talbert, and his favorite artist, Jerry Cultrain. When he got home, he sat for a few minutes in the Jeep considering the days events. He realized losing the big game was traumatic and created a deep feeling of despair, but when he heard about Lacie, his world crumbled.

Knowing and understanding his feelings, is important to Colton. It is one reason people find him so stable. He keeps his emotions in check, but when the emotions erupt, they explode with unexpected force.

Walking into the back door, he heard voices in the kitchen. His mom and dad were talking. "Hi Mom, Dad. I'm glad you're still up."

"We were waiting for you. Lacie called and wanted to remind you to be careful on your route Sunday morning," said Colton's mom.

Colton's dad, Adam, laughed, "That's one tough woman you have there, Colton. Lacie gets beat up and spends her recovery time thinking of others. She will make a great nurse."

"Not a nurse... a doctor! I'm trying to talk her into becoming a doctor," said Colton. "She is so smart, I know she will make a great doctor, but it's her decision."

"That's a wise attitude," said his mom. "Everyone has to make their own life decisions. If they always do what you want, they will end up blaming you if they fail."

Chapter 19

When Colton finished his meal, he excused himself and went to his room to call Lacie. They talked for over an hour. She said she had taken another pain pill, but overall she felt better. Their discussion ranged from Colton's disappointment with Friday's big game to her fears for Jenny's life.

"Let's promise to forget about Jenny and her creep boyfriend because they're nothing but trouble," suggested Colton.

"That's a promise," responded Lacie. "Call me after you get home from your newspaper deliveries. I think Mom needs me to help her, but I'll be able to take a break. Good luck and please avoid hitting those beautiful deer on The Point."

"Will do," Colton said.

After a chat with Seth he checked his Facebook page and was ready for bed. It was early by most people's standards, but he would need to be awake and ready to do his newspaper route at two in the morning.

Dressed in my best black suit, I headed downtown, to the Detroit Police Headquarters. Imagine me, Colton Blackwell, a Detroit Homicide Detective. It was hard work, but I made it. And today I join Detective Albert Doyle, my new partner.

I walked into the large room and saw Doyle talking to several other officers. He saw me and smiled. A friendly smile, not a smirk. I stepped toward him and he motioned for me to stay back for a moment.

He finished his chat and approached me with an open hand.

"Detective Blackwell," he said. "We have a murder to investigate."

As we walked to our car, Doyle caught me up on the details of the case. It was a domestic abuse gone wrong. The boyfriend was beating on his girl when the girl's best friend showed up. She tried to stop the fight, but the boyfriend attacked her with a butcher's knife. The coroner pronounced her dead at the scene and the CSI team is there now.

"I understand the scene is a mess, but at least the boyfriend is in custody. They found him hiding in the back yard, covered in blood."

"Sounds like an open and shut case. So why are we being called in?"

"His girlfriend, Jenny, says he didn't do it. She blames intruders. We need to investigate."

When we arrived, I could see the boyfriend in the back of a patrol car and Jenny was in the living room. I looked into the kitchen and saw the pool of blood surrounding Jenny's beautiful friend. I must have turned white, because Doyle asked, "First murder?"

"No." *I replied,* "She looks like my girlfriend back home. It's unnerving."

"Lacie?" *he asked.*

"Yes, Lacie."

We checked the crime scene, talked to the girlfriend, and then went outside to talk to the accused killer. He insisted it was someone else, but we read him his rights and took them both to the station.

The accused killer was Luke Hadderton. Tall, black hair, handsome and in good physical shape. I noticed something strange about him though. There was an emptiness in his eyes, and his face showed pain and anger.

When we presented him with the overwhelming evidence we found, including his fingerprints on the weapon, he laughed.

"Dumb bitch," *he mumbled.* "She deserved it. Never interrupt a man when he's beating his woman. It's bad form, and she got what was coming to her."

He burst into a chilling laugh.

Colton woke and reached for the ringing alarm clock. He turned it off and headed to bathroom. When he returned, he slipped into his work clothes and went downstairs where his mom had set the coffee maker, so there was a pot of hot coffee waiting. After filling his stainless coffee tumbler and a Thermos, he was ready to face his night of deliveries.

He couldn't get the sound of Luke's maniacal laughter out of his mind. A good detective novel should help. He made sure there was one of Patterson's audio novels on his phone before he went to bed last night, and he was looking forward to an entertaining listen.

***

Colton arrived at the storage unit, in Pigeon, before two-thirty in the morning. Both Joe and Rob, the other two drivers, were loading their newspapers. The papers arrived early.

Joe yelled to Colton, "Early papers today. I guess the advertisers are waiting for the big Thanksgiving edition. Have you put in your orders for Thanksgiving papers yet?"

"Yes. Dad helped me decide how many I needed. I might end up having to make two trips though."

"I use a trailer to load my store drops, and Rob uses his brother's pickup truck."

"Are the papers that big?" Colton asked.

"Sure are. Advertisers put in big ads and tons of Black Friday flyers."

Colton loaded his papers as Joe and Rob left to start their routes. After checking for new deliveries and cancellations, he put his headphones on and took off for his first delivery.

The James Patterson novel was exciting and as he drove through The Point, Colton kept his eye out for criminal activity. Other than marauding deer there was no unusual activity. Sheriff McNabb asked him to watch for the home burglars who have been breaking into vacation homes along Lake Huron. This criminal activity is one reason for the success of his new security company. Many homeowners on The Point leave for the winter and having an unprotected home is an invitation to burglars.

As Colton came to the end of the deliveries on The Point, he passed Mrs. Hoffstarter's and Doyle's homes and noticed that one of his old customers yard light was on. The customers, Max and Irene Clawson, were in Florida. The elderly couple left last week and would not be back until spring.

Colton approached the home, watching for signs of activity. He parked on the side of the road. Staying in the shadows, he approached from the side of the home without seeing any intruders. After reaching the side deck he dropped to his knees when he saw what looked like a woman laying next to the hot tub. He didn't want to startle her, but he wanted to know why she was using his customer's hot tub. She wasn't moving. As he approached, he studied the girl's face, and realized it was Jenny, dressed in a skimpy red dress and high heels. Her skin was a solid white, and it appeared the hot tub had turned red with blood. Blood dripped from her wrists into the hot tub. It was obvious, Jenny Stillmore was dead. *No one could lose that much blood and be alive*, he thought.

Colton's mind was in a fog. He felt ill, but not sick. There was a rolling feeling in his stomach. It felt the same as when he saw the murder on the beach, a few months ago.

He knows he will have to call the police. But doing so will entail spending the morning answering questions. The first call he made was to his Dad.

"Dad, I have a problem. I found Jenny Stillmore dead in a hot tub at Max and Irene Clawson's home. I'll call the police in a minute, but someone will have to help do my route."

Tears ran down his face as he said, "Yes, it's upsetting, but I've been through this before. I'm OK, Dad."

Colton gave his Dad the address and then dialed 911.

"This is Colton Blackwell. I've discovered a woman's body in a hot tub, here on The Point... No I didn't check for a pulse, but I know she's dead. I can tell because the hot tub is red with blood, and she is white as a ghost... No. I didn't check her pulse... Because I didn't want to contaminate the crime scene."

The dispatch officer said there would be someone on the scene in about fifteen minutes. "Don't leave, Colton," she advised.

"I'll be here," Colton promised.

Colton put his phone away when he remembered he had Doyle's business card in his billfold. He called him.

"Mr. Doyle," he began, "This is Colton Blackwell. I'm sorry for disturbing your evening, but I'm down the street about six houses east of you. Could you come down here? I found Jenny, the girl we told you about yesterday. She's dead... In a hot tub... Yes, I called the police, but I could use moral support. I hate having to deal with the police in situations like this. I'm afraid I might say the wrong thing and get myself in trouble."

Doyle said he would be there in a few minutes. "As soon as I can get dressed and make coffee."

Colton walked back to his Jeep and found his coffee mug. He took a big gulp and thought about how everything changed. *One minute you're doing your job as usual, and the next minute you're waiting for the police, watching a dead girl in a hot tub.* He took another drink and thought, *If I wasn't sure I was awake, this would make an awesome dream.*

He walked back to the hot tub and squatted down to study the horrific scene. His mind was racing with questions. Whispering he said, "I'm so sorry Jenny. Did someone do this to you or did you want to end your pain?"

He took a deep breath and wiped the tears forming in his eyes. "I promise, if someone did this to you, I'll try to find out who. You didn't deserve to die like this."

Doyle was standing behind Colton, listening to his words of comfort. He knelt down and put his hand on Colton's shoulder. "Son, did you feel her answer? Some detectives believe they can. I never had that experience, but I always ask the victim what happened."

Colton looked into Doyle's gentle eyes and said, "I think she told me someone else did this to her."

"That will be the question that needs answering."

Looking over the crime scene, Doyle asked, "Did you take a photograph?"

"No! It never crossed my mind. Do you think I should?"

"Yes. Take a couple from this angle and then from over there. Be sure you disturb nothing."

After Colton finished taking the pictures, Doyle suggested that they stand by their vehicles. "The police will be here soon." he said. "In fact I see flashing lights through the trees now."

As they walked to the road, two police cars, and an ambulance pulled up. Huron County Deputy Ned Wooddell approached Colton. "Where is she?" He asked.

Colton pointed to the hot tub and Ned turned to his partner and said, "Follow me."

He told Colton to stay put while they investigate. Colton watched as they walked toward Jenny.

Just as State Trooper Steve approached the Jeep, Colton's dad drove up. Colton walked over to his car and said, "Dad, I want you to meet Al Doyle, Lacie and I met him yesterday. He's a retired Detroit Policeman, and he's moved next door to Trudy. I called him for moral support. I don't want to make stupid mistakes and have the police think I had something to do with Jenny's death."

Adam and Doyle shook hands and spoke. Colton kept his eyes on the officers and knew Trooper Steve was eager to question him.

"Dad, can you take my Jeep to do the rest of the route? The directions are on the passenger seat. I'm not sure how long I'll be here."

Adam agreed. He gave Colton a big hug and took the keys from his hand. "I'll see you at home. Doyle, take care of my son."

Chapter 20

When Trooper Steve saw Colton's father drive away, he walked up to Colton and before he could ask who Doyle was, Doyle extended his hand and with a voice of authority he said, "Trooper, my name is Albert Doyle, a retired Detroit Homicide Detective. I am here at the request of my friend, Colton. After calling the police he remembered that I lived just a few houses west of here and felt a need to have someone, of knowledge, help him during this horrible time. I'm sure you understand how disturbing discovering a dead body is."

"I understand but I need to speak with Colton alone. Colton, come with me so we can talk in the patrol car."

Doyle stepped closer to Trooper Steve, and with his face inches away he said, "Officer, you will not interview Mr. Blackwell without an adult, such as myself or his parent, in his presence. Is that understood?"

The trooper stepped back. Colton could see rage flash across the Troopers face. "We'll see about that, Sir."

Trooper Steve turned and walked back to his vehicle. Colton could see he was shouting on the radio with someone. Perhaps his commander? When he returned he apologized to Doyle for any misunderstanding and suggested the three of them sit in his patrol car to talk.

Colton grinned all the way to the patrol car where he told Trooper Steve what he saw when he drove up to the house. He explained that he didn't touch or move anything. He explained how he knew the victim from school. Colton also advise the Trooper he and Lacie had seen Jenny and her boyfriend, Luke Hadderton, fighting in and around school.

"We saw Luke hitting Jenny. We think he was abusing her, but she wouldn't get help when we suggested she should," Colton added.

Trooper Steve typed notes as he asked questions. Doyle stopped Colton only when Steve asked why he felt a need to call Mr. Doyle.

"That's not a question you need to answer, Colton."

"Oh, I think Trooper Steve knows why. The trooper has a problem with teenagers. He thinks all teenagers are guilty of something. Perhaps he is projecting his own personal experiences as a youth, onto us," Colton said with a chuckle.

"Smart ass," quipped the trooper.

"That's enough, trooper. You needn't call my friend vulgar names," responded Doyle.

Colton watched as the EMS workers moved Jenny's body into the ambulance. Deputy Ned and his partner strung police tape around the hot tub. The yellow tape reminded Colton of all the murder mysteries he'd watched and listened to.

"Doesn't the Coroner have to come down to the scene?" he asked.

Trooper Steve and Doyle answered. "Go ahead, Steve," suggested Doyle.

"Around here, the Coroner only comes to the scene when needed. This is likely a suicide, so the crime scene investigators will be here later to sweep the area. Photographs get taken of the scene and any evidence gets tagged, bagged, and sent for processing."

The Trooper continued, "For now, you both can go home. If we have further questions, we will call."

Doyle thanked the trooper and walked with Colton to his car. Together they watched the ambulance drive away. Deputy Ned approached Colton and then stopped when he saw Doyle.

Colton said, "Ned, this is Albert Doyle. He's a retired Detroit

Detective and a good friend of mine."

Doyle smiled at hearing Colton's description. "Yes, a good friend."

He shook Ned's hand and complimented him on his good work. Laughing he suggested that he could find him a job in downtown Detroit.

"Hell, NO! We may have crime in our county, but at least when we go home, we feel safe."

"I understand. That's why I left Detroit and moved here. I want to retire in peace, but now I find myself involved in a murder."

"Who said anything about a murder?" asked Ned.

Colton watched as Doyle pumped for information. "Well, aren't all deaths considered murder, until proven otherwise. I mean, a young girl in her prime, what evidence is there that she would kill herself?"

"Her Facebook page. She posted a goodbye note," said Ned. After he said that, he realized that he might be telling too much. "But that's for the Sheriff and Coroner to decide. I gather the evidence."

Ned turned to Colton and added, "I am sorry you had to find Jenny like this. If you need help, you know my number." He turned to Doyle and thanked him for helping Colton.

Colton and Doyle stood next to their vehicles drinking coffee.

"Doyle, thank you for the help. I know you didn't want to get involved in a murder/suicide, but I trust your opinions, and I know I can learn from you."

"So, why not become a police officer?" asked Doyle.

"No... I want to run my security business. If I run across a good mystery, all the better. Besides, I have a knack for stumbling into mysteries."

"It's not luck or a knack; you're observant. Anyone else would have driven by without questioning why the lights were on. You, Colton, have a nose for mysteries. A sixth sense, of sorts."

Colton laughed and promised to keep Doyle informed of anything that comes up, and Doyle offered to help him whenever he's needed.

As Doyle got into his car he smiled. *Living here might be more fun than I expected,* he thought.

***

When Colton pulled into the driveway, he saw that his dad finished the route, so he checked his Jeep for any damage and then went into the back door.

"Mom... Dad? I'm home."

He found them sitting at the kitchen table.

His mother jumped up and gave him a big hug. "Colton, I'm so sorry you had to go through this. I hate when this stuff happens. Do they think she committed suicide? Or was it her worthless boyfriend who killed her?"

"The police said she posted a suicide note on Facebook, but I'm not sure," Colton said.

Colton's dad offered to make him breakfast, but Colton said he wasn't hungry yet. "My stomach is a little upset from the excitement. I'm going up to my room to call Lacie, and then I'm taking a nap."

Lacie had heard all about how Colton discovered Jenny's body in the hot tub.

"Don't tell me, Uncle Ned told you?" Colton asked.

"Yes, he told me. I'm so sorry you had to find her like that. I can't believe she killed herself instead of leaving Luke. That bastard drove her to this. He should be in jail," Lacie said.

Colton could tell that Lacie was angry at Luke. "Yes, he should pay for his actions. Did Ned say they had proof that Linda committed suicide?"

"Just that she posted a Facebook note."

Colton asked Lacie if Jenny friended her on Facebook because when he checked his page he discovered she was not one of his many

Facebook friends..

"Yes, she accepted my request last month. When I looked at her page, this morning she had posted a note, but someone took it down and put up a poem about forgiveness."

"Did you make a copy of that note?" asked Colton.

"Yes. I'll email it to you. How do the police know someone else didn't hack into her Facebook account and post that note?"

"You're good. You might make *detective first class* soon," laughed Colton.

Lacie asked if Colton listened to the radio report. She told him Jenny's name wasn't given, and the cause of death was *still under investigation.*

"They also didn't say who found her. So far, no one knows you were there."

"Well, that's good, I guess. Did they say anything about the funeral?" asked Colton.

"No, but I'm sure an obituary will be online soon."

While Colton and Lacie talked, Seth sent them messages. He guessed Colton found Jenny and wanted more information.

After talking to Lacie, Colton called him, and said, "So what's so urgent that you couldn't wait 'till I finished talking to Lacie?"

"Oh, were the two of you talking?"

"You know we were; she read the message you sent me, Seth," Colton said.

"Well, I am your business partner, so tell me what happened last night. Did you find Jenny? How did she die? Well...?" He begged.

Colton laughed. "Why don't you come over after lunch and we can talk? I want to go over some business items, anyway."

"You mean I have to wait to learn all the details? Damn, you're mean."

"Well, I found her in a hot tub on The Point, and it was a bloodbath. A real blood bath."

"Wow! I'll talk to you later this afternoon. How would two o'clock be?"

"That's fine. I need to rest now, so I'll see you then."

***

Colton was working in the garage office when Seth showed up. Eager to hear about Sunday morning's adventure, Seth's first words were; "Give me all the details and leave nothing out."

Colton told him everything from the moment he saw the hot tub.

Seth replied, "You know, I should drive with you, because there's always something happening when you're delivering those damn newspapers."

"Hey, I would rather I hadn't found Jenny, and I wish this was just a bad dream, but it's not."

"I'm sorry, I don't want to make light of her death, and I'm sure it was hard to handle. You know I can't stand seeing blood, so I wouldn't have been any help.."

"It was difficult, but I'm glad I called Albert Doyle."

Seth looked puzzled and asked who Doyle was.

"Lacie and I met him Saturday at Mrs. Hoffstarter's home. He's a retired Detroit Police Detective and a former restaurant owner who moved next door to Mrs. Hoffstarter, just a few doors west of where I found Jenny. I knew the police would end up thinking I did something wrong, so I asked Doyle to help me."

Seth laughed. "Did the police act like they always do?"

"Yes, but Doyle helped keep Trooper Steve under control. I like the way he handles people and I feel we can learn a lot from him."

"Speaking of police, Sheriff McNabb called me yesterday afternoon," Seth said. "It seems there was another robbery on The Point. I checked our security cameras, but we didn't have a camera near the house that the burglars broke into."

Colton thought for a moment, and then he asked, "What does

McNabb expect us to do?"

"He wants us to watch the area when you do your route. The robberies occur in the early morning and he thought we could set up a few cameras on the main road to watch for suspicious looking vehicles. The police can't do that, but we can, as long as the camera is on one of our customer's property."

"Any ideas where we should put the cameras?" Colton asked.

Seth opened his laptop and showed Colton a map of The Point area, showing where there are already cameras. "I marked the best areas in red. There are three places where we could catch traffic coming into and leaving The Point."

"Looks good, but how can we watch these 24 hours a day?"

"We don't have to because I can plug the camera data into my software for identifying threats."

"That sounds like something out of a spy novel. Since when do we have that kind of software?"

"I took software I found for free, and I rewrote it. I can specify the automobile or truck I want to watch for. When that vehicle comes into view, the camera sends a notification along with a live feed to my computer. It's sort of like magic."

"Yes. It sounds like magic. Have you tried it yet?"

"We use it in our business every day, Colton. Where have you been? When I installed the first security cameras on The Point, the deer kept causing the alarms to go off so I designed this software to identify deer and other non-humans. Now the alarms only go off if an unidentified person is in the video."

"Seth, I'm impressed."

The two continued their conversation until Colton's mother walked into the office. She had several business papers that needed signing and presented the two business owners with some good news.

"We are now making a profit and every new security system you install from now on, will only increase that profit. I understand, because of Jenny's death, you probably are not in the mood to celebrate, but I put a bottle of non-alcohol champagne in the refrigerator."

Colton opened the bottle and grabbed three plastic cups. "To our new business, and to Mom for keeping us on track," Colton said.

Seth told Colton's mom about what Sheriff McNabb asked them to do and she suggested that they be very careful. "Don't get involved trying to stop a robbery in progress; that's a job for the police."

Seth nodded his head in agreement. "I'll be careful, but I might have a hard time holding Colton back. He thinks after he acts."

"I do not! I think; then I make the wrong decision," Colton said with a chuckle. "Mom, I'll be careful."

Chapter 21

After working an hour alone in the garage, Colton stepped outside and saw his brothers in the backyard practicing with their archery equipment. He stood for a few moments watching and then got his equipment to join them.

Jason was ready to shoot an arrow at the Styrofoam target when Colton asked, "Do you two want me to show you how it's done?"

Jason shot the arrow into the heart of the Styrofoam deer, turned, and said, "Only if you can beat that."

Terry ran up to Colton and gave him a big hug. "You can show me how to shoot like that," he said. "I always end up shooting the deer in the butt."

The brothers practiced for an hour. Both Jason and Colton helped Terry improve his skills. He had several good shots and was excited to have his brothers spend time with him. Colton invited them into the garage where they sat around the table drinking Coke and talking about December bow hunting plans.

"Why didn't you go with Dad up north to hunt on opening day?" Jason asked.

"Dad asked me, but I was busy getting my business started and besides, I prefer to hunt with a bow."

Terry sighed, "I wish I could go with Dad."

"It won't be long until you can. Time just seems to fly by these days."

"That's for sure," said Jason. "It's gonna be Thanksgiving soon and then it'll be Christmas in just a flash. It's crazy how time flies."

"I can't wait for Christmas to get here," Terry said.

"Looking forward to seeing Santa?" asked Colton.

"No. Just the gifts. I asked for a new bike. A big one like Jason's."

"I hope you get one," Jason smiled and patted his brother on the back. "Then we can go down to the river together. But, be sure to ask Santa for a wet-suit too."

"Why?"

"You never know when I'll push you into the river for fun," Jason said with a wicked laugh.

"Don't worry, Terry. I'll save you from your mean brother."

Colton looked at his phone and realized it was getting near dinner time. The brothers made a mad dash into the kitchen where Cyndi had the table ready. After another great meal the family watched television and visited. Colton excused himself and went to his bedroom.

He knew it would be difficult to fall asleep tonight. Every time he closed his eyes he saw Jenny's lifeless body lying near the bloody hot tub. When he wasn't thinking about her, he was asking himself what mistakes he made at the football game. *Why didn't we win? Am I that bad of a player? Did Jenny kill herself or did Luke kill her?*

Feeling rested after waking early Monday morning while still dressed and laying on top of the bed covers, Colton's mind raced back to Jenny. He jumped up to check the Bad Axe radio station's website for an obituary, he found her picture plastered at the top of the page.

There was no mention of how she died. *Jenny died unexpectedly Sunday morning.* The obituary mentioned that her mother preceded her in death, along with an aunt, and grandparents. *She is survived by her father Joseph Stillmore, a younger sister Caroline Stillmore, an aunt Amanda Stillmore-Groun, and an uncle Ronald Stillmore.* The obituary continued; *Viewing will begin Monday from 3:00 p.m. to 8:00 p.m., at the Pigeon Funeral Home. Funeral service will take place at the Pigeon Funeral Home, Wednesday at noon, with a lunch at the Caseville American Eagles, after a graveside service in Caseville.*

Colton used the bathroom before anyone else was up, got dressed, and then went downstairs for breakfast. His mom was already at the stove. "Colton, wake your brothers and sister."

"I already woke them. I took my shower and then I made sure they were all up," Colton said as he poured himself a cup of hot coffee. He spotted coffee cake and asked if it was for now or later.

"It's for breakfast. I made it yesterday afternoon with Stephenie. She's getting interested in cooking and I'm glad. I could use another cook in this house."

"Mom, I can cook. It's just no one will eat what I cook."

"You're just like your dad. One excuse after another. I hope you end up being married to someone who refuses to cook. That will teach you."

Colton thought about what she said. He couldn't remember if Lacie liked to cook or not. After consideration, he replied, "If Lacie doesn't like to cook, then I'll learn how to. If Detective Doyle can become a master chef, then I guess I can learn to cook."

"Detective Doyle? Is that Trudy's new neighbor?"

"Yes. He also helped me Sunday with the police. I like him. He reminds me of the detectives I read about in my audiobooks. The nice ones, not the crazy ones."

It surprised Cyndi to hear about her son's new hero. "What do you know about this man?" she asked.

"I know that Trudy Hoffstarter has known him for many years and she likes him. You know she's a good judge of people so if she says he's a good man, he is."

Colton's mom laughed. "Good enough, then. When will we meet this super detective who can cook?"

"After Thanksgiving. I asked him to come over for dinner with Trudy, but he's helping make Thanksgiving dinner for those who don't have a family."

There was a rumble of feet and loud voices making their way to the kitchen. Colton's mom sighed. "They're here. Help me with these dishes."

All day Sunday, at their parents request, Colton's siblings avoided talking about him finding Jenny's body. Today they wanted to know everything about her death.

Colton sighed and gave them a limited version of the events.

Stephenie asked if he thought Jenny's sister would be at school today.

Colton's mom said, "I don't think so, Steph. I'm sure she'll be with her family at the funeral home. Colton, are you going to her viewing after school?"

"Yes. I asked Lacie to go with me. We're not going to the funeral though."

***

Colton watched as his siblings got on the bus. After they left, he called Lacie's uncle, Deputy Ned. He was eager to learn what Ned had to say about Jenny's death.

"Hi, Ned. This is Colton. Anything you can tell me about the investigation into Jenny's death?" he asked.

Ned told him that the coroner pronounced it a suicide and there will be no further investigation.

"Are you aware her boyfriend abused her?" Colton asked.

"They decided there isn't enough evidence to substantiate any abuse. Besides, Luke's father said he stayed at home, sleeping," reported Ned.

Colton thanked Ned and told him about the job Sheriff McNabb asked him and Seth to do.

"McNabb told me all about it, and I'll be around The Point while you do your route Tuesday morning."

Colton was thankful there will be the backup for him and Seth. "That's great. I'll try to stay out of trouble and I promise I won't try to capture any crooks by myself."

"You better not, because if you do, I might just kick your butts and throw you in jail."

"On what charges, Ned?"

"Stupidity!"

Colton kept thinking about Jenny as he pulled into the school parking lot. He made his way to his locker and sat down on the floor, to wait for Lacie. When he saw her, he jumped up and walked toward her. She put her arms out and gave him a big hug.

"I'm so glad to see you. Did Ned talk to you about the investigation?" she asked.

"Yes, and I bet he told you too," Colton said. It amazed him how much Ned and Lacie talk.

"Yes, he told me. He's my source for all the local news." She laughed and suggested they go somewhere private to talk. The halls got crowded and before they could move, a mass of students bombarded him with one question and then another. If it wasn't about the football game, it was about Jenny's death, and by the time Colton and Lacie could talk, the bell rang for first hour classes.

"We can talk in art class," suggested Lacie. They agreed and went their separate ways.

They didn't mention Colton's name in the news, yet everyone knew he found Jenny. Her death became bigger news than the football team's loss and Lacie's assault on Friday. Few students knew Jenny, but when they heard she committed suicide, they all shared their opinion.

During first hour the office advised students that if they needed help to deal with Jenny's death, there would be professional grief counselors in the office all morning.

"Don't think the grief you are experiencing is abnormal," the announcer said, "We all suffer a loss when one of our friends and fellow students have passed. Please, if you are having any trouble, seek help and remember there is no shame in asking for assistance."

Colton couldn't wait for his third hour chemistry class to end. Mrs. Quick was in a foul mood and kept insisting it was Colton's fault that everyone asked him questions about Jenny's death. He considered having a word with her after class, but decided that it would be a waste of time.

Lacie was sitting with Beth and Jerry in the art room. Someone had already placed Colton's art project on the table.

He sat down and smiled. "Does this mean you expect me to work on my art today?" he asked Lacie.

"Not me. All of our work was on the table when we arrived. Mr. Swansear put them out."

After taking attendance, Mr. Swansear talked about suicide, and how he went through a rough period in his life, when he considered it an option. The students sat in silence.

It was during a time when his mother had passed. His father became angry with him because he was a "needy ten-year-old" who should be able to take care of himself.

"After months of feeling guilty about my mom's death, and my father's anger toward me, I decided to hang myself in the garage. It seemed like the only choice I had."

"I sat on the box I had set in the center of the room, an old electric cord hanging down from the rafter. Crying my heart out I felt so alone because no one cared if I lived or died."

"That's when my dad walked in. He took one look at what I was about to do, ran, and fell to his knees. He reached his arms out and held me. At that moment he realized the pain I was in, and that I needed him now, more than ever before. Together we survived our grief. We helped each other survive our loss."

The art students were in tears as was their teacher. Colton rubbed tears from his eyes and said. "Thank you for sharing that, Mr. Swansear. We're glad you are here now, to help us."

Without speaking, the students worked on their projects. Mr. Swansear turned his stereo on and said, "It's too gloomy in here, so let's listen to some rock music. It was his favorite playlist of early 1980's music. The students again smiled even though it wasn't their first choice for background music.

Lacie and Colton planned to visit the funeral home after school, to pay their respect to Jenny's family. Beth had already told Seth that she wouldn't go because she doesn't like funerals or anything to do with death. She explained, "I realize it's a part of living, but I can't handle it. I don't know why, and I don't want to know."

"That's OK, Beth," Lacie said. "It's not like she was close to any of us, but I want closure."

***

After seventh hour Seth and Lacie met Colton at the side entrance. He drove up to the curb and Seth opened the door for Lacie and climbed into the back seat of the Jeep.

The three friends considered the events that brought them to this moment. Lacie was first to break the silence. "It feels like more than a few days since Luke assaulted me in Caro. I wonder if that was the last straw for Jenny. If only I would have kept my nose out of their business."

To change the subject and mood, Seth asked Colton if he would miss football practice.

"Yes, at first, and I must find another way to stay in shape. Perhaps I should join the basketball team."

Lacie burst out laughing. "Seth, he's pulling your leg. Colton hates playing basketball. Or, at least he keeps telling me he does."

"He does," Seth snickered. "He hates it because I've been able to beat him ever since we were little kids. I always made more baskets than him."

Colton pulled into the parking lot of the Pigeon Funeral home. He turned the engine off and together they walked down the sidewalk.

"You know, Seth, I never beat you because I wanted to protect your huge ego."

"My ego? You wanted to protect my ego?"

"Yes."

As they approached the funeral home doors, they checked each other to make sure nothing was out of place. "OK, here we go," said Lacie.

The smell of flowers was the first thing Colton noticed. As his eyes adjusted, he could see the casket and family members gathered around it. He wasn't sure which man was Jenny's father. The woman could be her Aunt Amanda, and he knew the young girl was Caroline because he had seen her before.

Lacie commented, "I don't see Luke, so that makes it a little easier."

Colton guided the group to the guest book and suggested they each sign it. He took an envelope and pulled a twenty out of his pocket for a memorial and checked the donation box next to the food bank.

Colton looked at the names in the guest book, and Luke had not signed the book. He thought, *No way to tell if he was here, since he could may have forgotten to sign the book.*

"Well," said Seth, "I guess we should to go up to the casket. You can lead, Colton."

"No. You lead, I'll follow Lacie."

Lacie grabbed Seth's right arm and Colton's left hand and said, "Together, or not at all, boys."

The three walked toward the casket. A tall thin man approached them with his hand out. "I'm Joseph Stillmore, Jenny's father, and this is my daughter Caroline."

Colton shook his hand and said, "I'm Colton Blackwell."

"Ah, yes," Mr. Stillmore said, "You found my girl."

"Yes, Sir. I am so sorry for your loss. We wanted to pay our respects to Jenny."

Lacie interjected, "Jenny was such a beautiful girl. We had classes together. We weren't close, but we talked many times."

"And you are?"

"Oh, sorry. I'm Lacie Wooddell and this is Seth, Seth Seamoore."

"Aren't the two of you owners of that new security company drumming up business on The Point?" Mr. Stillmore asked.

"Yes we are." It surprised Seth that he recognized their business. Then he remembered the flyers he mailed to over a thousand homes around the area.

"Well," continued Mr. Stillmore, "I wish you the best of luck." He turned to another guest and left the three standing in front of the casket.

Lacie was first to speak, "Jenny looks happy."

"Yes she does," came a voice behind her.

It was Caroline, Jenny's eleven-year-old sister. She continued. "Jenny didn't commit suicide. Colton, find the person who did this, because my sister would never kill herself."

Lacie took Caroline aside, and whispered, "Honey, we all have our opinions about what happened to your sister, but I think we should talk about this outside. We don't want to create a scene, do we?"

"Thank you Lacie." She turned to Colton, "Can we talk outside for a few minutes?"

Colton agreed. Before she headed for the door, Caroline walked up to her dad. "Daddy, I'm going outside for a minute. I'm having trouble breathing with all the flowers in here."

"OK, but don't stay out too long, and wear your jacket, it's getting cold. Did you bring your allergy medicine, Honey?"

"Yes, Daddy."

Lacie and Caroline walked out first. Colton and Seth stood for a while and then they left the funeral home. The two girls were sitting on a bench. Colton approached them and said to Caroline, "Why don't you believe the police report?"

"My sister was not depressed. She told me Saturday morning that something good was coming out of all the bad things in her life. I don't know what she meant, but she was happier than I've ever seen her. She said she was moving to Detroit to live with our aunt. She wanted to leave The Point and start over with her life. Not end it!"

Colton knelt down and took Caroline's hand. "Did you tell the police this?"

"Yes, they said sometimes people who are suicidal become happy when they reach a decision to end it all, but they didn't know her like I do... or did." She cried and Lacie put her arm around her.

Colton stood. "I promise I will do everything I can to find out what happened. I'm so sorry, but we have to get going. Do you have my sister's cell phone number?"

"I think so, why?"

"I can get your cell phone number from her then. What I want you to do is look around for anything that will help us know what your sister was doing. It could be anything. Messages, Facebook, even a diary or letter. Be careful not to tell anyone what we are doing; just keep your eyes open for clues. I'll call if I have more questions. Again, tell no one what we're doing. Promise?"

"Promise!"

Caroline walked back into the funeral home. When the three teens saw her walk through the wooden door, they walked toward the Jeep.

Colton drove Lacie home first, then he and Seth drove back to school to pick up his car.

"I'll meet you in an hour at the garage. OK?" he asked Seth.

"Yes, and I'll bring the equipment. It shouldn't take more than an hour to set the trap, and when we're done, we can go out for dinner."

Chapter 22

Seth was on time, and Colton was ready to go. They put the security cameras in the back of Colton's Jeep and set out for The Point.

"Have you decided where we should put the cameras?" asked Colton.

"Jim Owens installed a security system at a home next to Mrs. Hoffstarter that would work. He has a mailbox and we could install a camera looking down the main road. I looked on Google Maps and it would work. The other is down further west, and perhaps one on the south shore."

"Mrs. Hoffstarter's neighbor is Albert Doyle, the retired police detective I told you about. Let's do his first."

Seth agreed. In a few minutes they were in Doyle's driveway. Colton went to the side door and rang the bell.

Mr. Doyle opened the door. "Colton, how can I help you?"

Colton explained the situation to Doyle and then he yelled for Seth to come meet Mr. Doyle. The technology Seth was using fascinated Doyle, and the two talked for a few minutes about the security camera Seth would install.

"Where did you find software capable of identifying types of vehicles?" he asked.

"I found a free security program with face recognition, and I rewrote the code to include more than just faces. The system notifies me when a vehicle or person I'm looking for comes into view. Then I get images of it sent to my phone. I can have the software call the police, but that could be a problem if my program mistook a home owner or delivery company as an intruder."

"Yes it would cause problems. Like reporting a false fire alarm. The fire department can make you pay for their trouble. And if the police keep getting called in error, soon they will refuse to respond."

Doyle watched as Seth set two cameras on his mailbox. One looking east for vehicles coming into The Point subdivision, and the other could see a mile down the road in the opposite direction. Turning to Colton, he said, "When do you think these robbers will strike?"

"If they stay on the same schedule, they will break into another home tomorrow morning. That's why we're setting the cameras up tonight."

Colton studied the two camera views and suggested that they may only need one other camera. "From this location we can cover a two mile area. The third camera should be two miles west. If we see them turning toward the South Shore, we could to track them down."

Seth thought for a moment and agreed. "Well, that will save us a lot of time and energy. Mr. Doyle, you have the perfect location."

Doyle laughed. "I move here because of the perfect location, and I looked forward to a nice quiet retirement at my lake cottage. Instead I'm greeted with a dead girl in the hot tub, and now a security trap to catch home burglars. It's just like being back on the force in Detroit, but with a beautiful lake view." '

"Welcome to The Point, Mr. Doyle," laughed Seth. "If you spend time around Colton, you'll run into all kinds of tense situations."

Doyle laughed and then turned serious. "Seth and Colton, just make sure the two of you avoid contact with the robbers. Watch for them, then call the police. When I was on the police force, we always waited for backup before we approached a dangerous situation The one time I didn't wait, I almost died."

Colton told Doyle that the police would be in the area all morning. "They're part of the trap, and we will be careful."

After setting up a third camera, Colton and Seth drove to Caseville for dinner at Lefty's Drive Inn, a throwback 1950's diner with the best footlongs in the county.

Sitting in a booth, the two talked, only as best friends can do.

"I want to say I'm sorry about the other night in Caro," Colton said, as a look of shame flashed across his face.

"Look, I said it was OK. And it is! I know you; you keep everything inside and when the pressure reaches its boiling point, you pop your cork."

"I pop my cork?"

"Yup. Just like a fine bottle of bubbly."

Colton laughed and took a bite of his footlong. "Trade you, some of my onion rings for chili fries."

"Great idea. Just don't eat them all, like you always do."

"Nag, Nag, Nag."

***

By the time Colton arrived home, it was past seven p.m.. His siblings were doing their homework and his Mom and Dad were at the kitchen table, talking.

His mom asked, "Colton, are you sure you're OK? It was very traumatic finding Jenny yesterday morning,"

"It was, but going to the funeral home helped, because she looked so peaceful. That helps replace the image left in my mind yesterday. Besides, I have a new mission to catch burglars tonight with Seth."

Colton's dad's face grew grim. "Don't tell me you're up to something dangerous again."

"OK. I won't tell you that. Dad, I know how you feel, but Sheriff McNabb asked us to do this tonight, because burglars are breaking into the homes of summer residents, and McNabb detected a pattern to these break-ins. He's convinced they will strike early tomorrow morning."

"What do you have to do?"

"We set cameras up along the main road, and then we'll look for moving vans or trucks that enter The Point. If we spot a van pulling into a driveway, we will contact the police and they will take it from there." Colton didn't think they would be in any danger, and he was trying as hard as he could to assure his parents of this.

"Well, be careful."

Colton's Mom reached across the table and took her son's hands. "We are proud of you, and we trust you. Please stay away from any danger."

"Thank you, Mom, Dad. I won't do anything stupid; I promise."

Colton's mother suggested he talk to his siblings. "They may want to hear all about Jenny's death. Colton, please be careful what you say; they're young and impressionable. This kind of event is hard to understand for them, and for us adults."

"I got it, Mom. Sensitive and understanding?"

"Yes. And if you can, move the conversation to sports, when possible," added his Dad.

After being grilled with questions and going through all the reasons the Loons lost the game Friday, Colton and his brothers and sister were ready for bed, and he didn't have to answer questions about Jenny's death.

***

When Colton's alarm clock rang, he was already awake and dressed for the Tuesday morning newspaper delivery. Throughout the night he kept thinking about finding Jenny's lifeless body near the hot tub. Sleep eluded Colton, but the image of her hands hanging over the edge with blood dripping into the hot tub, became burned forever into his mind and heart.

Instead of dressing for work, Colton wore school clothes and sent a message to Seth to do the same. If they run into the burglars, he figured they may not have time to change clothes before school.

As he passed through the kitchen, he grabbed two cold Cokes and two big candy bars left over from Halloween.

Seth parked his Charger next to Colton's Jeep and was standing in the driveway with a mug of coffee in one hand and a bag in the other.

"I have a ton of candy here." Seth said as he jumped into the passenger side of the Jeep. "My mom couldn't give it all away to the kids, so I'll share it with you." He grinned when he saw the candy bars in Colton's hand.

"Sorry, Seth; I brought two huge candy bars for us, but you never know, I might get hungry for more." Colton had a twinkle in his eyes as he dropped one candy bar into Seth's candy bag.

On their way to the storage building in Pigeon, Seth reported what the security cameras displayed. "There was a lot of traffic up to midnight, but then it died down. There were no large trucks or vans, and only a few pickup trucks and a motor home left The Point."

"Well, we might not see a robbery tonight. It seems odd they would rob homes on a regular pattern, like Sheriff McNabb suggested," replied Colton. "I've been trying to figure out how they know who went south for the winter?"

Colton thought for a moment. "Unless... perhaps they have access to the list of customers leaving for the winter, like the list I get from my newspaper. The other newspapers would have a list too, and if the robbers had one of those lists, they would know which houses are unoccupied."

"How would they get their hands on the list?" asked Seth.

"Good question." Colton turned into the storage shed and saw the other newspaper delivery men loading their papers. The company delivery truck was early, and they left the papers stacked in the storage shed.

Colton appreciated Seth's help. Together they had the Jeep loaded and ready for the first delivery in less than four minutes; a record for Colton.

The two friends talked about the football game, their girlfriends, deer hunting, their business, and Jenny's death.

"Colton, do you think we might have pushed Jenny into committing suicide?"

"No way. Lacie gave her information to help her get out of the abusive relationship, so Jenny knew she didn't have to put up with Luke's crap. And besides, her sister said she intended to move to Detroit to get away from him, and she appeared happy. To be honest, I think Luke killed her, and made it look like a suicide."

"That's what I've been thinking, but how do we prove it?"

"We need to do our detective work."

"Sounds good," said Seth

"The only problem is we're not the police. We can't drag his ass downtown to interrogate him in a small musty room with no window, just a desk with two chairs, a bright light, and a two-way mirror."

Seth laughed at the image Colton described. "Well, we have to use our detective minds. We'll think of something."

Colton was half done with the route on The Point when Seth got excited and pointed to the screen on his laptop.

"Get your crap together, Seth. What do you see?"

Seth was so excited he couldn't speak. "The robbers just pulled into the house next to Mr. Doyle. They have a big white moving van. It looks like a rental van."

Colton took his phone out and dialed Detective Ned's personal number.

"Ned. We spotted them. They're on the north side of the main drive. The house is Mr. and Mrs. Washingham. They left for Arizona two weeks ago. I got the notice last week."

Colton gave Ned the address, but Ned said he was in Caseville, and it would be at least fifteen minutes before he could get to The Point. "Keep your eyes on them, but don't get close. Don't let them see you. Do you understand, Colton?"

"Got it, Ned. We'll finish the route, then we'll stop and stay back from the Washingham house. No lights, no noise. We'll park on the side of the road, out of view. Is that good enough?"

Deputy Ned said, "Perfect. I'm calling for backup. I'm sure I'll be there before they arrive. They will not approach until I give the signal."

It took ten minutes for Colton and Seth to finish the route up to Doyle's house. They drove the last five hundred feet without headlights, so no one could see them.

Colton pulled off the road in front of Doyle's. There were several pine trees separating the two properties.

"This is as far as we go," Colton whispered. "Now we wait for Ned and his backup."

"Only one problem. I have to pee," whispered Seth.

"No. Hold it in!" insisted Colton. "We can't take the chance. When I open the door, the light goes on."

Seth reached for the dome light, snapped the cover off, and removed the bulb.

"There, it won't light up, now." He insisted, as he opened his door. "Like I said, I have to pee, now."

With great care, Seth walked toward the trees. Standing behind a large pine, he unzipped his jeans and watered the ground. He sighed with relief.

A large hand wrapped around his face from behind, and he felt a gun pushing into his spine. A deep voice said, "Don't move, or you're dead. Why are you here?"

"I have to pee. Just let me go and I'll be done and gone in a flash."

"No way, you're not going anywhere." the man said.

"Well, let me finish and zip up my jeans."

"OK! But no funny business."

Seth didn't know what to do. If he tried to get away, he'd die. If he didn't get away, he might be a hostage when the police get here. Decisions, Decisions...

A thud sound came from behind. Seth turned around as the

robber dropped to the ground. There stood Al Doyle with a huge grin on his face and a cast iron fry pan in his hand.

"Here, hold my fry pan while I duct tape his hands and mouth. We don't want him to wake up yelling to his friends, inside the house."

Seth watched as Doyle worked. "You weren't afraid he would shoot me in the back?"

"No. I figured his finger would only shoot blanks," Doyle said. "Besides, I'm an expert with a fry pan."

Doyle bent down and grabbed the man's limp arm. "Let's pull him to the Jeep. I don't want to stand out here. They might come looking for him."

Colton almost lost it when he saw Doyle and Seth pulling a body up to the road.

Seth had a huge smile on his face as He and Doyle laid the robber's body next to the Jeep. Colton saw a car with its headlight off, approaching from the other direction. It was Deputy Ned, and behind him were two other county deputies.

Ned walked toward the Jeep. When he saw the man taped up, laying on the road, he turned to Doyle and said in a whisper, "What the hell?"

"Fry pan." Doyle said. "I hit him with one because he had my friend, Seth, hogtied."

"And what was Seth doing?" Ned asked, almost laughing.

"Peeing on my trees. That's what he was doing!" said Doyle.

To avoid laughing, Ned turned to the other officers. "OK, men. Let's round up the robbers."

The men, with their hands next to their guns, walked up to the door. It took less than five minutes for the officers to escort two men from the house. As they did, Colton turned his headlights on so he could see the action.

Doyle yelled to Ned. "The one we caught is awake now. I'm sure he wants a ride with his friends."

Ned walked over to the Jeep. Doyle and Seth helped the man get onto his feet. The deputy laughed when he saw the robbers hands taped behind him with duct tape.

"Nice handcuffs, Doyle."

"I learned that trick when I was a homicide detective in Detroit." Doyle said.

"Impressive," said the Deputy, as he ripped the tape from the robber's mouth.

Colton cringed. He could almost feel the man's beard and lips ripping off with the tape.

"Hurts, doesn't it?" Ned asked the robber. Ned read the man his rights and lead him toward the patrol car. When the robbers were all loaded into the cars, he walked back to the Jeep.

"Well, thank you for your help, men. Colton, I'll let you know what we find, but I'm sure these men are the robbers we've been looking for. Deputy Mike and Chad will search the home for prints, photograph the damage, and then take your statements. I'm taking these three crooks to Bad Axe."

"Ned. I think I recognized the youngest robber, with the long hair. He's a substitute driver for the newspaper company, and I recall one of the other drivers saying he got the job because his girlfriend works in the circulation office. If that's true, they would have access to the list of customers who were leaving for the winter."

"Good lead," Ned said. "I'll look into it. Well, thanks again. And Mr. Doyle, welcome to the neighborhood."

It only took a few minutes for Deputy Chad to take statements from Colton, Seth, and Doyle.

After he recorded Colton's he said, "We're done here for now. If the sheriff needs more, he'll contact you. Now I have to help Deputy Mike finish up the robbery scene."

Doyle picked up his fry pan and said he was heading home. "I've got friends stopping in for breakfast, and I'm sure you boys need to finish your deliveries."

"We sure do," replied Colton. "Before you go, thank you for saving

Seth."

"No problem. My fear of facing a boring retirement was unjustified. I had more fun than I deserve tonight!"

Chapter 23

The morning sunrise was beautiful, with hundreds of giant windmills dotting the horizon. Colton and Seth pulled into the school parking lot before the first bus arrived.

Colton took another sip of his cold coffee and put his hand into Seth's trick-or-treat bag of candy and asked, "Well... what's the agenda for today?"

"Good question. I wish we had time to shower."

Colton agreed. "Now you know how I feel every morning after I deliver papers. I never have time to go home and change, or shower."

"I'm telling you, Colton, quit the job. Our business will make us rich, so you won't have to drive around delivering newspapers." Seth was serious. In his mind, Colton was wasting time he should devote to the business.

"If my route becomes a problem, I will quit. Until then, don't worry. My job is enjoyable because it gives me time to unwind, so I can listen to my books and think about my problems. I do some of my best thinking when I'm doing the route."

"Understood; I won't bring it up again," Seth promised. "Now that football is over, what will you be doing with your after school time?"

"I'll be working on our business with you, and I want to look into Jenny's death. It still feels off, because her clothing wasn't spattered with blood even though both of her wrists were cut, and there was blood in the water but no blood on the steps. It doesn't look like a suicide."

"Do you think it was Luke who killed her?"

"He's my first guess, but how do we prove it?"

Seth thought for a moment. "Too bad we aren't policemen; we could drag his ass into a room and beat the truth out of him."

"Seth, you've been watching too many old movies. They don't beat suspects anymore; they question them."

"We can't even do that."

Colton and Seth walked across the lot and into the school after they saw the bus carrying Lacie and Beth pull into the school lot.

"I'll see you later, Seth. I want to tell Lacie about our adventure this morning."

Seth smiled. "I'm sure she knows all about it, already."

"She might have heard Ned's version, but I'm sure she'll want to hear the truth."

Colton felt strange walking through the halls. There were no congratulations or back slaps. With the loss on Saturday, the students had nothing to say. He wanted to just scream, YES WE LOST... GET OVER IT.

As Lacie approached, he noticed a visible bruise on her face. Colton tried not to mention it, but he couldn't help himself. He put his hand up to her face and touched her hair.

"You look beautiful, today."

"Thank you, but I know the bruise still shows even though I tried makeup which didn't cover it."

"It's not that bad." He tried to look like he believed what he was saying, but Lacie knew better.

"I know how it looks."

Lacie's face turned serious. "So, tell me all about the robbery this morning. Uncle Ned called, but he wouldn't give me the details. He said the two of you made a new agreement, and I don't get all the news anymore. What's up with that?"

"I told Ned that it was important that he respects my privacy. I want to tell you when I do something, so it's not his place to tell people what I'm doing." Colton was having a hard time saying what he meant. He heard his words, and they didn't convey what he was feeling.

"OK. So tell me what happened."

Colton told Lacie everything about the morning's adventure. He even told her how Seth got kidnapped by one robber and Mr. Doyle rescued him. Lacie kissed Colton on the side of his face when the bell rang.

"I'm glad you and Seth didn't get hurt. I'll see you in art class."

"Sounds like a plan," Colton said as he turned toward his first hour class with a smile on his face.

Connie Jackson noticed the smile when Colton walked into their history class. It was contagious, and when he sat down next to her, she broke into a smile.

"What's going on. Did you do something funny in the hallway?"

"No. Why?"

"That grin goes from one ear to the other. And it looks suspicious."

Colton laughed. "Connie, I feel good even though we lost the big game. I spent the night helping the police catch nasty robbers, and even though Jennie died last Sunday, my life is good."

"Too deep for me. I'm just happy I found my iPad this morning. You know how much they charge us if we lose those things?" She asked.

"Yes. And thank you for not poking me with your pencil."

"I kind of understand what you meant by that being an abuse. It's like when I pinch my sister and don't let go. Or when guys say nasty things about each other. If your actions or words hurt another person, it's wrong. Mrs. Dunn helped us understand what bullying and abuse is, and so did you."

"See! Something else to make our life good."

Mr. Dinger, in a hearty voice yelled, "Colton, can you and Connie stop talking? I'm trying to take attendance."

"Sorry, sir."

***

The conversations in school centered on the football team's loss and Jenny's funeral tomorrow. Colton and Lacie agreed that they would not attend the funeral since they already visited the funeral home and the buzz around school was that only a few students planned to attend.

During art class, Lacie summed it up when she said, "Jenny didn't have many friends. I talked to a girl who said she was friends with Jenny before she met Luke. She said Jenny was outgoing and sweet, but she became distant after she began dating him."

Jerry Cultrain nodded in agreement. "I knew her in junior high. She was a sweetheart. But when Luke got his claws into her, she turned away from all her old friends. Perhaps she didn't want us to know what that creep was doing to her."

Beth wasn't quite as sure about why Jenny changed. "People change. I don't know many kids who are the same as they were in junior high."

As they talked about Jenny, Colton became aware most of his friends believed she had killed herself. Seth and Lacie knew how he felt, but the others didn't. He decided that it would be best to keep his feelings to himself.

After seventh hour Colton said goodbye to Lacie at her bus and then stopped into the locker room to talk to Coach Talbert.

Coach was glad to see him. They talked about the game and Coach tried to lift the Colton's spirits by telling him how good the team played Saturday. Colton wasn't sure about that. "If I played a good game, why didn't the Loons win?"

"Colton, both teams can't win. That being said, both teams played well. Accept it and move on."

Aden walked in while Coach was talking and said he agreed with

Coach Talbert. He told Coach he was trying out for basketball. Talbert wasn't the basketball coach, but Colton's decision not to tryout for basketball surprised him.

Colton explained, "I'm not great at shooting baskets, but the biggest reason is, I've started a business with Seth and we need time to build our customer base. This winter will be a good time for that."

After talking about basketball, business, the robbers on The Point, Aden's Camaro and girlfriend, Jenny's death, and the weather, Colton and Aden headed home.

Colton told Aden he was glad he got his scholarship to play college football.

"Colton, you'll get a football scholarship next year."

"I won't be applying for one. I plan to get my degree through online courses. There's so much I want to do and going off to college for four years isn't one of them."

"Wow. That's not what I ever expected you to say, Colton. You're good at football. I figured you wanted what I wanted."

"Aden, it works for you, but it won't work for me. I've already got a half year of college credits, and if I keep going, I could have a degree in two years. In the meantime, I'm having fun with my new business."

The two shook hands and walked to their vehicles.

***

Since Thanksgiving was only a week away, Colton's mom was in the holiday spirit. When he walked into the house, he noticed pumpkins setting on the kitchen table ready to become pies. Several small pumpkins and fall leaves graced the fireplace mantel with a few Christmas decorations scattered around the house. It made him feel warm inside and helped ease his stress.

"Colton, it's nice having you home early. Are you going to miss football practice?"

"No. I'll be spending more time getting the business in order. Seth said we're up to ten paying customers and his dad has found three more business owners who want our security system installed." Colton grabbed a box of crackers and stood in front of the refrigerator.

"You can eat cheese, but remember you should exercise now that football is over. You don't want to keep eating like you've been, without exercising."

"I will. I remember last year, and I don't want to get out of shape either."

Your brothers and sister are home. The bus just stopped."

Colton walked to the door and opened it. "Welcome my friends."

Terry screamed with delight. "Colton, can we practice basketball? Are you going to be on the team? When are we going deer hunting?"

Before Colton could answer, Terry ran to the bathroom to pee.

Jason laughed and hugged his older brother. "So, when are we going deer hunting?"

"The first of December. We'll go into the woods near The Point."

"Can we hunt deer on The Point?"

"Not on The Point, but Dad knows the owner of a large private 100 acre wooded lot and he got permission for us to bow hunt there. I'm not sure of the day, yet. I hope we can hunt on a Saturday, because if we can't, then we have to skip school."

"Skip School? That sounds even better!"

Colton's mom blocked that idea. "No! Well... only if he must." She gave Colton a stern look. "Make sure you can hunt on a Saturday."

Seth pulled into the driveway and walked into the garage office. Colton excused himself. "Mom, I'll try to finish by dinner time. If not, may Seth and I eat in the garage?"

"Yes, there will be enough for both of you. Check the paperwork in the basket on the desk. Two of them need your signature."

"OK. Thanks, Mom." Colton rushed out the door. Seth was standing in the doorway, waiting for him, and together they went into the office.

The two had a very productive afternoon.

***

Colton and Seth completed their work before dinner. He asked if his friend wanted to stay, but Seth declined, because he was taking Beth to Bay City for dinner and a movie.

"Sounds like fun. I'll see you in the morning," Colton said as he headed toward the house.

After a hearty dinner, Colton went into the living room to watch the evening news. Stephenie followed and sat next to Colton on the couch.

"Colton," She whispered. "Look at this Email message." She handed her cell phone to him.

The message was from Jenny's sister, Caroline. It read, "The funeral was sad. I wanted to let you know I found Jenny's diary and I'll bring it to school tomorrow. Tell Colton to read it. I am positive Luke killed my sister. I want him to pay!"

"Did you email back?"

"Yes, I said I would see her at school and I'll give you the diary, after school."

"OK. Stephenie… please don't talk about this in school and tell Caroline not tell anyone what we're doing. If Luke is a killer, we don't know what he would do to any of us."

"I'll be careful. Are you going to watch the news? It's so boring. I'm going to my room to do homework."

Colton enjoyed a restful evening at home. He considered Seth's comments about quitting the paper route. Tonight he admitted to himself that it was nice not having to deliver papers. When he started the job he needed the money, and he discovered he enjoyed being able to drive, make money, and listen to audiobooks. Without the job, he never would find the time for his books.

Besides, he considered, *I would have missed the thrilling events on The Point.*

After checking his Email and Facebook page, Colton called Lacie to talk about Jenny's death. Lacie didn't want Colton to confront Luke, out of concern for his safety.

"You know he has a temper. If you try to talk to him about her death, he will blame you and start a fight."

At first Colton said he wasn't afraid of Luke, but upon consideration of past events, he decided Lacie was right.

"I won't talk to him until I'm holding some kind of proof. I wonder if he has an alibi. Perhaps I can ask Ned, tomorrow."

"Good idea. Just don't tell him what you're doing," Lacie suggested. She was aware her uncle Ned told the Sheriff everything he heard. "I have an idea, Colton. Why don't you talk to Mr. Doyle about your investigation? When you get the diary, you could have him look it over with you. Since he was a homicide detective, perhaps he could help you gather evidence."

"Excellent idea. I'll call him tomorrow, but I won't be able to meet him until Thursday afternoon. Would you like to join me?"

Lacie took a moment to answer. "Yes, but you can drop me off at Mrs. Hoffstarter. I'd like to visit with her while you men talk about Jenny."

"Lacie, have I told you how much I love you?"

"Yes, but you can tell me again. It makes me feel good."

Chapter 24

After a good night's sleep, Colton was eager to begin his investigation. Convinced that Luke murdered Jenny, Colton must now find the proof.

After blazing through a first hour history test, Colton spent the morning considering ways to investigate Jenny's murder.

During art class, he asked to use the restroom. While out of the room, he called Deputy Ned's cell number.

"Ned, I have a question. Did the police look into where Luke was when Jenny died?"

Ned sighed and asked, "Are you still convinced someone killed Jenny?"

"Well... yes I do. It doesn't add up, considering how I saw Luke hit Jenny." Colton didn't want to admit his feelings on the case, but there was no way around.

"Luke had an alibi. He was in the custody of the Sheriff for two hours and his mother picked him up and took him home around midnight. A state trooper arrested him in Bad Axe for hitting a man at the gas station. As I understand, Luke dropped Jenny off at her home on The Point, and by ten o'clock he was in our holding cell. Luke didn't get released until midnight. The coroner says Jenny died Saturday night at about twelve. The coroner doesn't believe Luke had enough time to kill her."

"Damn! It appears I'm wrong," Colton admitted. He hated when he was wrong.

"Yes... you are not perfect, Colton. So stop trying to make every tragedy into a murder case. Jenny was unhappy, perhaps because of how Luke treated her, but he did not kill her."

When Colton returned from the restroom, the teacher asked what took so long. Colton shrugged his shoulder and didn't respond.

Lacie could tell that Ned said something Colton didn't want to hear. "Are you going to tell me what he said?"

"Luke didn't do it, and I need to reconsider my case."

Colton explained why Luke had a good alibi. Jerry had been listening to the conversation and asked, "Does this mean Jenny committed suicide?"

"No! It means Luke didn't kill her, and I'm still convinced someone else had a hand in her death. There are so many questions. I mean... why would she get dressed in high heels and a sexy red dress to kill herself, and how could she cut one wrist and then the other wrist without getting blood on the steps where she was laying? It all looks wrong," Colton insisted.

Lacie understood Colton's frustration. She put her hand over his and asked, "Who else would want to kill Jenny?"

Colton looked down at their hands. He turned his, so they were holding hands. He considered for a moment and said, "I think her diary may answer those questions."

The art teacher walked toward the couple prompting Colton to work on his painting, which needed a great deal of attention.

***

At the end of the last hour, Colton met Lacie by the locker room doors. He offered to give her a ride to Pigeon where she works a few hours as a nurse's aid.

During their drive to Pigeon, the couple talked about Thanksgiving, which was only one week away.

"Are you still joining our family?" Colton asked.

"I wouldn't miss it for anything. Mrs. Hoffstarter is still coming, isn't she?"

"She is. I asked Mom to call her to make sure because we won't see her Saturday. I'm delivering part of the Thanksgiving paper Saturday afternoon."

Lacie laughed. "Yes, we can. I keep losing track of my days. With this job three days a week, and my online class work, I feel like time is going too fast."

"That I can relate to. I guess we're both overworked."

Colton pulled up to the hospital doors and stopped. "Have a good day at work. Remember, it's only a few days until the weekend and then next week will be shorter because of Thanksgiving."

"It can't get here soon enough," Lacie said.

Colton got out of the Jeep and opened Lacie's door. He helped her out and gave her a huge hug, and a passionate kiss. "We can talk later."

When Colton pulled into his driveway, he saw his brothers in the backyard target practicing with their bows. He watched for a few minutes and then slipped into the office.

Stephenie came running into the office with Jenny's diary.

"I didn't look at it, like you suggested, and Caroline needs it back tomorrow because she's afraid her dad might notice it's gone. Can I take it back tomorrow?

Colton thought for a moment and said, "Yes! I'll read through it and scan the important pages."

Sitting at his desk he read the diary. It covered the last two months. After reading half of the pages, he took his phone out and looked at the photographs of the scene of Jenny's death. The pain associated with his seeing her like that, came rushing back. He would never be the same.

Colton had witnessed a murder before, but it was at night and he didn't see the victim up close. As he looked at the gruesome photographs, he picked up the office phone and dialed Doyle's number.

"Mr. Doyle, it's Colton here. I was wondering if we could discuss

Jenny's death tomorrow afternoon. I have her diary and I need professional help in my investigation."

Doyle asked about Luke and Colton responded, "Ned Wooddell, the sheriff's deputy, told me Luke has a good alibi. If it was murder, someone else is the killer."

Doyle said, "I would love to help you. A little excitement would be welcome."

Colton agreed to meet at Doyle's home after three p.m. He spent the rest of the afternoon copying Jenny's diary. He copied two pages at a time and saved them as a PDF document. He also printed them since he wasn't sure Doyle could open the digital file.

***

Colton finished his evening dinner and retired to his room. He took Jenny's diary with him. The diary had many gloomy observations, and he soon found himself absorbed in Jenny's life. After reading the entire diary, he took a highlighter and marked his copy, highlighting sections he wanted to discuss with Doyle.

Since Colton had to be up early for his route, he went to bed before nine. When the alarm clock buzzed, he realized that he had slept for six straight hours. He was eager to get to work.

Colton dressed for school (just in case), grabbed a snack, some hot coffee, and in no time he was on the road. The route took less time than normal and Colton attributed this to the fact that there were another fifteen customers who were heading south for the winter and the papers were smaller than usual.

Colton didn't drive home even though he finished early. Instead, he drove to school and sat in his Jeep listening to his audiobook. The only cars in the parking lot belonged to school personnel and teachers. When the buses arrived, he walked to the front doors and waited for Lacie.

He sat with a group of guys in front of the school office, talking about sports and parties. It amazed Colton how many students are into drinking, smoking, and drugs; two of them bragged about how sick they got on booze the night before. Colton mused to himself, *It's no wonder they have bad grades and are always in trouble. I don't see the fun in drinking until I puke.*

When he saw Lacie walking through the school doors, he rushed to greet her as she grinned in surprise.

"This is nice, so why are you in such a good mood?" She asked.

"Because I spent the night thinking of you."

Hand-in-hand the couple walked to their lockers. Colton picked up his book for first hour and walked over to Lacie's locker. "One week 'til turkey day. Are you as excited as I am?"

Lacie laughed. "You're just like a little kid at Christmas. Yes, I'm looking forward to Thanksgiving and I'm looking forward to spending time with Mrs. Hoffstarter."

"Yes, we'll have a great time, and I want to ask her some questions about my investigation. I will drop off the pages from Jenny's diary so she can read them before Thanksgiving."

Frustration flashed across Lacie's face. "Why can't we enjoy the holiday? I mean, everything shouldn't always revolve around your investigations, or business, or football."

Colton looked down, then his eyes moved to meet Lacie's icy blue eyes. "You're right. I get so involved that I don't consider how my actions impact you. I will only bring up Jenny's death, if Mrs. Hoffstarter does."

"Thank you. Now I'm looking forward to a great Thanksgiving day."

During art class, Jerry asked about his investigation. Colton had decided not to share Jenny's diary with any of the other students, so he shrugged and said he had nothing new to report.

"Too bad man," Jerry replied. "It's always interesting when you have a hot case to share."

"Not today, Jerry. Not today."

***

The bell rang at the end of seventh hour P.E. class. Colton caught up with Lacie.

"You are going with me to see Mr. Doyle, aren't you?"

She looked surprised. "No… I forgot… sorry… I have to help Mom."

He gave her a quick kiss and told her he would call and tell her what Doyle says about Jenny's diary.

"Be careful to avoid hitting any deer. Mom said they're moving around a lot because of the hunters."

"They're always moving around on The Point, since they feel safe there."

From school Colton headed straight for The Point. He didn't want to be late for his meeting with Doyle. As he drove past the Washingham home, he could see police tape laying on the ground. They removed the robbers van, but the sheriff's men didn't do a great job of clearing the crime scene.

He turned into Doyle's driveway and parked next to his beautiful black Buick Enclave. As Colton walked around Doyle's S.U.V. he looked in the driver's window and took a deep breath. *Wow, this is even nicer than my Jeep. Oh, well… Someday I'll have one of my own.*

He rang the doorbell and Mr. Doyle, dressed in a Tiger's sweatshirt and jeans, greeted him. Colton could tell his clothes were not from Walmart. *Perhaps he shops at a designer store in Detroit,* he considered.

"Colton, come on in. I saw you admiring the new Buick I purchased when I moved up from Detroit. It's the first personal car I've owned in many years."

"It's a beautiful vehicle; makes my Jeep look old," Colton said with embarrassment in his voice.

"Your Jeep looks fine. Do you drink coffee? I made a fresh pot and you're welcome to a cup, and I also have cookies I made for a party I'm hosting for a few new friends."

Colton accepted a cup of coffee and took one cookie. His eyes kept wandering around Doyle's beautiful home. It was like Mrs. Hoffstarter's home, but Doyle's had more masculine features. The large kitchen featured a counter with several leather chairs.

Colton sat in one and felt at home. "This is nice, Doyle. It reminded me of a man-cave; like the one Dad and I created in our garage. I use ours as the office for our new business."

"Thank you. Every day the place gets a little closer to what I want. I had a large home in Detroit, but most of the furniture was old and dark. This house is modern and needed what they call *cottage accents*."

Doyle looked around the room. "Now I sound like a decorator. To be honest, I had someone else help me do this. I can be creative in the kitchen, but not at decorating a home. I know what I like and I could convey that to a professional decorator who knew how achieve it."

"It looks great," Colton said as he took another cookie. "Here is a copy I made of Jenny's diary. I read it and highlighted areas I found interesting and relevant."

Doyle picked up the pages and read. As he read, Colton walked to the large picture windows and admired the view of Lake Huron. While standing by the windows he felt something rub against his legs. It was a rusty brown and black Bloodhound, sniffing his leg and watching his every move with great curiosity.

"What's your dog's name," Colton asked.

"Copper," replied Doyle. "He's a Bloodhound, but he needs to smell everything, so take care."

Colton sat down on the plush yellow and orange rug and played with Copper. He liked dogs, but never had one as a pet. Chickens were as close to a pet as his parents would allow, and after the family ate them he didn't want more.

Doyle walked into the family room and sat in a large leather chair.

"I can tell Copper likes you since he always stays in his room when strangers visit."

"What do you think of Jenny's diary?"

"It's obvious she was being abused. But I wonder if there was another abuser. The way she talks about Luke and at other times about, *Him*. As if there was another man involved," Doyle observed.

"That's what I felt when I read it, and from what the police say, Luke has a good alibi."

"Only if you trust parents to be honest about where their child was. I'm sure they would protect him."

Colton thought for a moment and said, "The police seem to believe his parents."

"Yes, but they were not looking for a killer. The police assumed suicide all along."

Colton thought about what Doyle said as he scratched Copper behind the ears.

Doyle laughed as he watched Colton, "You keep that up and Copper will be your friend forever."

"I hope so," said Colton. "If Luke didn't kill Jenny, who did?"

"That's the million dollar question. Let's go over what we have for clues." Doyle walked back to the counter and Colton followed him. On the counter were five-by-seven prints of the photographs Colton took at the crime scene.

It was hard to look at them as the memories rushed back into Colton's mind. Doyle took a black marker and wrote on a large white sheet of paper. He wrote Jenny's name over her photograph. Then he wrote Luke's name next to her.

"We know Luke was abusing Jenny. Have you ever seen Jenny with someone else?" asked Doyle.

"No. According to her diary he was her boyfriend for the past two years, but that's as far back as the diary goes. She could have had a boyfriend before, but how would we know that?" Colton asked. "How will we be able to investigate this?"

Doyle thought for a moment, sipped coffee, and took a bite of his cookie. "If we were the police, we would talk to her parents and all of her friends. Since we aren't the police, here's what we'll do. I will investigate Jenny's and Luke's family. I can get information from the police and public records."

"What should I do?" Colton asked.

"I want you to talk to students at school. Find anyone who knows if Jenny had other boyfriends before Luke. Be careful, Colton. You don't want Luke to become aware you're snooping around," Doyle warned.

Copper put his paws on Colton's knees and looked at him with his big droopy eyes. It was as if he was repeating Doyle's warning.

Chapter 25

After driving home, Colton called Lacie and asked if she was still enjoying her new part-time job at the hospital.

"You know I am because I keep telling you I love helping the nurses and patients, and Mom told me I have *the touch*," she added.

"Your mom is right."

"Thank you," Lacie responded. "Now tell me what Mr. Doyle thinks of Jenny's diary."

"He agrees there must be another person who abused Jenny, and he wants us to ask around school about Jenny's past boyfriends." Hoping Lacie would volunteer to help him, he said, "You're good at getting people to share and you are friends with more girls at school than I am."

"Yes. I'll help you, and I would make you beg more, but I have homework to do tonight."

Colton felt relief when she accepted. "Thank you, with luck we'll find someone who knows something important."

"I hope so, and I was wondering if you think it would be smart to say we're planning a memorial for the school yearbook? That would give us an excuse for asking questions."

"Great idea; you're so smart."

"Yes, I am. I'll see you in the morning. Love ya!" Lacie said.

Before dinner Colton asked Stephenie about Jenny's diary. "Did she say anything when you gave it back?"

"No, but she acted strange."

"What do you mean?" asked Colton.

"She's been in an odd mood... sad about her sister dying, but today something else was bothering her. When I asked her, she told me to keep my nose out of her business."

"Then don't bother her, because there may be trouble at home or something."

Colton's mom called everyone in for dinner. The conversation around the table included plans for Thanksgiving next Thursday and Christmas. Terry and Jason listed the hundreds of things they needed for Christmas presents, and Stephenie asked for a new telephone.

"I want one that isn't someone's old phone, but it doesn't have to be expensive; just new," she said.

"Colton, what do you need?" asked his dad.

Colton laughed. The past several years Christmas were lean, with his dad being laid off and the bills piling up, there were few gifts around the tree.

"I'm just thankful for what I have; family, friends, and my Jeep. You've given me enough this year."

"That's nice, Colton," replied his dad. "I'll give your gifts to the kids down the road."

Terry jumped up and yelled, "No, give his gifts to us; we need Colton's gifts."

"Terry, we need to talk about what Christmas is about, because it's not about you getting all the gifts."

"I'm sorry Mom."

While his brothers and sister learned the true meaning of Christmas, Colton excused himself and went to bed. Sitting at his computer he checked the audiobooks on his phone and selected a new Baldacci novel. Lacie had convinced him to listen to the Evanovich series with Stephanie Plum, but Colton was looking for raw excitement.

I need some hard action, he thought. a*nd John Palmer fits the bill.*

Colton woke early and realized he didn't have a route to do this morning. His mind raced with images from the novel he listened to and Jenny's death, so he got ready for school. His mom was up and asked why he was up so early.

"I thought I had a route, and then I couldn't get back to sleep,

"I know the feeling. As you get older, it gets harder to sleep."

There was a light snow on the ground when Colton reached school. The sun was trying to come out as he sat in the Jeep, parked in the school lot... thinking about Jenny's death.

Luke pulled his car up next to Colton's Jeep and got out. Colton lowered his window as Luke approached.

"I want to tell you how sorry I am about Jenny," Colton said.

"You know, you'll pay for what you and your bitch did to her," Luke threatened.

"We did nothing to her. You're the one who beat the crap out of her," Colton replied.

Luke slammed his fist down on the hood of the Jeep and walked away. Colton got out and checked the hood for damage. He yelled after Luke, "You're lucky my Jeep is tougher than your stupid fist."

Luke looked back, laughed, and replied with several choice words and sign language. Colton gathered his backpack and walked into the school.

***

Colton met Lacie at the front door and walked with her to his locker. After telling Lacie about his run-in with Luke, Colton asked if she wanted to change their plans to question students about Jenny.

"Look, I'm not afraid of Luke. If he tries something again, I'll scream my lungs out and everyone will realize what a bully he is."

Colton frowned. "Please, be careful and use our cover story."

"I will. And you be careful too. It sounds like Luke may want to fight with you, too."

Colton considered Lacie's comment. Seth mentioned a few weeks ago that the two of them should learn self defense. Today the idea sounds good.

"I'll be careful." Colton gave her a tight hug and a tender kiss on the lips. "We can talk in art class. Good luck."

Colton walked to history class, stopping to talk with students about Jenny. He mentioned the memorial for the yearbook and asked what they remember about her. One boy, Joey, said he was her friend in sixth grade. She moved to Pigeon from somewhere near Detroit during the middle of the school year.

"We became friends, but I never went in her house or anything like that; we talked a lot. She was hot, but too high-class for me to ask her out."

"What do you mean?" asked Colton.

"Well, she was beautiful, and I was a pimply, skinny nerd, and I think she thought of me as a safe friend. I had a lot of hot dreams about her if you know what I mean."

Colton nodded his head, wrote a few notes, and asked if Joey had any idea who Jenny dated since then.

"Nope, after sixth grade she found other friends. I saw her with that Luke guy a lot, and I believe she could do better than him."

Colton agreed and walked into Mr. Dinger's history class.

The day progressed with varied results. Only one girl said she was close enough to Jenny to have spent time at her house. Carly Brown told about her experience with Jenny over the past two years.

Colton walked into the art room and observed Lacie standing in the hall talking to Carly. The bell rang and Lacie joined Colton and Jerry at their table.

Colton was eager to share with Lacie what they discovered about Jenny. "Well?" He asked. "What did you learn?"

Lacie walked to the storage shelf and grabbed their paintings, paint, and brushes. "Not right now; we can talk about this later, in private." She nodded toward Jerry, suggesting he was listening.

Jerry seemed confused by the conversation. "Whoa. What's going on here? Colton, you got another mystery going and you're not telling me about it?"

Lacie sat down and started on her painting. "No, Jerry. We're trying to put together a memorial in the yearbook for Jenny. Both Colton and I have been asking students for information on her."

Jerry said, "So you two are investigating Jenny by talking to her friends? Sneaky!"

Beth was listening to the conversation and moved to the trio's table. "Can I join you?" she asked.

"Yes." said Jerry. "But don't ask too many questions. These two don't want us listening to them."

Lacie handed Colton the notes she took during her conversations with students, and Colton gave her, his. They read them and then asked if Jerry or Beth wanted to see them.

"No!" Jerry responded. "I have better things to do."

Beth took the two notebooks and read through them. She handed the notes back, turned to Colton and said, "I heard two guys talking to Luke about you and Lacie investigating Jenny's death, and he looked angry. Have you seen him today?"

"Yes! This morning he hit my Jeep with his hand; there was no damage, but I will try to avoid him."

Lacie said, "You better because I don't want you getting in trouble today."

"Don't worry… there won't be any trouble."

Colton and Lacie discussed their notes. They agreed Jenny did not have another boyfriend in this school. If someone else was abusing her, he had to be from another school or not in school. The two agreed to avoid asking any more questions today.

***

Colton was late for his seventh hour P.E. class because the office called him to speak with District Attorney Bagley on the phone. Mr. Bagley wanted to let Colton know his Latino friend, Tony Lopez and his family, now have their green cards and work permits so they can live and work in Huron County.

"Will they ever be able to apply for citizenship?" Colton asked.

"Yes, they can apply, but if you and Seth hadn't revealed their situation the Lopez family would have been deported. You should be proud of your effort, Colton." Mr. Bagley said. "I also want to let you know the robbery suspects are on their way to jail, so thank you for your help in catching them."

Colton was happy for Joey and appreciated Mr. Bagley's comments.

Mrs. Downer gave him an excuse slip to take to Coach Talbert, and he walked down the hall to the locker room. After changing into his gym clothing, he walked across the hall and into the hallway leading to the gym doors.

"Hey, Colton," came a yell.

Colton turned around to see who called him; it was Luke standing a few feet behind him, holding a knife.

"Why the knife, Luke? I'm not fighting, so just walk away," Colton warned.

"You should be so lucky, because I hear you and your bitch are asking a thousand questions about Jenny and Me. I told you to keep your nose out of my business."

Colton started toward the gym doors and Luke rushed at him. Colton turned and defended himself from the knife. He batted his arm against Luke's hand and the knife landed on the floor. As Luke bent down to get it, Colton hit him aside the head and kicked the knife down the hallway.

Coach Talbert was standing in the hallway and he stepped on the knife. He bent down, picked it up, and yelled, "Stop fighting, NOW!"

Colton backed up with his hands up. Luke turned to face Coach and said, "He tried to knife me. I was just heading back to class, and he started a fight. He's been after me ever since my girlfriend died."

"That's a pile of crap, Coach. It's his knife, and I was heading into class. I have an excuse from the office for being late." Colton pulled the slip out of his pocket and handed it toward Coach Talbert.

The coach stepped toward Colton and took the slip. He pulled his cell phone from his pants pocket and called the office. "Mrs. Downer, send the principal down to the locker room. There was a fight here and also send someone to watch my class."

Coach put his phone away and said, "Boys, you are both in deep trouble."

The principal rushed down the hallway and stopped next to Coach Talbert. "What happened, Coach," he said.

The coach explained what he saw and handed the knife to the principal. "I don't know whose knife it is, and I've never seen it before. Do we need to call the police?"

"We can decide later. Mr. Dinger has a free period, so Mrs. Downer told him to watch your class?" The principal said. "Let's go to the office. Boys, move it. We need to sort this out."

Colton and Luke walked down the hall and turned toward the office. The Coach and Mr. Zeller walked behind them. Mr. Dinger passed them, nodded his head and walked into the gym.

In the office, Mr. Zeller said, "You two can sit here while I talk to Coach Talbert. Don't try leaving and no fighting either."

Luke spoke first. "So, why are you asking all the questions?"

Colton laughed. "Now you ask. Why the hell didn't you ask before you got us into trouble with your damn knife?"

"Sorry, I got pissed but I still want to know."

"I don't think Jenny killed herself; I think someone else killed her."

"You think I killed her, don't you?" Luke stood and moved toward Colton.

"No. I know you didn't. I can tell you loved her, in your own crazed way, and besides, you have a good alibi. So sit down and chill out."

"Who do you think killed her?" asked Luke.

"That's what we're trying to discover. We figure it's someone she's been seeing other than you. I don't know who, but in her diary she talks about someone else. She wrote about HIM. No name, just HIM or HE."

A knowing look rushed across Luke's face just as Coach and Mr. Zeller opened the principal's door. "Come on in, boys," said Mr. Zeller.

The principal held out the pocket knife, now in a plastic envelope, and asked who's knife it was. Both Colton and Luke denied ownership.

"I talked to the police and they will keep the knife and Coach Talbert's statement, in case we cannot reach an understanding. For now, you are both suspended for two weeks. If one of you fails to confess to starting this fight before the two weeks are up, I will decide whether you can come back to our school. This is serious and without cooperation you could still end up going to jail."

Colton protested but the Principal cut him off. "No excuses! Get your things and leave the building. I will call your parents and when you are ready to talk, have your parents call the office. Do you understand?"

Both Luke and Colton said, "Yes, sir."

Colton went back to the locker room and changed into his school clothing. He gathered his things from the locker and headed out to his Jeep. Luke was standing next to the Jeep.

"Enough already, Luke. I'm not fighting you."

"Don't go all bat-shit crazy, Colton. I want to tell you I will find the bastard who killed my Jenny and I will kill him." Luke had a crazed look in his eyes.

"Do you know who it was?" Colton asked.

"I might know." Luke jumped into his car and squealed his tires as he drove out of the parking lot.

Colton sat in his Jeep for several minutes. He sent a text to Lacie as tears ran down his face. *This will not end well,* he thought.

Chapter 26

After talking to Mr. Zeller, the school principal, Colton's mother called her husband, Adam. She told him what Mr. Zeller said and asked if he wanted to come home before Colton arrived.

Adam replied, "No. I trust Colton. Tell him we'll talk when I get home."

Cyndi walked around the kitchen considering what she would say to her son. In the past few months Colton has found himself in several dangerous situations, but this is the first time his adventures have threatened his education, and she worried.

Colton stopped in front of the white two-story farmhouse. He loved his home and family and would do anything to not have to face his parents today. Having their respect is one of Colton's most valued assets, but now he's let them down. Even though he didn't cause the altercation at school, he's facing the consequences.

After building up his courage, he turned into the driveway and parked in front of the garage. He thought, *I could just go into the office and work.* He turned the Jeep engine off and sat staring at the garage door. *I have to face them.*

He took a deep breath and his cellphone rang. The call was from Lacie. "Hi, you got my message?" he asked.

Colton sensed Lacie had been crying, and she wanted to know everything. He was more eager to talk to her than his parents, however when she asked what his parents said about the suspension, he realized that he was avoiding them. "No, I haven't had time to talk to them."

Lacie understood how his emotions and said, "You need courage, don't you? Are you afraid what they will say? Colton, they love you and they trust you to tell the truth.."

"I let them down, and I hate that."

"Go into the house and face them. Call me later and we can talk." She ended the call.

Colton grabbed his backpack and gym bag. As he walked toward the house, the back door opened. His mom was standing in the doorway, smiling. She walked down the steps and said, "I know why you're home early, and your dad and I still love you." She opened her arms for a hug.

"Mom, I'm so sorry," Colton said as he dropped his bags and reached his arms out to accept the hug.

"Come on, you will make me cry, so let's go inside," she said. "You can tell me all about it. I told your dad, and he's not upset, but he wants to talk after he gets home."

Colton spent the evening going over the events leading to his suspension from school. His dad questioned how Colton will prove his innocence.

Adam asked, "Doesn't the school use security cameras to monitor the doors and hallways?"

Colton wasn't sure. "I can find out Monday. I am meeting Mr. Doyle tomorrow, so I'm sure he'll make suggestions."

"You trust Doyle, don't you?" Colton's dad inquired.

"I sure do. I've talked with him several times and he's great. He reminds me a lot of you, only older and with a background in law. I told you he's a retired Detroit Police Detective, didn't I?"

"You did, and he's a chef, business owner, and drives a brand new Buick Enclave, but those things don't make a man good," Adam warned.

"I know that, but I'm sure I mentioned that Mrs. Hoffstarter told me he's *a wonderful man*."

"Well... in that case he is a wonderful man." Adam laughed and got up from the table for a coffee refill.

"So, son, what are your plans for the next two weeks?"

"I have to figure out how I can convince Mr. Zeller it was Luke who started the fight," Colton said. He wasn't sure he should mention Jenny's death, but said, "I'm sure you don't want to hear I'm still trying to find Jenny's killer."

"Damn, Colton, is that why you got into a fight with Luke?"

"Yes. After he attacked me I told him I didn't think he killed her and he should have asked what I thought before he started the fight." Colton walked to the coffee maker. He filled his cup and said, "Luke implied he knows who killed Jenny. I wish he had given me a name, so I could tell the police."

"It sounds like Luke is a hot-head, so I it wouldn't surprise me if he ends up killing someone," Adam said.

"Yes, he might hurt someone. I'm lucky it wasn't me."

Colton spent a few hours chatting on the phone and internet with his friends. They felt Colton would be able to prove he didn't start the fight. Seth suggested getting a copy of the security camera recording, and Colton agreed. Jerry suggested some strong-arm ways to torture Luke into fessing up to his crimes. No one agreed with him.

Before it got too late, Colton called Doyle.

"Colton, how can I help you?" asked Doyle.

Colton told Doyle what happened at school and asked if he could stop at his home after delivering newspapers Saturday afternoon. His usual delivery day is Sunday morning, but with the Thanksgiving holiday coming, he will deliver the Black Friday advertisement section to all the stores on Saturday. Sunday he will deliver the news section to the stores and the entire enormous paper to each of his subscribers.

***

Colton had a restless night, dreaming about Friday's fight. He didn't set his alarm, but still got up before six. After showering, he joined his mom in the kitchen. His dad left early for work.

"Do you want me to wake the kids up?" he asked his mother.

"No, I'm not ready for them, yet. I still have to make breakfast and organize the list of chores for today," Cyndi said. As she checked the coffeemaker, she continued, "and what time are you picking up your papers?"

"Three o'clock this afternoon. I will drop them off at the stores before I meet with Mr. Doyle."

"I have business reports for you in the office. Will Seth be coming by this morning. Your new business is getting busy, and Jim installed seven new security systems last week with five more ordered for next week," she said.

The coffee maker sputtered and stopped brewing. Cyndi filled her cup and sat down.

Colton took a cup from the cupboard. "That's great, Mom. Seth will be here by eight o'clock, so we'll go over the paperwork before our business meeting." Colton filled his mug with coffee and sat down next to his mom.

"Are there any chores you want me to do for you?" Colton asked.

"No..." She sighed. Her mind wasn't on their conversation. Colton could tell she was in deep thought, and he figured it was thoughts of his problems.

"Mom, I will be careful. This whole thing with Luke was a fluke. I have to prove he started it and I'll be back in school."

"It's not that, Colton. I was thinking about Thanksgiving. There is so much to do, and since I'm working on your business, I'm not getting it all done."

"Any suggestions how we can solve that?" Colton asked.

"Yes. Hire a cleaning woman, cook, and secretary to help. Then I'll lie around all day yelling out orders while I eat chocolates."

Colton laughed. "I can almost see you doing that. You know, Mom, I think you need a vacation. It's too bad You and Dad couldn't go to Florida like my customers do."

"Why can't we?" Cyndi asked.

Colton smiled. "Tell you what, I'll watch the kids and you and dad can go after the holidays... during winter break."

"Where are we going," asked Stephenie as she walked into the kitchen followed by her younger brothers.

"Mom and Dad might go to Florida for a vacation," Colton replied.

"Mom, we want to go too! Please?" pleaded Jason. "Can we go to Disneyland?"

Terry jumped up and down and screamed, "We're going to Disneyland? Yay!"

Cyndi looked over to Colton and smiled. "I guess we're going to Disneyland?"

"Sorry, Mom. I'll keep the house warm and safe while you're gone."

***

Colton and Seth spent the morning going over business plans. They decided to mail an advertisement flyer twice a month and after a few months they will consider other forms of advertising. Since the business is now making money, they feel it's important to keep growing.

At lunchtime Seth and Colton drove to Pigeon and picked up a pizza for themselves and his mom and siblings. They called Lacie and Beth, but they both had other commitments..

After playing two video games, Colton announced it was time for him to do his paper route. He asked Seth if he wanted to go with him to meet Doyle.

"Sorry, I need to get our equipment order finished and then Dad wants me to meet with some men from his Lions club. They're watching football this afternoon."

"Sounds exciting, but I'm picking up my papers in Pigeon." Colton said as he walked out the garage toward his Jeep. He turned around and walked back into the garage.

"I forgot to get a shovel. The one from my Jeep is missing, and the forecast is for several inches of snow today and tonight. I wouldn't want to get stuck without a shovel."

Seth agreed and asked what happened to the one in the Jeep?

Colton said he noticed it had disappeared when they stopped in Pigeon for Pizza. "I'm sure Dad took it for his car and forgot to tell me. It has a short handle and fits his trunk better than this one." After putting the shovel in the back of the Jeep, Colton drove off, leaving Seth in the office.

The newspapers and the other drivers were already at the storage shed. As they loaded their papers, the drivers made small talk about the weather and how large the papers were. Colton finished loading and drove to his first store drop. He would sell over four hundred newspapers at his retail outlets this Sunday. Everyone wants the special advertising sections and Colton is eager to deliver.

When he finished his store drops, Colton drove to The Point. He pulled his Jeep into Doyle's driveway and walked to the side door. As he stood on the beautiful deck, Colton looked out across Lake Huron and watched a freighter making its way down to Detroit.

Doyle opened the door and suggested he come in before the storm hits. "You won't have a nice evening for driving tonight," he said.

"I'm just glad I have a four-wheel-drive Jeep, and a shovel." Colton walked into the kitchen and bent down to pet Copper. The Bloodhound was eager to have his ears scratched and Colton obliged.

Doyle offered Colton a flavored coffee, which he accepted. As the two men talked about the case, Colton kept his eyes on the lake. In the distance he could see dark streaks of snow squalls and he kept thinking of the SS Edmund Fitzgerald and how it sank during a November snow storm.

"Your mind is a thousand miles away, Colton. Did you hear anything I said?"

"Sorry, Doyle, I find it relaxing here, and I was thinking of the freighters I saw heading south-east, to Detroit."

"Good eye. I follow them on an app I have that shows where the ships are. There is a gale warning for Lake Huron and the ships are heading to port," He said.

The two men got down to the business of Colton's school suspension and Jenny's murder. Colton started by saying, "After talking to kids in school, I think the killer might be someone from outside school. Luke seems to know who it was, but he wouldn't say. He threatened to kill whoever it was! That's more serious than a fight."

Doyle took a deep breath, "I hope he doesn't do something stupid. I made calls to my friends in Detroit and I may have discovered something relevant about Jenny's family. To get the details, though, I have to drive to Detroit. If we get the security video from the school on Monday morning, we can drive there. My friends in the Detroit Homicide Department said they will help with the video and give us the information they have about Jenny's relatives."

"Why can't they tell you over the phone?" Colton asked.

"Because they want me to visit them." Doyle chuckled. He walked over to Copper and said to him. "Do you want to come with us, Copper? I won't let them put you in their jail again. I promise."

"Again?" asked Colton.

"The homicide department gave me Copper as a goodbye gift, and for a week they kept him in a holding cell until my farewell party." Doyle said. "As I understand it, the holding cell worked out great, but Copper didn't like the smells and got quite upset."

Colton considered the offer and said he would go to Detroit, but he wondered if Seth would also like to go.

"Call and ask him," suggested Doyle. "While you do, I'll take a quick pit stop."

Getting out of school on a Monday sounded great, so Seth didn't hesitate to accept. "Wow! We will be at the Detroit Police Headquarters?" He wanted to make sure he wasn't hearing things.

"Yes. Doyle said he can get information about Jenny's family, and he wants to get a copy of the school's surveillance video from last Friday."

"I would love to see that video. Do you think it shows anything?" asked Seth.

"No." Colton knew the camera didn't cover the hallway where the fight broke out. If anything was on the video, it would only be the two guys walking toward the gym. He told Seth to meet him at the office on Monday and the two of them could drive to Mr. Doyle's house.

Doyle was standing behind Colton listening. "Sounds like Seth will join us Monday?" he asked.

"Yes. What time should we meet you?"

"Be here at eight. We can stop into the school and get the video. I would love to take the knife, but that might be impossible," Doyle said. He stood silent for a moment. "Call your friend, Ned. You know, the county deputy. Ask him to get the knife for us so we can take it to Detroit for analysis. I bet we can get fingerprints from it."

"Great, because I never touched it. I hit Luke's arm, and it fell to the ground. Coach Talbert and Principal Don Zeller touched it. Will we be able to get their fingerprints?"

"All teachers have their prints on file with Michigan. I can get a copy."

Colton reached into his jeans pocket and pulled out his cell phone. He punched Ned's number and waited. "Ned, this is Colton. No. I'm fine, but I need your help again. Mr. Doyle wants to know if you could get the knife used in the fight Friday."

Doyle could hear Ned objecting. He motioned to Colton to let him talk to Ned.

"Ned, Doyle wants to talk to you," Colton said, passing the phone to Doyle.

"Deputy Ned. We're heading to the Detroit Police building on Monday. The State Police have a forensic lab there and I want them to check the knife for fingerprints."

Ned wasn't comfortable letting an outsider handle the evidence. To ease his concerns, Doyle said, "Put the knife in a sealed evidence bag and the State Police will verify and keep the chain of evidence unbroken."

Ned agreed to the offer and suggested they pick it up in Bad Axe on their way to Detroit.

It was getting near dinner time, so Colton thanked Doyle for his help, said goodbye to him and Copper, and headed for home.

Chapter 27

The alarm rang and Colton rolled out of bed. As he got dressed for his route, he kept considering yesterday's visit with Doyle. Questions filled his mind. *I wonder what information Detroit discovered about Jenny's family? Could the killer be a family member? I wonder if the video has anything of use on it? Will the fingerprints clear me? I wonder if Luke knows who killed Jenny.* He stopped worrying to concentrate on his work. *Tomorrow I might find the answers*, he concluded.

When he stepped outside, wind and snow blasted his face. Over three inches of snow covered the Jeep and driveway. He heard the forecast calling for the possibility of snow, but this is insane. *I hate snow;* he cursed.

Upon arriving at the Pigeon storage locker, he saw the other two drivers waiting for the truck. Colton got out to talk with Rob and Joey.

"Any idea when the truck will get here?" Colton asked.

Rob said, "I called, and they said the printing press broke. They aren't sure when it will get fixed, so we wait."

Joey laughed, coughed, and had another drag on his cigarette. "It's two-thirty now. The last time they broke the press, they arrived five hours late. We could be here all night and then we still must get the papers delivered."

Rob suggested a game of cards, Joey said he wanted to take a nap, and Colton said, "I'll listen to my audiobook."

They each walked to their vehicle and waited. Colton grabbed the heavy coat and blanket he kept in the jeep for emergencies and considered running the Jeep for heat but didn't because it would use too much gas.

The Baldacci novel made the hours tick by faster, but his book got interrupted by a honking horn and Colton turned around as the company truck pulled up next to the storage shed. He checked the time, and the truck arrived three hours late, and by four o'clock he had the Jeep loaded.

Rob yelled, "Good luck with your deliveries and have a good Thanksgiving. At least the snow stopped!"

"Thanks Rob. It's amazing how big these newspapers are?" Colton yelled back. "My Jeep will never be the same."

The deliveries went slow, at first. It took Colton a while to figure out how fast he could drive, and how to avoid slipping into the ditch when he stopped to deliver a paper. After an hour of deliveries he was at The Point Market. He turned into the driveway when he noticed two police cars and several other people standing around the newspaper rack.

Colton drove up and stopped. He got out and walked over to talk with Deputy Ned, who was walking toward him.

"What happened, Ned?" he asked.

"Colton. We've been waiting for you," Ned said. "Luke Hadderton got killed this morning and I need you tell me what happened?"

"What? How would I know what happened? I just got here."

Trooper Steve walked up to Colton and said, "Well kid, you did it now. I wouldn't have taken you for a killer, but we never know, do we?"

"Killer? What the hell are you two saying. I didn't kill Luke. Jesus, why would you say anything like that?" Colton was livid. His route was tiring, and he was on-edge from listening to the killings in the Baldacci novel. The whole moment seemed like it came straight from the novel, but it was real.

Ned told Steve to back off and asked Colton where he was at two thirty this morning?

"Is that when the coroner thinks Luke died?" Colton asked.

"Yes, give or take, that's the time. Now tell me everything that happened," said Ned. He was trying to make it as easy as he could for Colton to tell the truth. He didn't think Colton would kill anyone, but Luke is a hot head, and if there was a fight, it may have been self-defense.

Colton walked with Ned toward his Police car, and Ned suggested sitting in the car because it was snowing again. As he warmed his hands, Colton explained where he was since the last time they talked.

"You're saying the papers were late, and you didn't get started with your deliveries until after four? Do you have anyone who can corroborate that?"

"Yes, to both questions." Colton pulled out his cellphone and hit Roy's number. "This is Roy, another driver. We parked together all morning."

"Roy. Colton here. Could you tell the police where I was this morning?"

Ned took the phone and talked at length with Roy. After speaking with him, Colton had him talk with Joey.

Ned finished talking to Joey and asked, "Colton, can you tell me where your shovel is?"

"If you mean my short farm shovel, it was in my Jeep until yesterday morning when it disappeared, and I had to find another one. The new one is in the Jeep. Why do you want to know about my shovel?"

Ned realized Colton couldn't be Luke's killer. "We found it next to Luke's body; it was the weapon used to killed him. At least we think it was."

Colton looked toward his newspaper stand and watched the Crime Investigators work. They were taking fingerprints from the newspaper rack and molds of foot and tire prints in the snow. "Is his body still there?"

"No. The coroner took the body. They will do an autopsy to determine the cause of death. There is a wound on the back of the head, but that injury looked superficial. The coroner wasn't positive what killed him, but he was positive about the time of death, and now I know there's no way you could have been his killer."

"Thank God and thank you. I also need to prove I didn't start the fight with him in school Friday," Colton said.

"We'll do that because I got the OK to send the knife to Detroit with Doyle, and I have a copy of the surveillance video, which you can pick them up tomorrow."

Colton wondered, "Did you see the video?"

"Yes. The two of you are on it, but not the fight. I don't think it will help you," Ned said as he finished typing Colton's statement into the laptop.

Trooper Steve approached Ned's car. "Well, are you taking him to Bad Axe?" he asked.

"Nope," said Ned. "Colton has an ironclad alibi. I checked it out and there's no way he did this. It looks like someone tried very hard to pin this on him, but they couldn't know Colton's papers were three hours late, and he wasn't here at his usual time."

Steve bent down to see Colton. He said, "Lucky for you kid, why does this crap seem to follow you around?"

"If I knew, I'd tell you, Sir."

When Colton reached home, he told his parents what happened to Luke. They were both concerned about his safety and his Dad wondered how he could prove he didn't start the fight at school with Luke. "Dad... Mom, Seth and I are going to Detroit tomorrow with Doyle. He talked to the homicide department and they are going to help us with evidence. I'm not sure what they can do, but Doyle thinks it's worth a try. Besides, I will enjoy being in their building.

"Well be careful, and you're sure you can trust this Doyle?" Colton's mom asked.

"Honey I met him and he seems to be on the level, besides he's a good friend of Trudy Hoffstarter."

"OK, if you say so. But Colton, be careful," His mom added.

After lunch, Colton spent Sunday with his brothers, shooting at the deer target. He tried not to think about the death of Jenny and Luke, but it kept creeping into his mind, until after dinner when he watched television and then went to bed early.

***

By Monday morning the snow had melted. Colton sat at the kitchen table while he waited for Seth to arrive. Adam left early for work and Colton's mom was downstairs doing the laundry.

All day Sunday the local radio station gave continuing reports about Luke's killing, but there was no mention of Colton's involvement. The police requested, "If you know of any information regarding this murder, please call the Sheriff's office today." There was even a report on TV-12's evening news, where the report started out with the headline, "Death Hits Small Town Again."

Seth walked up to the porch and rang the bell. He saw Colton sitting at the table and since Colton didn't respond, he walked into the room and yelled, "Hey, you ready?"

Colton jumped and almost fell off his chair. "Damn, you scared the crap out of me."

"You were deep in a trance and didn't hear the doorbell."

"I'm ready. Ned said we can stop in Bad Axe and pick up both the knife and the school video," Colton said.

"Great. Do we need to drive over to Doyle's or is he picking us up?"

Colton grabbed his coat and said, "You drive."

Doyle was ready and waiting in the garage where he told Seth to park his Charger next to the Buick Enclave. Seth called shotgun and jumped into the front seat as Colton climbed into the back and admired the luxury when he sat down. *Wow!* He thought. *This is super nice.*

"Great S.U.V." said Seth.

Doyle laughed, "It's OK. I'm not used to big luxury vehicles since I always drove a four door Ford. Big car… like police cars."

"Right, you were a police detective."

"Yes. Now I'm a retired detective."

Colton asked where Copper was and Doyle told him Mrs. Hoffstarter volunteered to watch him. "I hope he doesn't cause her any problems."

Doyle drove through Bad Axe and pulled into McDonalds' drive-through. "Anything you guys need. I'm up for a large coffee."

"I'll have coffee," said Colton. Seth ordered a big breakfast with apple juice and coffee.

The next stop was the sheriff's office. Doyle and Colton went in, leaving Seth to finish his breakfast. Doyle warned him not to get food on the leather. He then laughed as they walked to the office doors.

There was a small sealed package at the front desk with Doyle's name on it. A young blond officer stood by the counter and said, "I need your identification before I can let you have this."

Doyle pulled out his badge, and the girl marked down the name and number. "Please sign this evidence form and remember you're responsible and must keep it secure."

Colton couldn't believe the hoops they made Doyle crawl through. *It's just a video and pocket knife,* he thought.

On the way out Doyle explained why it was important to follow the rules. "The evidence must never be out of the hands of an official. If it does, the evidence becomes tainted. I've seen many cases lost because the police were sloppy and couldn't prove someone hadn't tampered with the evidence."

"I'm learning," said Colton. He realized just how much he needed to learn.

Doyle had Colton and Seth in stitches all the way to Detroit. He told them many humorous stories about his time as a detective.

"You should write a book about your adventures," noted Seth.

Doyle grinned with pride and said. "Perhaps. It's fun to remember the happy times, but it's too bad the bad times outweigh them. If I wrote a book I'd have to talk about those sad events too. I don't think I want to relive them, therefore, I'll just enjoy the adventures of today and tomorrow."

Seth suggested that if Doyle spends time with Colton, he'll find himself involved in many adventures. "He's a magnet for trouble," Seth said.

"I get that feeling, Seth, but I'm not missing Detroit anymore. For a while I feared The Point would be too tranquil for me, but so far it's been one adventure after another."

Doyle exited I-75 Downtown Detroit and drove to 1310 3rd Ave., where he found a parking space. He gathered the evidence package and Seth grabbed his laptop. The three walked to the front entrance.

Looking up at the impressive building, Colton asked, "Were you stationed in this building?"

"No," Doyle answered, "this is a new building. Over the years the police department has gone through many changes. The new State Police crime lab is here and some of my old Homicide pals have offices here."

They walked into the lobby and two men in dark suits walked toward them. The older man with gray hair, a bushy mustache, and a large round belly, opened his arms and said, "You old Irish bum. What did you do, stop eating?"

Doyle laughed. "Maxwell Brown. How the hell have you been? Last time I saw you was at my restaurant the day I signed the final sales papers. I didn't expect to see you here."

"I wouldn't miss your coming home celebration."

"And no, I'm still eating and cooking. Just not as much."

The two men laughed and Max gave Doyle a hug and introduced him to Lieutenant Detective Howard Smithers. Smithers was a thin man who stood over six feet tall. He had a full head of blond hair and was young enough to be their son.

"Max told me all the tall tales about your adventures with the Department, Doyle. I see you've brought the evidence and your two young friends."

"Yes, Sir. This is Colton Blackwell, football star and a young detective from Pigeon and his friend and business partner is Seth Seamoore. These two young men started a security and detective business, and it's because of them I'm turning to you for help." Doyle said.

Lieutenant Smithers shook Colton and Seth's hands and said, "It's great to meet the two of you. We've heard of your adventures and wanted to thank you for your help a few months ago, when you put away more major drug dealers in one sting than four of our men did all fall."

It surprised Colton that the Detroit Police appreciated their effort so he said, "Thank you sir, but we stumbled on those dealers by accident."

"It's all about the results." Smithers turned to Doyle and said, "We're glad to help you any way we can, so come on up to the Homicide Squad Room where there are more officers who want to meet you."

***

Colton and Seth followed the homicide detectives. The group took an elevator up several floors, and when the doors opened another group of officers threw confetti and sang, "For he's a jolly good fellow."

Turning to Max, Doyle laughed and asked, "What the hell is this?"

"We knew you'd never be able to stay away from being a detective, since Homicide is in your Irish blood and it's great having you back."

"Thank you, but my return is premature as I'm just helping my detective friend, Colton. So, enough of this celebrating; let's get down

Death On The Point - BLOOD BATH

to business."

Doyle and Colton gave the knife to the Michigan State Police forensic investigator and followed him into the lab while Seth worked with a video specialist on the school's security video.

The software the specialist used amazed Seth, and in less than an hour they were ready to present their findings. They returned to the central office and waited.

Colton and Doyle returned from the crime lab and Doyle suggested Seth report his findings first.

Seth stood and said, "We went over the video and by enlarging the image of Luke walking into the hallway, we could see the knife in his hands." He then showed the group a printout of Luke with the knife in his hand.

The video specialist added, "I will certify that this evidence shows Luke was the attacker and brought the weapon into the fight."

Colton let out a sigh of relief. Without evidence he wouldn't be able to prove his innocence to Principal Zeller. He then stood and reported that the State Police found Luke's fingerprints on the knife. The Huron County Sheriff had his fingerprints on file and they were a perfect match.

Doyle stood and opened the folder given to him by Lieutenant Smithers. "I've looked over this material. But first I would like Colton to present the case details for you."

"Doyle, I've never done this before."

"Colton, you're a natural. Tell us what has happened so far."

"It started in school when my girlfriend and I observed that Jenny Stillmore was being abused by her boyfriend, Luke Hadderton. We tried to get help for Jenny but that effort ended when Luke beat up my girlfriend, and the next day I found Jenny's dead body in a hot tub on The Point."

"The Police deemed Jenny's death to be a suicide, but after studying the photo I took of the scene, I suspected foul play." Colton showed the crime scene photo of Jenny. The officers passed it around. "I noticed that there was no blood on the ledge. How could Jenny cut both wrists and avoid getting blood on the ledge or on her dress? I believe it's impossible, and it also looks like the cuts are too precise. I would have expected the cuts to be haphazard."

Colton continued, "My investigation began by talking to students at school. Luke had a good alibi, so I knew someone besides him was having a relationship with Jenny. That person could be the killer, but none of the other students could tell us who it was. When Luke found out about my investigation, he attacked me in the school hallway. After I told him I thought someone else killed his girlfriend, he acted like he knew who it was."

"Two days later Luke lay dead next to one of my newspaper stops. Whoever killed him tried to frame me because they stole a shovel from my Jeep and placed his body to look like I hit him with the shovel. The killer had no way of knowing I would be three hours late, due to a printing press breakdown, and at the time of death I was with two other drivers waiting for our newspapers."

"As it stands now, I think one person killed both Jenny and Luke. That person is unknown, but I suspect he was having an abusive relationship with Jenny."

Doyle congratulated Colton on his presentation. Lieutenant Smithers said Colton's detective skills were impressive.

"Now for my part." Doyle began, "I asked Lieutenant Smithers to find everything he could on Jenny's family. Many abused girls come from homes where the father abused the mother, so it is a known pattern of behavior." Doyle opened the envelope and revealed that Jenny's mother died after being beaten. "The father was a suspect, but there was not enough evidence to press charges. He owns a large construction company in Detroit. He is the owner but has a general manager who handles the day-to-day work."

"What about other family members?" Colton asked.

"Her uncle Ronald has been in fights, but there is nothing to show his involvement here," Doyle reported. "The uncle works for his brother, is unmarried, seems to be a loner, and he is a heavy drinker. He has two drunk driving and several assault charges on his record."

"So, what do we do now?" asked Colton.

Lieutenant Smithers said, "We will send this information to the State Police and the Huron County Sheriff. You will allow them to investigate, and I don't want you involved any further. It's time for the police to take the lead; they will find the killer of those two teenagers."

On the way home, Doyle treated Colton and Seth to a dinner at his former restaurant in Troy. The beautiful building and the way the staff showed their respect for Doyle impressed them.

After getting home Colton called Lacie and told her about the trip to Detroit. She said everyone at school is rooting for his quick return.

"I will call the sheriff tomorrow morning and then he needs to send Mr. Zeller the proof we found. I'm not sure when I can go back to school but I don't expect to return until after Thanksgiving."

Lacie wished him luck and suggested he get lots of rest for his Tuesday morning route. "Colton," she added. "Please don't find another body and promise me you won't get into more trouble."

Colton laughed. "I promise. You understand it's not my fault."

"I know."

Colton ended the call and listened to his audiobook until he fell asleep.

Chapter 28

The newspapers were back to their normal size, and it wasn't long before Colton finished the route, but he missed the last-minute race to school. Today, the drive home seemed anticlimactic and when he walked into the kitchen and sat across from his mom, she said, "You appear to be down in the dumps."

"I am, Mom. I should be in school instead of sitting here. This is so crappy."

"Perhaps if you eat breakfast and work on your business, you'll perk up," Cyndi stood and walked to the stove. She returned with several pancakes and a large cup of coffee. "We received two more orders for security systems. It's amazing how fast your business is growing. Most businesses take forever to get off the ground, and here you and Seth are with over twenty paying customers."

"That's because Seth is so amazing. Do you realize he planned this business over two months ago? I'm lucky he's my partner, and I hope I can contribute enough."

"Don't worry, Colton, you're doing your share."

After breakfast Colton talked to Sheriff McNabb and Deputy Ned. They received the evidence and forwarded the results to the high school principal. Colton asked his mom to call the school and find out when he can return.

"I'm not calling today, Colton. Mr. Zeller will need to show the evidence to the Superintendent and perhaps even the School Board so they can decide what to do. I'll call him tomorrow morning, so don't plan on returning until after Thanksgiving."

Seth and Lacie kept Colton informed about the happenings in school. During lunch they did a video chat on Facebook. Colton missed being with his friends and seeing them in school without him made it worse.

After school, Seth stopped into the office to order more equipment, and Jim also dropped in. He informed Colton and Seth that a customer on The Point asked if they would like to install a system at his factories in Lapeer and Romeo.

"Wow. Did you get his phone number?" Colton asked.

Jim handed him a business card and Colton recognized the name. "He was one of our first customers so I guess he's impressed with our service."

"That's what he told me," said Jim. "He suggested calling him in January, after the holidays."

Seth looked at the business card. "Do you feel we can do this big of a job, Jim?"

"It will take a few more workers, but I have a list of guys with electrical experience who would love this kind of work."

In an excited tone Colton said, "We should try to land this job and look for more because if we want to grow this company, we need to think big. I would love to have two crews installing security systems full time."

Seth agreed and Jim said he would line up workers in case they land the contract. The meeting lasted until dinner time, then Seth said he had a dinner date with Beth and Colton wanted to spend time with his family.

"Are you going to call Lacie before dinner?" asked Seth.

"Yes, I missed being with her in school. I wonder what it will be like when she's in college and I'm here working on our business?"

Seth considered what Colton said. "It sounds like you're intending to skipping college. Is that your plan?"

"No. I plan on finishing college online. It will only take a few years because I have credits now, and I signed up for business classes next semester."

Seth laughed. "That's been my plan all along; in fact, I've earned over six credits."

"Damn, I better get working. I can't let you graduate from college first."

***

The call to Lacie got forwarded to her voicemail, and Colton remembered she was at work in the hospital and wouldn't be out until after six. He left a message asking her to call him when she got home.

"Mom," Colton called as he walked into the kitchen. "We may get a job in Lapeer. Jim says it's a large factory and they want our security system."

"That's great news, but don't underbid the job. The goal is to make money and the larger the job the more money you could lose."

"Before we bid the job, I'll let you study the offer. I hope you realize we would run in circles without you, Mom."

"Yes, I'm aware of that," she said. "And I want you to know how much I love the job. I studied business after high school and now I remember why. Please call your brothers and sister to dinner, and since your dad just drove in the driveway and dinner will be ready in fifteen minutes."

Over the dinner table the family talked about the Thanksgiving plans. Stephenie volunteered to help her mom cook, provided she didn't have to clear the table and wash dishes.

"We'll see about that," her Dad told her.

"I would cook but you all might get sick," added Terry.

Jason said he would help with dishes.

When Colton's phone buzzed, he took the call in the living room because it was Lacie. "Hi, I hope work went well," he said. "I missed you today."

Lacie laughed. "I thought the video chat was nice, but I could record the entire morning for you."

"That won't be necessary. Mom's calling Mr. Zeller in the morning, and the Sheriff sent him the proof of my innocence so he may let me return before the two-week suspension is over."

"Wonderful," Lacie said in a soft voice.

"What's the matter? You sound like you're down in the dumps."

"I'm a little sad."

"Why?" Colton asked.

"One resident in long-term, Mr. Gurter, died today while I was in his room."

"Was he old and sick?"

"Yes, that's why he was in long term care. I got upset because they called the doctor and he did nothing to save his life. Colton, they let him die!"

Colton could tell that Lacie was crying, and he wasn't sure what he should say, or if he should say anything at all. After consideration he said, "Perhaps the doctor did what Mr. Gurter wanted. I'm sure if Mr. Gurter was young and healthy he would want to continue living, but if he was in pain, he might not want the doctors to keep him alive."

Lacie thought about what Colton said. "You mean like a Living Will?"

"I think they call it that; did you ask your Mom about it?"

"Not yet, but I should talk to her since I'm sure she must have experienced the same feelings."

"I'm sure she has, Lacie. You're such a caring person, and I love you for that," Colton said.

"Tomorrow is only a half day so would you like to do something with me?" Colton asked.

"I can't. Mom wants me to go with her to Bay City. We're visiting my aunt in the hospital."

"I'm sorry and I hope she gets well soon," Colton said. "What time do you want me to pick you up on Thanksgiving?"

"Oh God. I almost forgot to ask you something."

"What?"

"Can my mom come with me to Thanksgiving dinner at your parents house? Before you answer, I should tell you that I already asked her to come."

"Then you know the answer. Mom is cooking a bird big enough to feed an army, and I've seen your mom eat, and she's not an army." Colton then asked, "What about picking up Trudy. She's expecting us to pick her up at one o'clock, and Mom plans on having dinner at two."

"Pick us up at noon, and then you and I can drive over to Trudy's house. I'm sure my mom will love helping your Mom with dinner while we're gone."

"Sounds like a plan. I love you and I'll talk to you tomorrow in school," Colton said. "On my phone that is."

***

Colton spent Tuesday evening watching television with the family. Since there wasn't a route to do on Wednesday and he wasn't allowed to attend school, he stayed up and watched the late shows.

When he awoke it was past nine, and he heard his mom in the kitchen. He showered, got dressed, and joined her.

"Did you call Mr. Zeller about my suspension?"

"Yes, but you won't like what he said."

"What did he say?" Colton asked.

"He wants you to complete the two-week suspension before you can go back to school."

"Did he say why?" Colton wasn't as upset as his mother expected he would be.

"You're taking this well," she said. "You won't like what he said, though."

She took a deep breath and said, "According to him it's against school rules to change a suspension once it's handed out. Also, he said you need to rethink your actions both in and out of school because he's concerned that you're setting a bad example for other students."

That made Colton angry. "What action is he talking about? I don't drink and do drugs like many of my classmates, so what am I doing that would set a bad example?"

"You will need to ask him that yourself."

Colton grabbed his coat and started toward the door. "Mom, I'm going to the school, and I'll ask him that question, now!"

"Colton, whatever you do, don't get angry at him because it won't help if you make him even more upset."

"I'll be fine," Colton said as he walked out the door. While driving, he considered what he would say., and each scenario sounded angry. *I am angry*, he realized. *Perhaps I should listen to him after which I can tell the bastard off! No, I can't talk like that, because he's only doing his job.*

Colton parked in front of the school and they buzzed him through the doors. He walked up to Miss Downers desk.

"Is Mr. Zeller available? I need to talk with him," Colton asked.

Miss Downer picked up her phone and after she talked for a few minutes, she told Colton to go back to his office.

Colton walked up to the door as Mr. Zeller opened it. "Come in Colton. I'm sure your mother told you what my decision was, so how can I help you?"

"Sir, I don't understand why you feel I am a bad influence on my classmates. Would you explain what I did to deserve that?"

"Come in," the principal said. He showed Colton to a chair, and he sat behind his desk.

"Ever since this year began, you've involved yourself in one criminal event or another. Those drug dealers and your silly investigation into the death of that man on the beach. The Board of Education doesn't consider it appropriate that you became involved in these activities."

Colton's blood was boiling, but he didn't lose control of his anger. "And I'm sure Jenny and Luke's death upset them?"

"Yes, another tragic event you needed to avoid. You are a smart student, but I'm not sure you possess common sense. Why do you let yourself get involved in these crimes? And what makes you believe you can start a business while you are still in school?"

"Mr. Zeller. Let's talk about the crimes I helped to solve. I helped a Latino family who were being held as slaves by a man who was molesting a young girl. I witnessed a murder, and no one listened; perhaps I should have ignored the plight of the Latino family and I should never have told people what I saw that night on the beach. Lacie and I didn't have to help Jenny when we witnessed Luke beating and abusing her either, and I didn't let Luke attack me, did I? Tell me how I could have avoided it? How could I not do what I did in these situations?"

Mr. Zeller listened as Colton continued. "As for setting an example for the students, is the Board of Education aware you ignored the plight of Jenny? We told the school office, Coach Talbert, the police, and you about it. What did you do? You want us to report abuse and bullying when we witness it, but you turned a blind eye when we told you. Further, as for my starting a business; that, sir, is none of your damn business!"

Colton didn't believe what he said, and the expression on the principal's face showed his surprise.

Both men sat silent for a few moments. Colton smiled and said, "Sorry about that last comment, but it is up us and our parents what we do after school. Seth and I have a 4.0 grade point average. We're good students and we're old enough to know of what we can and cannot do."

Mr. Zeller reached for the thermos of coffee on his desk. He shuffled a few papers then his eyes turned back to Colton. He said, "I know we don't always get things right. I knew of Jenny's problem, and I tried to talk to her father but he told me to stay out of their business. It is my business to protect our students from harm, and that's why I worry about how you handle yourself with these cases."

"I understand that, and my parents also worry; they also trust me."

Mr. Zeller smiled. "Yes, your mom was vocal about her trust when I talked to her. I can see where you get your fire from."

"Oh yes... Mom. Did I tell you she is helping us manage the security business? She's smart and a great mother."

"So, how much money did you lose so far?"

"Our business has lost no money. We make a good profit and employ three people besides Seth and I. This week we're bidding on a security system for two factories in the city. It wouldn't surprise me if we have a full time installation crew before Easter," Colton said.

"OK! Like I said, we don't always get things right. I can't change the rules about the suspension, but I can make sure it doesn't show up on your records. Most of the big colleges disapprove of suspensions on the records of applicants. Have you any idea where you're going to college? I know it's early but my Alma Mater, M.S.U., would be a great place to go, considering your football skills."

Colton smiled. "You know how I follow my path? Well Seth and I are not attending a major College. We plan to do all of our college classes online, and we figure we'll be able to graduate from college shortly after we finish high school." Colton added that statement to get Mr. Zeller's reaction. There was none.

Mr. Zeller flipped his desk calendar to December. "Great. Then I'll see you on Monday, December first.

"Oops. I can't be here that day; bow hunting opens again on the first day of December, and I'm hunting with my younger brother, Jason. I promised him, so is Tuesday OK?"

"We will see you Tuesday. Good luck hunting and please avoid getting into more trouble."

Chapter 29

Colton drove home from his meeting with Mr. Zeller. He went into the house and told his mom about the conversation.
"It sounds like it ended well; at least you weren't given another two weeks suspension."

Colton laughed and agreed. "I guess I'll have a week off, so do you need anything done around the house?"

"Not that I can think of," She said as she grabbed her coat. "I have to go shopping in Pigeon, you can mind the telephone. If it's a business call, the phone will ring here. I had Jim Owens set it up this morning."

"That's great; have fun shopping."

"Yes, sure. I'll have lots of fun shopping," she said as she walked out to her S-10 pickup.

Colton sat for a few moments. He wanted to call the County Sheriff to find out the progress of their investigation, but then he reconsidered. *I should keep out of this. At least for a while.*

He had enough coffee and found a can of Coke. As he sipped his drink, he continued to think about Luke's murder. *Who is the killer? Someone who was also abusing Jenny. Perhaps her father or uncle? That would be disgusting if it was sexual abuse. But why did they kill Jenny? What's the motive?*

The sound of the bus and the voices of his brothers and sister interrupted Colton's thoughts. The kids ran into the kitchen talking about school, sports, hunting, and kitties. It was Steph who was talking about kittens because she wanted one and knew her mom would never allow her to have one in the house.

"Colton, why is mom against pets?" she asked.

"I don't know, but I remember she wouldn't let me have a dog when I wanted one. Chickens in the shed are OK, and for a while we had two cows… but no pets."

Jason and Terry helped with the groceries when their mom got home. They made several trips and acted like it was too much work, causing Colton to laugh at them, which they didn't appreciate.

After dinner Colton again went to bed early. There would be a newspaper delivery tomorrow, Thanksgiving morning. Colton wished he didn't have to, but he knew it was his job, and he would also have to deliver papers on Sunday. *Sometimes this job is a drag*, he thought. *Perhaps when I make more money from the business, I'll consider giving it up. But until then…"*

There were no dreams during the night. At least he remembered none. *Perhaps the bad events are over*, he thought. *No! It's just a lull before the storm.*

There were no problems with the route. The roads were clear and because there were many customers gone, it took less time to finish.

Colton finished the last delivery and was home by six o'clock. He went to his room and took a nap. When his dad yelled for him to get out of bed, he couldn't believe it was almost ten o'clock.

He took a shower and put on dress clothes. Downstairs everyone, including his dad, were busy getting the house ready for guests. The Thanksgiving parade was on with no one watching, and he didn't take time to watch because he had to pick up Lacie.

Stephenie and Mom were busy cooking. It is nice to see the two of them sharing. Mom was explaining every step she made, then she had Steph take over. They were making rolls and Steph was beaming with pride when she saw the result of her efforts.

Colton grabbed a quick breakfast and excused himself. He rang Lacie and said he would be there soon. She welcomed his call because she also was running late. "I don't know what happened, but I overslept and so did Mom. We'll be ready at noon," she advised.

"In that case, I'll be there at noon, and you have an hour to finish."

Colton sat at the table and continued to watch the cooks work their magic while he drank coffee.

Before noon, Colton picked Lacie and her mom, Barb, up and they returned home with him. Lacie stayed in the Jeep as Colton walked Mrs. Wooddell into the house. Colton's mom greeted her and told him he should get going. "You don't want to keep Trudy waiting," she advised.

Trudy was waiting for Lacie and Colton's arrival. She walked out the door as Colton drove up to the garage door. He jumped out to help her and Lacie got out so Trudy could sit in the front seat of the Jeep.

"For heaven's sake, Lacie. I can sit in the back seat."

"The front is better. I still have newspapers piled in the back and it's a little drafty," advised Colton.

"Well, I don't want to put you out." Trudy held onto Colton's arm as she pulled herself into the front seat. "It's a bit of a climb, isn't it?"

"Yes. It is easier getting out, though," said Colton.

Lacie and Trudy talked about the nice weather as Colton concentrated on avoiding the deer walking across the road. Trudy laughed when one deer stopped in the middle of the road and wouldn't move until Colton honked the horn and threatened to run it over."

Trudy suggested that the homeowners association should try to move the deer off the peninsula. "They should do something because every time I plant flowers or garden plants, the deer eat them. They aren't afraid of anything or anyone."

As Colton drove up to his family's home Trudy remarked how quaint the white farmhouse was. "It reminds me of my childhood in Romeo. We lived on a small produce farm, and my dad sold his crop at the Eastern Market and my brothers and sisters and I worked in the fields until we went off to college. It was a wonderful childhood, and now I miss the closeness of family. My children and grandchildren don't know what family means."

"You're a part of our family now, Trudy," Colton remarked.

"Thank you," she said as she worked her way out of the seat. She was careful with each step, and Colton could see her age was showing. He remembered his grandfather used a walker toward the end of his life.

The house filled with laughter as Trudy was greeted in the kitchen by Cyndi, Lacie and her mother, and Stephenie. The girls were all helping with dinner and they sent the boys into the living room. "Watch the parade or the pre-football show," Cyndi instructed. The boys did as instructed and enjoyed the sports break, while the girls cooked, visited and drank ice tea and wine.

Lacie walked into the living room and announced that dinner will begin in ten minutes. "I have instructions to make sure you all wash up before we eat; even you, Colton," she added with a smile.

After offering a prayer and passing the food around, the conversation settled on how thankful they were to have each other.

No one left the table hungry, and the boys didn't get upset when Adam asked them to clean up the kitchen. He told Stephenie she didn't have to do dishes since she did such a wonderful job helping her mother.

"I had fun," she said, beaming with pride.

Barb Wooddell and Trudy also said they had fun.

Barb said since Lacie's dad died a few years ago, she finds holidays difficult. "Adam and Cyndi, today I enjoyed myself because you are such great friends, and Trudy you're amazing."

***

Colton and Lacie took Trudy home first. She grew tired, so they walked her to the door and said goodbye. On the way home Lacie talked about how much her mother enjoyed the dinner.

"I'm glad Mom spent the day with us. Last year she worked during the holidays to avoid the pain. I think she is getting over her grief," Lacie said.

"That's great. Perhaps we should introduce her to Doyle. Does your mom like Bloodhounds?"

"You're kidding, aren't you?"

"Perhaps."

Colton and Lacie went back to the farm and picked up her mother, was also tired and didn't talk much during the ride home. Colton asked Lacie if she wanted to go to Bad Axe for the Black Friday sales. She suggested going Saturday to avoid all the shoppers. "They'll have the same special sales," she said.

"Good idea. I have a list of gifts to buy for my family, so how about I pick you up at nine and we can have breakfast at Big Boy?"

Lacie turned to her mother and asked if she wanted to go with them Saturday.

"No, you two have fun. I'm doing my shopping next week in Bay City, since my sister should be well enough to go with me, and she needs someone to help her."

Lacie smiled at Colton. "It's a date."

Lacie helped her mother out of the Jeep and they walked into the house together.

After they waved to him, Colton backed out of the driveway and headed home.

The Blackwell family were sitting around the TV set. Colton mentioned that he was getting a little hungry again and asked about making a turkey sandwich.

Cyndi suggested that if anyone wants dinner, they will have to help themselves to the leftovers. "And those who make a mess, shall also clean the mess," she warned.

***

Colton completed his route Friday morning with no problems. He also finished the Baldacci novel Hour Game and was ready to start the third Stephanie Plum novel. Lacie said she already read Three to Get Deadly, and she said it's funny and exciting. After the tense Baldacci novel which began with a woman found murdered in the woods and a young teenage couple shot to death in their car while making out, he felt a need for some humor.

Black Friday for the Blackwell family ended up being an outdoor fun day. Colton and his brothers practiced basketball and shot arrows at the poor Styrofoam deer. Jason won the archery competition and Colton let Terry win several basketball games of HORSE.

For afternoon entertainment Colton and Seth worked on their business and they calculated three jobs for Pigeon business owners and wrote a bid for each.

Seth acted like he had a big secret to share all afternoon. Finally he said, "Colton, I have good news to share."

Colton looked up from his paperwork and said, "Well, what is it?"

Seth continued, "Remember the police technician I worked with in Detroit?" He waited for Colton's reply. Seth was playing with Colton and Colton didn't like being toyed with.

"He had the software you used to see the knife in Luke's hand?" Colton asked.

"Yes! Him. I loaned him a copy of the software I've been using for our security business because he wanted to test it. He sent me an email request, and I figured it was OK."

Colton was listening while Seth took his time sharing the facts. "Are you done or is there more to this story?" Colton asked.

"The city of Detroit wants to pay us a load of money to rent that software. A *boat load of money*! I mean lots of money!"

"And?"

"We have to find a lawyer and make a deal. We might get rich sooner than we expected, Colton."

"Don't you mean, you might get rich, since it's your software."

"No. It's our software. If it wasn't for our business, I never would have written the code so trust me, *WE* might get rich."

Colton didn't know what to say. He stood and shook his best friend's hand. "How much money is a boat load?"

Seth laughed. "Hell if I know, but we're about to find out."

The two partners discussed finding a lawyer, and they agreed to let Seth's dad suggest one and help with the legal questions. They also agreed not to tell anyone other than their parents. If it doesn't amount to anything they won't disappoint their friends.

Upon completing their work, the two played a video game, drank several cans of Coke, and finished a leftover pizza that had been in the refrigerator for quite some time. When Seth questioned its age, Colton said it wasn't green, but it was old. They decided the microwave would kill any germs.

Seth left before dinner time and Colton stayed behind. He took the paper Doyle drew out with Jenny's photograph and the suspects marked along the side. Doyle had a big question mark next to both Luke and Jenny. *The question was, what's the motive for these killings?*

Colton sat and thought about the case. Somewhere there was an answer. *But where?*

Chapter 30

Saturday morning Colton only had coffee for breakfast. When he told the family he and Lacie were going to Bad Axe to shop for Christmas gifts, his brothers wanted to tag along.

"Mom, help me out here. It's a breakfast date and I would love to have my little brothers with me, but I'm sure Lacie wouldn't." Colton stumbled for an excuse.

"Boys, it's Saturday and you have chores to do. Let Colton go shopping and perhaps he'll buy you something nice for Christmas." She looked at Colton and winked. "Have fun."

Lacie was ready when he arrived. Colton told her how his mom told his brothers he would buy them a nice Christmas gift. "Now I have to get them something."

"Didn't you plan on buying them a gift?"

"Yes, I got them compound hunting bows for Christmas, but I gave them their presents a few days ago."

"Well, that's not your mother's fault. How would she know?"

"She saw me give them the archery bows." Colton said. "Oh, well… they are my brothers so I suppose I can find them something else, but it takes a lot of thought and my brain is tiring from all this stress."

The Jeep turned into the Big Boy parking lot. "Look at all the cars."

Lacie suggested they go to another restaurant, but Colton said there should be room for two more in Big Boys. "We might have to wait and I'm hungry."

As soon as they walked in, two groups left the restaurant. Colton and Lacie sat in a booth next to the breakfast buffet, which they couldn't resist so they both ordered the buffet.

While eating Colton kept shopping on his phone for gift ideas. Lacie had enough and said, "Colton, either the phone goes or I go, and since I'm not done eating, put the phone away."

Colton put the phone face down and apologized. The conversation turned to the great time they had Thanksgiving, and ideas for gifts.

The shopping started at Ace Hardware for a gift for his dad and mom, moved to the Jewelry store for Steph's gift, and then to Dunham's Sports. While in Dunham's, Colton picked out two gifts for Jason and Terry. He noticed Lacie looking at some shirts and workout tights and made a mental note to come back alone.

The last stop was Walmart. Because the parking lot was full, Colton parked away from the crowd. "Are you OK walking this far?" he asked

"It's fine, but be sure you lock the doors because we don't want our gifts stolen."

Colton locked the Jeep and together they walked into Walmart. The two spent an hour in the store and ended up buying nothing. Lacie was looking at quilts for her mom, but everything was in the wrong colors, and Colton didn't know what he wanted. He spent most of his time checking out the video games, cell phones, and computers. Together they looked through the book, music, and movie departments.

Colton laughed as they walked out the store, "At least we didn't have to wait in a long check-out line."

At first Colton didn't see his Jeep. His heart raced as he imagined it being stolen, then he relaxed upon seeing that a larger van was hiding the Jeep.

Lacie screamed when she saw the Jeep. Someone used spray paint and wrote: YOU WILL DIE, across driver's side. The other side repeated those words and added swear words.

Colton grabbed his phone and dialed the sheriff's office. Within fifteen minutes, Ned drove up to the Jeep and walked around it. His face was grim as he got on the police radio and talked to the Sheriff.

"Colton. How long were you in the store?"

Lacie answered, "We spent an hour in Walmart. It happened while we were shopping."

Ned had Colton drive the Jeep to the County Sheriff's Office to fill out paperwork. When he arrived at the police station, Ned approached the Jeep and said, "I talked to the body shop here in town and they will clean off the paint while we wait. If you let the paint dry, you might need a new paint job."

Lacie and Colton followed Ned into the station. Looking out the glass door of the office, Colton watched as his Jeep drove away. "I hope this works," he said, turning toward Ned. "Did the Walmart security camera catch anything?"

"Yes, I have it here." Ned turned the monitor so Colton could see. "Look! See the guy walking between the cars with the spray can? Does he look like anyone you know?"

The man was thin, wore blue jeans and a brown work coat. He also wore a stocking mask over his face. Colton watched the man in the video spray paint his Jeep.

"No. I don't know who it is, but he sure is mad at me, isn't he?"

Ned turned the video off and said, "I wonder if this has anything to do with Jenny and Luke's deaths. We had Jenny's father and his brother in here yesterday, and the sheriff questioned them. They both are about the same build as the guy in the video."

"Do you think one of them killed Luke?" Colton asked. He wanted this investigation to reach an end as soon as possible.

Sheriff McNabb walked in before Ned could answer. "Ned, is this the video from Walmart?"

"Yes, Sir."

"Let me look at it," McNabb said. He watched the video for a few minutes and turned to Colton. "Boy, you pissed off this guy, didn't you? Ned, doesn't he look like that skinny brother of the dead girls father? Shoot, he looks like the same guy, so let's see where he was today and check the other footage from Walmart. He got to the store in some kind of vehicle."

Ned stood and gathered his things. "It would be great if we captured a picture of his license plate."

The sheriff laughed. "Hell yes! That would be great. Better than ice cream on apple pie." He turned to Colton. "Well son, how you doing? Not much fun getting your Jeep all screwed with, is it?"

"No," Colton said. He wasn't sure what to say to the sheriff. "Do you think they will try to kill me?" He glanced through the window at Lacie. She was sitting alone, and in his mind the threat was real, and he feared for himself and Her.

The sheriff put his hand over Colton's shoulder and said, "Yes, they might try to kill you, but we won't let them… will we?"

"I hope not."

The sheriff walked around the office talking to a female officer about another case, so Colton walked out to be with Lacie and she trembled.

"Are you cold," Colton asked.

"No, but I am frightened."

***

Colton gave Lacie a hug and glanced outside as his Jeep stopped in front of the office.

"Lacie, my Jeep is back, and look… they got the paint off!" he shouted.

Together they walked outside. The repairman got out of the driver's seat and smiled. "You're one lucky bastard, Mr. Blackwell. Whoever did this used cheap Walmart spray paint and you must have just waxed your Jeep. The paint washed off with little trouble. We used paint remover, but we diluted it and didn't have to scrub too hard.

Sometimes when we scrub hard, the car's paint comes off too."

"It looks great. Will the insurance pay for this?"

The repairman handed Colton the bill. "Well, if they don't, you can send us the money. OK?"

"I will. Thank you," Colton said as he took the keys from the repairman. He returned to the police station to tell the Sheriff about the Jeep.

The officer at the front desk said, "He left a minute ago. I'll tell him you got the Jeep back. He asked me to remind you to stay away from trouble and while you do your route tonight, he'll have deputies watching out for you."

That offer comforted Colton a little, but he planned to call Seth later to see if he would go on the route with him. Perhaps they could take their baseball bats for protection.

Colton dropped Lacie off and spent the evening watching television. It was his mother's turn to select a movie, and they watched a Holiday Romance. Colton wouldn't admit it, but he enjoyed the movie.

Before going to bed his mom and dad asked him to be careful. "If you see Jenny's dad or uncle, don't confront them; just leave and call the police. You don't need more trouble," said his dad.

Colton promised them he wouldn't do anything stupid. "Besides, Seth will be with me."

Seth was eager to help with the route and he brought his bats with him. "What are the odds of us having to use these?" he asked.

When they arrived at the storage unit in Pigeon, the papers were already there. Within a few minutes the two were delivering newspapers as they discussed the murder case. Seth wanted to hear everything the Sheriff said, and Colton was eager to share.

Driving through the woods Colton kept feeling like he was being watched. "Do you feel that?" he asked Seth.

"Feel what?"

"It might be the police watching, but I swear someone is out there."

Seth laughed. "Your nerves are getting to you."

Colton pulled up to The Point Market. "This is where Luke died," he told Seth.

"OK. Why are we here?"

"I have to put papers in the newspaper rack."

Colton drove up to the rack and opened the back of the Jeep to pull out a bundle of newspapers. Seth walked around the rack. "Where was his body?"

"You're standing on the spot. The killer struck him from behind and Luke fell into the newspaper rack. There was blood all over."

Seth stepped back and looked around. There was nothing but woods. "Damn. That's creepy, let's get going," He said as he jumped into the Jeep.

Colton finished the rack and started the Jeep. Before they could drive away, the bright lights of a vehicle stopped in front.

"Shit!" yelled Seth. "Let's get the hell out of here."

Colton laughed. "Look at the top of the car. It's a police vehicle."

The car drove up and a young female deputy officer opened her window. She smiled and said, "You must be Colton. I see you have had no problems tonight."

"No problems, other than the scare you gave Seth, here."

"I wasn't scared," Seth yelled back at the officer. "Just startled by the lights."

"Sorry about that," she said. "How much longer do you have?"

"About an hour."

"OK. I'll be around in case you have any problems. Otherwise, have a nice day." The officer said.

After the police car drove away Seth said, "She's quite the looker for a police woman."

Colton stopped, placed a newspaper into a mailbox, and said, "That's sexist of you. What should a police woman look like?"

"It was just a stupid comment. I was joking."

"I know you were. You were also correct about her being *quite the looker*."

They laughed and continued the route. It was still dark when Seth's Charger left the Blackwell driveway and turned on the road. Colton went into the kitchen and then straight to his room. The family would be up in less than an hour and he was too tired to face them.

***

Colton lay in bed thinking about Luke and Jenny's murder. *If I talk to Jenny's dad and uncle, perhaps one of them will confess... Not a good idea.* He concluded.

He heard talking coming from downstairs and sensed someone was looking at him. Pulling the blanket down to peek at the door he saw Terry standing in the doorway watching.

"Terry, what are you doing?"

"I was waiting for you to wake up. Mom said not to wake you, but she didn't say I couldn't watch you. Can I come in?" he asked.

"Sure you can. I'm awake now."

Terry sat on the side of the bed and they talked about anything and everything. Before long Jason was at the door. "Mom said you guys should come down for brunch. What are you talking about?"

"We were talking about you, Jason."

"What? What did I do?"

Terry laughed and said, "Nothing, silly. Colton is just teasing. He got us more Christmas gifts yesterday."

"Where are they?" Jason looked for the gifts.

"Santa has them and he'll bring them when he brings your other gifts."

Jason smiled at Colton. "I can wait, but Mom can't. We better get downstairs or she'll be mad at me."

After brunch, Adam asked his sons if they would like to help put Christmas lights and decorations out in the yard.

"Last year we didn't have enough money to decorate, but now we can," he said.

Colton thought it was a great idea, but he wondered where the old lights were.

"I threw them away and bought new ones. I got new strings of LED lights, a blow up Santa with a reindeer, and a small nativity scene to go on the porch."

It surprised Cyndi to discover her husband bought decorations without speaking to her first. "How much did you spend on these decorations?" she asked.

"Less than three hundred, but they will last a lifetime. I got them on sale before Thanksgiving. Honey, I realize you missed the lights last year, so I wanted to surprise you."

Terry was the first to say. "Dad, you're the one who always wants the lights put up."

"Yes dear," added Cyndi. "Terry is right, but I'll enjoy them. So come on guys, get busy!"

It took all afternoon to complete the lights. Colton and Jason wrestled with the large blow-up Santa, but they got it to stay up. It was amazing how many lights they had to string around the pine trees and shrubs. Adam calculated down to the last light. He changed the flood lights to LED colored lights and Steph helped set Jesus into his manger.

After dinner the family had a grand lighting ceremony. Adam spoke first. "Before we turn the lights on, I want to thank my family for understanding my desire for decorations."

"We already know the story, Dad. You grew up without lights in a log cabin in the woods and had to walk ten miles in the snow to school," Colton laughed at his words.

His mom also laughed. "Colton, that's my story."

"Enough talk already," said Jason. "Turn the lights on so we can go back in the house where it's warm."

With that, Adam plugged the cord in and the yard glowed with white and blue lights. Santa was waving his arm and Jesus was basking in the light of the eastern star.

"Wow! Dad, everything is so awesome," said Terry.

Everyone agreed and then suggested they warm up in the house. Cyndi said she put hot chocolate and cookies on the table and it was a mad dash toward the kitchen.

Chapter 31

Monday morning the Blackwell house filled with the sounds of children getting ready for school. After the Thanksgiving break they hated the thought of school, but when Cyndi said it would soon be Christmas, the complaining stopped.

Colton wasn't as lucky. He wanted to go to school but faced another week of sitting around the house. As he watched his siblings load their backpacks, he sipped his coffee and sulked like a lost puppy.

His mom noticed his condition and scolded, "Are you going to be like this all day?"

"I don't know. Perhaps."

"If you are, you can stay in the garage. For heaven's sake, what will you do when you're out of school. Most normal teenagers relish the thought of not having to go to school."

Jason piped up and said, "Mom, Colton's not normal."

Colton gave his brother a stern look. "Watch it, Jason. We haven't gone hunting yet."

Before Jason could return the barb, the bus pulled up to the end of the driveway. "Bye mom. Have fun, Colton. See you when we get home."

"Bye," Colton whispered as he grabbed his coat and told his mom he would take her advice and go to the garage office.

During the day Colton kept in touch with Lacie. Every hour he called her or sent a message. At noon she sent him a message, "Please stop calling. I'm getting in trouble with the teachers."

Colton understood her message and decided to just concentrate on his business or perhaps a video game or two. Once he stopped thinking about his problems, time flew by quicker. Before he knew it, the bus was stopping and his siblings were running into the house.

Jason came out to the garage to talk about Monday's hunting trip. They discussed where they will hunt, what they will wear, and how early they will be in the woods. Both are excited about their first hunt together. They walked across the driveway to the house where Cyndi was busy in the kitchen and Stephenie was sitting at the table doing her homework while watching her mother cook.

Colton sat down next to her and asked, "How is school going?"

"Good, but Caroline looked like someone hit her at home. She had big bruises on her arms. She tried to hide them and told me she fell, but I remember how you looked when that guy beat you up in the garage."

"Did you tell anyone?"

"Who would I tell?" Steph asked.

"The teacher or Mrs. Robbett, the principal," Colton suggested.

"No, I didn't tell because Caroline asked me not to. She asked what you were doing, and I told her about you and Jason going hunting on Monday morning. She doesn't think you should kill deer, either."

"Steph, try not to tell her anything about me. I can't say why, but I don't want her family to know what I'm up to. Understood?"

"OK. Can you help me with these math questions. I want to get done so I can play."

After dinner Colton went to his room early to talk to Seth, Jerry, and Lacie. When he told Lacie what Stephenie said about Caroline, she said, "You need to tell someone. Caroline's in danger of ending up like her sister."

"I'm already on the family hit list, Lacie. If they found out, I turned them in for abusing her, there's no telling what would happen."

"Now you worry about yourself?"

"OK. When I hang up, I'll call Mrs. Robbett. I think I have her phone number." He checked his phone, and it was there. "Yes I have it so I'll call you back after I talk to her."

Mrs. Robbett didn't expect to hear from her favorite student. When Colton explained what his sister saw, she became silent, speaking only to ask questions.

"Colton, we know that Caroline has been suffering from grief, but I never considered abuse. As you said, if someone abused her sister, it is possible she is in danger too. Tell your sister not to mention this, and we will look into it and get help for Caroline if she needs it."

"Thank you Mrs. Robbett. Having seen what happened to Jenny, I couldn't live with myself if I did nothing about Caroline."

"You did what is right, and I'm glad you called. Thank you."

Colton called Lacie back and explained what Mrs. Robbett told him.

"I'm proud of you, Colton, but go to bed because that route of yours is coming up soon and I still have homework to do. I'll talk to you tomorrow."

***

Tuesday's route was a breeze. A freezing breeze with over three inches of snow. No one tried to hurt his jeep, including the deer, but he noticed plenty of police cars following him.

When he finished with the route, Colton stopped at Main Street Cafe in Pigeon because he saw Deputy Ned's patrol car out front. Ned liked his donuts and often visited the restaurant.

Colton sat at Ned's table and the two talked at length. Ned was not eager to share the information he had regarding the Stillmore brothers, but Colton coaxed enough to learn what was happening.

"The sheriff has been trying to talk to the Jenny's uncle, Ronald Stillmore, but he keeps himself in Detroit and only comes up here on the weekends. We think he's trying to avoid us," reported Ned.

Colton told Ned about Caroline and Ned said he would keep his eyes open. "Kids are sacred. They should never be treated like that.

God, I hope she's not being abused."

"So do I," agreed Colton. "I'll be glad when this is over, because Jason and I are going hunting on Monday and it would be nice if we didn't have to worry."

"Well, if you let us know where you are, we'll try to cover your butts," joked Ned.

"Last question, Ned, does the sheriff suspect anyone else in Luke's murder?"

Ned didn't speak for a moment. "No... it's a dead end. He is out there, but we're unsure who he is. Could be one of the Stillmore brothers, or someone we never heard of, so we're at a loss... for now."

Ned paid for Colton's breakfast. As they left Main Street Cafe, Colton noticed a vehicle he saw earlier on his route; it was a newer white van, and he made a mental note of the license and asked Ned it he could run it to see who it belonged to.

"I can't run a license plate without a good reason," said Ned.

"How about because I believe he's the guy who painted my van and killed Luke?"

Ned wrote the plate number in his notebook and said he would try to get approval from the sheriff. "I'll call you if I learn anything, but I wouldn't expect much."

***

The rest of Colton's day dragged on. Seth and Lacie told him their teachers are threatening to take their phones away if he called them. He could only send messages and then wait until they replied.

The only enjoyment he had was when his brothers rushed into the garage office and wanted to know if he would help them practice shooting the styrofoam deer. Colton grabbed his bow and spent two hours in the backyard. Colton got the highest score, Jason was a close second and Terry was far behind.

"I quit. Why can't I shoot like you, Colton?" Terry asked.

"Terry, you're good for your age. When you get to be my age, you'll be better than I am. Just keep shooting, and, trust me, you will get better," Colton promised.

Jason added, "When I was Terry's age, I couldn't shoot as well as he does, but I kept trying."

The back door opened and their mom called them in for dinner. They put their equipment away and ran for the house. Terry promised Colton he would keep trying.

After dinner Colton spent an hour talking to Lacie on the phone. She suggested he get away from his route, business, and the murder case. "Tomorrow you'll sit around again with nothing to do. If I were you I'd find something interesting to keep myself busy."

After a restless night Colton woke ready for action. There was no action. Nothing planned, nothing to do but sit in the office all day. *This is getting old*, he thought.

He watched his siblings get ready for school and sat at the kitchen table until his mom kicked him out of the house. Around nine o'clock Jim Owen drove up to the office to pick up security equipment and supplies. He had three installations planned for the day.

"Jim, would it bother you to have me with you? You could show me what you do and I might help."

"I take it you're bored?" Jim asked.

"Yes! What do you say?"

"If you want to tag along, it's OK with me. I'll even let you buy me lunch."

Jim didn't let Colton spend the day watching him. Instead he made him do the bulk of the work. Together they got all the installations done, and they did a layout for a job at one factory in Bad Axe.

When they got back to the office, it was past dinner time.

Jim congratulated his boss. "I didn't expect you to be as helpful as you were, Colton. In fact you impressed me."

"Not half as impressed as I was of your work. I'm so glad Seth hired you to help us. I enjoyed learning the job today, and I had fun."

Jim asked if Colton wanted to help Thursday and Colton declined. "I have my route to do, but if I get bored later, I'll let you know."

Colton's mom offered to heat the leftovers for his dinner, but he decided to drive into Caseville for a cheeseburger at Lefty's Diner. He called Lacie and then Seth, hoping one of them would be his guest. Neither could get away so he drove to Caseville alone.

He drove into the parking lot and stopped. While walking into the diner, he noticed the white van driving past. The driver was wearing a hooded sweatshirt so he couldn't see who it was. A strange feeling of dread creeped up on him.

After ordering, he called Ned and asked if they found out who the van belonged to.

"Colton, it's Ronald Stillmore's van. I need to talk to you. Are you at home?"

"No, I'm in Lefty's Diner having eating dinner," Colton replied.

"Don't leave. I'm a mile away and I'll meet you there."

Colton's meal arrived at the same moment Ned walked through the doors. Ned sat down and ordered coffee. "Yesterday you mentioned Jenny's sister, Caroline. I wanted you to know the school, social services, and the sheriff questioned her and her father."

Colton grew excited by the news. "What did they find out?"

"Caroline told them her Uncle *was messing with her*. He hit her two times and forced her to do *a nasty thing*. Her father got upset and said Ronald might have been doing the same to Jenny."

Colton took a bite of his burger and thought for a moment before asking, "Why don't the police arrest Ronald?"

"Give us time. We haven't been able to find him because he's living in that white van and hiding it at night. We'll catch him, but I wanted to let you know he's out there and he might be after you. He knows you got help for Caroline so you need to be careful."

"Ned, I have my route to do tonight, Friday night, and Sunday. I can't miss it so I'll take my chances," Colton said.

"Can Seth go with you?"

"Not tonight, he's in Bay City. Tomorrow he might help, but I know he'll help me Sunday."

"I'll make sure there are plenty of patrol cars watching you. Just be careful."

Colton didn't tell his parents about Ronald and the danger he was facing. Instead he went to bed early to get as much rest as possible.

***

In his dreams Colton saw dark figures walking in the snow-covered woods. There were white vans passing him as he walked between the trees. Ghostly images of a young woman dressed in red and her lover moved in and out of the fog. A scary clown with blood dripping from his hands stood motionless next to a tree.

He woke tired and bewildered. *Is Ronald going to strike this morning?* He asked himself.

The temperature was in the teens when he started the Jeep. Driving to Pigeon he saw no other vehicles on the road. His papers were ready for him and the other drivers were already on their routes. After loading his newspapers he decided not to listen to an audiobook. *I don't want distractions. If Ronald strikes, I'll need all my wits to escape,* he thought.

Ronald didn't strike. It was a boring three hours of deliveries and Colton was cold and tired. Upon delivering his last paper, he headed home to rest. There would be no school for him again today, so he planned to sleep in late.

Cyndi woke her son at nine a.m. and asked if he wanted to help Jim Owens again. "He's outside and would like your help," she said.

"Tell him I'll be there in a few minutes." As he walked into the bathroom he called out, "Mom, put a bagel in the toaster for me. I'm taking a quick shower."

Colton was glad Jim asked for help. Together they spent the entire day, working and talking. Even though it was hard work, he felt relaxed. Colton enjoyed Jim's company, and he was learning about his business, from the bottom up.

After dinner he talked to Lacie and decided not to mention Ronald. Instead they talked about what was happening in school and at the hospital.

"You sound tired," Lacie said.

"I am. I worked all day with Jim Owens and I think he had me do all the physical jobs because I worked my butt off."

"You need to exercise more. Without sports, you'll get out of shape and I'll have to start looking for a new boyfriend." Lacie laughed.

"Don't do that, I promise I'll stay in shape."

"Colton, you're perfect. Even if you were out of shape, you would be perfect. Of course you're more perfect as you are right now."

Colton laughed. He realized he needed exercise to stay in shape, now that football season is over, but Lacie's comment hit home, even if she was joking.

Lacie asked what he planned to do Friday and Saturday, and Colton said he wasn't sure. "I plan on working with Jim on Friday, and Seth is going with his parents Saturday, and you'll be gone, so I guess it's just me and the family."

"That sounds like fun. I have to get going, I love you Colton," Lacie said.

"I love you too, Lacie. Please drive carefully tomorrow and tell your mom I said HI."

When Colton's alarm clock rang he was already up and ready for his Friday deliveries. The weather forecast was for freezing rain and he knew it might be a late delivery.

The papers were already at the storage shed and the other drivers were loaded and gone. *So much for being early*, Colton thought. He did the route without any problems. The police were watching him and it gave him a degree of comfort. There was no sign of Ronald, and Deputy Ned said his van had not been seen in the area.

Colton was home before Jim arrived, so he had breakfast with his mom and waited. Jim was please to have a helper for another day. He commented that if Colton keeps helping, the company will have a record number of security installations.

It was hard work and Colton was tired and achy at the end of the day, but he felt great. Jim was a good teacher and friend. By working with him, Colton gained knowledge and skills needed to succeed in his business. Most of all, he was proud of his work.

He talked to both Lacie and Seth before going to bed early. He was exhausted and his sleep was deep, without dreams.

Terry woke him at eight, Saturday morning. He wanted to know if they could practice archery after he finished his morning chores. With nothing planned for the day, Colton offered to help his brothers and sister do their Saturday morning chores, but he mostly worked in the yard and garden.

There was a roar of celebration when Cyndi announced that all of the chores were done. Terry and Jason ran out to the yard and wanted to practice archery. Colton was eager to have some fun, so for the next five hours they shot the poor Styrofoam deer full of arrows.

After lunch the family watched a movie selected by Stephanie, and then a movie selected by Terry and Jason. By bedtime, everyone was exhausted, including Colton. He went to his room and called Lacie. She was driving back from Bay City with her mom and told him to be careful on the route.

"I will. I wish we had time to do something together this weekend."

"So do I, but Mom needs my help and I can't say no," Lacie whispered softly, so her mom wouldn't hear her comment.

"I understand. I'll call tomorrow after the route. Seth is going with me, so the route will be less boring." Colton said.

After saying goodbye to Lacie, Colton called Seth and confirmed that he will be ready. Seth assured Colton he would drive with him,

Colton told Seth that there was a good chance they might have a run-in with Ronald, and Seth asked, "If Ronald wants to do something, what is he waiting for?".

"I don't know," replied Colton. "It's hard to get in the mind of a crazed maniac, child molesting killer."

"OK! I see where you're coming from. I'll be there at three o'clock, but should I bring anything, besides my coffee and baseball bats?" Seth asked.

"Do you still have any Halloween candy left?"

"Yes, I'll bring it," laughed Seth

Colton spent the reminder of Saturday night listening to another audiobook.

Chapter 32

Seth knocked on the door instead of ringing the doorbell. He didn't want to wake the entire Blackwell family, but Colton was not waiting for him outside. When the door opened, it wasn't Colton who greeted him; it was Colton's dad. In the background Seth heard Colton's voice saying, "I'll be there in a minute, Dad. Tell Seth to start the Jeep. The keys are on the rack by the door."

Adam handed Seth the keys and asked, "Did you hear what he said?"

"Yes, and have a nice morning, Mr. Blackwell."

"I hope to, once you two are out of here," Adam said.

Colton apologized for being late. "I guess I did more than I thought yesterday. I slept right through my alarm."

The two teens jumped in the Jeep and started down the road toward Pigeon. The large delivery truck was unloading the papers into the storage shed, so Colton drove behind the truck and together he and Seth loaded newspapers into the back of the Jeep.

Colton checked the list of starts and stops and sped toward the start of his route.

Seth asked Colton how he liked working with Jim Owens, and Colton replied, "He's a great guy. It surprised me how fast he can install a security system. In fact, I learned a lot from him. You taught him well, Seth."

As the two delivered papers they discussed Ronald Stillmore. Seth kept looking into the shadows, wondering when he would jump out with a gun. "Do you think he wants to kill you?"

Death On The Point - BLOOD BATH

"I don't know. I think the guy is crazy. Anyone who would spray paint my Jeep is not normal, and if he killed Jenny and Luke... well I hope he hangs."

"They don't hang killers; they give them life in prison," remarked Seth.

"Hanging would be too good for him, anyway."

Seth laughed at Colton's remark. "You hate this creep, don't you?"

"Yes, I do. He has made my life hell. I can't do anything without worrying he'll pop his head up like a crazed clown."

"Oh, funny... like Ronald the clown?" Seth asked.

"Something like that," agreed Colton.

They were just about finished with The Point deliveries when Colton noticed a vehicle parked on the side of the road with only its interior lights on. "I wonder if that's the police," he said.

As the Jeep approached the vehicle, its headlights came on. Colton could see it was a pickup truck or a van. The vehicle's lights were on high as it drove toward him.

"What should I do?" Colton asked.

There wasn't time for Seth to answer. The van stopped alongside the Jeep. It was Ronald Stillmore; his window was down, and he laughed at Colton.

"Hey. I see you and your buddy have the cops watching you. They can't help. I can kill you whenever I want."

"You don't want to do that," said Colton.

"Yes I do!" Ronald said as he pulled his hand out from under his coat and pointed something at Colton.

"BANG" he yelled, pointing his finger.

"YOUR DEAD!"

Both Colton and Seth ducked... Ronald laughed... a maniacal laughed. Colton thought it sounded like the Joker in a Batman movie. Seth later said it was the devil himself.

Ronald drove off and one of the county patrol cars chased him.

Colton could see the van driving into the woods with the Deputy on its tail.

Let's get out of here while we can, Colton insisted. They finished their last few deliveries on The Point and headed for Caseville. Feeling nervous, Colton and Seth completed the route, saying almost nothing as they both considered how close they had come to death.

They went into the Blackwell home to have breakfast. Cyndi made eggs, bacon and toast for them and listened to their tale. As they talked, Colton could see his mom cringing.

"Mom, they will catch this creep, and then it will all be over," he said.

Colton's dad hugged his wife. "He's fine, honey. Everything will be OK."

"I know I worry, but that's what mothers do. And damn it Colton, you would worry anyone. I pray they catch this Ronald soon."

Seth assured Mrs. Blackwell that the police were there and if something bad happened, they would have covered them. "It's not Colton's fault that this creep is after him. It's impossible to say what crazy ideas fill Ronald's head. The man is *nuts*! Totally out of his head, *nuts*!"

Seth's comments didn't ease Cyndi's fears.

***

Colton and Seth went to the office to talk. Colton saw his brother heading to the office and Colton asked Seth not to tell his brothers about Ronald or what happened during the route.

"We're going hunting in the morning and I want it to be fun. I don't want to have Jason worrying about some clown jumping out of the woods with a gun."

After Seth headed home, Jason helped Colton put hunting gear in the Jeep, to prepare for an early morning hunt.

"Don't we need a license?" Jason asked.

Colton pulled two hunting permits out of his pocket, and he

handed Jason his permit and showed him how to pin it on his hunting jacket.

"We have to dress warm, so wear an extra sweatshirt under your jacket. Once we get into the woods, we can find a good spot and wait. I hope we see a deer, but there are no guarantees."

Jason said it would be OK even if they see no deer. "Being able to hunt with you will be fun enough," he told his big brother.

Cyndi had a feast set with dinner featuring roast chicken with potatoes and carrots, squash, green beans, and apple pie with ice cream for dessert.

Cyndi mentioned that Colton should find an activity to help him keep in shape, and he told the family he's considering trying out for the baseball team in the spring.

Adam laughed and said, "Now you're talking about a real sport."

"Colton told us you were a great baseball player, Dad." Jason was proud of his dad and wanted to tell him "I wish I could play like you did."

"You can; it takes a love for the game and a lot of practice," his dad replied.

***

Monday morning Jason was knocking on Colton's bedroom door. In a whisper he called, "Colton, you're late. We have to go now!"

Colton looked at his alarm clock and there was fifteen minutes left before it would ring. Jason was eager!

"Go downstairs and make yourself a bowl of cereal. I'll be down in a minute," he said as he rolled out of bed. "Jason, did you shower with the scent-free soap I put on the shower shelf?"

"Yes, and I don't stink anymore."

"Good! I'll shower and meet you in the kitchen."

Colton knows how important it is to avoid giving off a human scent when bow hunting. If deer smell the hunter, they will run. With a gun you can shoot the deer from further away than you can with a bow.

Jason finished his breakfast and was sitting when Colton walked into the kitchen. "Are we ready to go?" he asked his older brother.

"Settle down; I want to eat too and it won't be light for another two hours. We have lots of time to get to the woods and find our spot," Colton advised.

It didn't take Colton long to finish his cereal. While the two sat, he checked his phone and asked Jason to grab something to take with them to eat later. "Grab two energy bars for each of us. Do you want to take a mug of coffee?"

"Yuck... No... Can you make me some hot chocolate?"

"Good idea so I'll get two insulated mugs down from the cupboard." Colton made his coffee and poured hot water into one mug for his brother. Soon they had lunch ready.

"OK. Time to go hunting for that big buck. Are you ready?"

Jason jumped up and down, "Yes... Yes! Let's go!"

Together they walked to the Jeep. Colton cleaned the snow that had accumulated on the windshield, jumped behind the wheel, and said, "There, we're ready. Buckle up and think positive. We will get a deer today."

It took less than ten minutes to reach the hundred acre wooded plot where they would be hunting. It was along M-25 and was private. Today there will be a few hunters, but the owner limits who can hunt on his land.

Colton parked next to two pickup trucks. He helped Jason with his bow and arrows and checked his coat. "You look like a professional hunter. We will bring our drinks and some energy bars with us. I found a spot last week where we can sit together and hunt. It faces a nice opening. The landowner planted food for the deer during the summer and the deer might come back looking for more."

Colton and Jason walked along the path. The woods were dense in some areas with a mix of different tree types. When they reached the clearing, Jason exclaimed, "I bet this is the spot, isn't it?"

Colton chuckled and agreed that it was a good spot. They walked over to some small pine trees and settled in for the morning. Jason sat down on a small plastic tarp he had in his pocket and they adjusted their bows and arrows. "You keep an eye on that side of the opening and I'll watch this side," Colton instructed.

The sun was rising to the east, and in the wooded plot, a pink light glistened from behind the branches and the moon worked its way down the western horizon. It would take another hour before the sky would brighten. Colton told Jason the deer will move around soon.

Jason became excited and pointed to his side of the clearing where two small doe stood at the edge of the woods. Colton put his finger to his mouth to stay silent, and then he whispered, "We'll wait for a nice buck."

A frown formed on Jason's face but he understood. The brothers didn't have a doe permit. "Look for the antlers. They can be button horns or full racks. When you don't see antlers, we don't shoot. I know you're eager, Jason, but you said it was being here that was important."

Jason smiled, "It is, and I'm having fun."

There were no other deer walking across the clearing so Jason asked if he could get something more to eat. The energy bars were gone, and the sun was at high noon. Colton suggested they walk back to the Jeep together. "We should drive over to Lefty's Diner for lunch. Does that sound good to you?"

"It sure does. I'm getting cold too."

They gathered their gear and walked back toward the entrance, and when they reached the Jeep, Colton opened the back of the door to put his bow away.

Someone yelled from across the road. "Hey! I'm back, Colton, so are you ready to die?"

When Colton turned to look. he saw Ronald with his crossbow pointed at him and he reached for his phone. The phone dropped into the snow and Colton bent down to retrieve it. He heard the arrow and felt a flash of pain in his back. The arrow entered his left butt cheek and passed into the right cheek. The pain was overwhelming, and he dropped to his knees.

"You will die!" Colton heard Ronald's maniacal laugh and Jason's panicked scream. He turned to Jason to tell him to run, but Jason had his bow set and he shot toward Ronald. The shot hit Ronald in the groin and pinned him against the large oak tree he was standing in front of. A spot of blood was forming on the crotch of his jeans, and Jason shot again, this time hitting under his right armpit. Another arrow hit under the left armpit and a third arrow nailed his boot to the base of the tree. Ronald was screaming and couldn't move.

Colton shouted into his phone, "Ned, we're south of The Point on M-25... Ronald is here and I need an ambulance."

Colton heard the police siren before he passed out. Jason was holding his brother in his arms, tears running down his face. "I'm sorry Colton, I'm sorry," He cried.

Deputy Ned and his partner, Deputy Mike Hoard, ran up to Colton. When Ned saw Ronald pinned to the tree he laughed. "Jason is that Colton's handy work?" He pointed to Ronald.

Colton regained consciousness in time to hear Jason say, "I wanted to hit him. I tried real hard, but I kept missing."

Colton looked at Ronald pinned onto the tree and smiled. "Jason, you were great, and you don't have to tell anyone you missed, because you didn't... you didn't miss."

Ned called out, "Mike, keep Ronald Stillmore covered because he'll try to run if he gets loose."

As Ned checked Colton's wounds he saw that there was not a lot of bleeding. "Colton, we can't take the arrow out, because if we do it'll bleed more. When the paramedics get here..." Before he could finish, the ambulance pulled up next to Colton's Jeep.

Ned talked to the driver and the other two paramedics pulled the stretcher from the back of the vehicle, and the driver stepped out and asked Ned if he had a cutter.

Colton, in a shallow voice said. "In my hunting bag. There's a cutter I used to snip arrows."

Ned reached in the bag and pulled out the wire cutter. "That's what we need." The paramedic gave Colton a shot for the pain and said, "Colton, this is going to hurt, but we need to cut the arrow's ends off and then get you on the stretcher."

Holding the arrow the paramedic squeezed the cutters and snipped off one end. Colton's blood curdling scream made everyone jump. The paramedic, Bill Carson, smiled and asked, "Did that hurt?"

The second snip of the arrow didn't hurt as bad because the medication was working. As they moved Colton onto the stretcher another pickup truck screeched to a stop, and Joseph Stillmore, Jenny's father, jumped out. He took one look at his brother and then turned to Colton. "Did my brother do this to you?" he asked.

"Yes," replied Deputy Ned.

Joseph waked across the street and stood in front of Ronald. "You stupid ass, what the hell kind of man are you?"

Mike and a state trooper had freed Ronald and cuffed his hands behind his back. As they escorted him to the police car Joseph followed. Ronald turned his head to look back and yelled to his brother, "Joe, you know I will tell them how you killed your wife because that way you and I can hang together... side-by-side. That's the kind of man I am, you bastard."

Ronald laughed, that maniacal laugh. Deputy Ned told Joseph to meet them in Bad Axe. "I believe there's more to come, because I heard about your wife's death and the lack of evidence and no eyewitness. It looks like your brother will turn your life into hell, too."

✳✳✳

After an hour in the emergency room, they moved Colton to a hospital room. Late Monday afternoon he laid in bed talking to his mom and dad. Both of his parents were grateful the injuries were not worse.

"The doctor said you were lucky," his mom said.

"Is Jason OK?" Colton asked because he feared Jason would become traumatized by what happened.

"Are you kidding? He's proud that he saved his big brother," Cyndi said. "Ned told us what happened and how Jason kept shooting arrows. Any idea how he could do that without hurting Ronald?"

"I think he was being guided by someone upstairs, Mom. I'm glad he didn't kill him, because that would be hard to live with, and now he has bragging rights without the guilt."

Lacie's mom, Mrs. Wooddell, RN, came into the room. "Colton, there is a line of people who want to visit. Should I send them away, or do you feel up to seeing them?"

Colton didn't know what to say. In his mind the answer depended on who wanted to visit, so he asked, "Who's here?"

"Your friends and classmates. They heard about your injury and they want to help. You know son, there are many people who care about you," She said.

Colton's mom and dad gave him a hug and said they would be back in the morning. You can visit with your friends since we need to pick up the kids," advised his dad. "Honey, how about dinner at Main Street Cafe?"

"That would be nice. We love you Colton, and we'll see you tomorrow."

Colton's nurse allowed only four visitors at a time, and it was a parade of students, teachers, neighbors and the police.

Seth and Beth were glad their friend was doing well. Beth asked Colton if he visited with Lacie yet, and Colton said he didn't know where she was. He had hoped she would be the first to visit but she might be out doing something more important.

Beth assure him that Lacie would show up and visit soon.

Aden thought it was funny that Colton got shot with an arrow in his butt cheeks, and he kept making jokes.

"You know, Colton," Aden said, "you will be the butt of a lot of jokes."

"Hilarious, Aden. I'm sure I will hear a lot of butt jokes. I'm glad it's not a more serious injury."

"I hear your brother shot the killer in the nuts? That must have hurt like hell." said the Loon's tackle, Bill Crawley.

"Not exactly in the nuts. The arrow hit his scrotum, but it hit nothing of value," laughed Colton. "It amazed me that only one arrow hit Ronald. And that was a flesh wound. Yet my little brother still stopped the bastard."

Coach Talbert talked about how proud he was that Colton didn't look the other way when Jenny and her sister needed help. And Mr. Zeller told him he is looking forward to his return to school. "I'm proud of you, Colton."

There was only one visitor left. Lacie stood outside the door, waiting for her mom to let her talk to Colton, but she had to give Colton his medication and check his wound, first. Lacie watched the tender care her mom was giving.

"Colton, I'm sorry but visiting hours are over," she announced.

"But, I didn't have time to talk to Lacie," Colton protested.

"Oh? In that case, Lacie, you can visit as long as you like."

Lacie walked into the room and sat in the chair next to Colton's bed. She reached her hand out and took his. "Hi. Are you feeling well enough to talk?" she asked.

"I've talked all afternoon and they've given me pain killers, so it doesn't hurt much." He shifted his weight on the bed and grimaced. "Perhaps I spoke too soon."

"I can see it hurts. Did the doctor say there would be permanent damage back there?"

"No, everything will work just fine, but I need to tell you something."

"First, I want to say something to you," Lacie insisted.

Lacie stood and stepped closer to Colton's bed. "Is there room for me to sit on the edge?" she asked.

Colton moved to the side and Lacie sat, holding his hands. "Colton, I've decided that since you are apt to keep getting injured like this, I cannot become a nurse."

"What? I thought nursing was your dream job?"

"It was, but now I realize you will need a doctor to look after you."

Colton laughed, "You want to become a doctor? Wonderful. You will be the best doctor in the area."

Lacie stretched out and laid on her side while she faced Colton. "Now it's your turn."

"I have been considering my future too, and even though I love my newspaper route, I've decided I like being in business and being with you more. Monday I'm giving Metro Newspaper my notice so now I'll be yours full time!"

Lacie smiled. "Does this mean you'll be giving up your detective work, too?"

"Hey, one step at a time."

She put her arm around his neck. "I love you so much, Colton."

"I love you too, Lacie."

If you liked this book, you will love Duane's other novels.

In Search Of Elysium
A touching sci-fi adventure for all ages!
Kevin Carpenter is learning disabled. In a touching adventure he leads his friends on a search for God, taking them deep into space, in search of a planet called Elysium.

Death on the Point
No. 1 - The Blackwell Series
Colton Blackwell, a football star and teenage detective, stars in this fast moving mystery series; a humorous and romantic novel filled with action and adventure

Blood Bath
No. 2 - The Blackwell Series
Colton Blackwell is faced with another murder.
The humor, romance, and adventure continues.

Deadly Sixteen
No. 1 - The Spirit Walker Series
This reincarnation story takes you through the history of Detroit, Michigan, investigating a 300 year murder mystery.

Doyle Mysteries
No. 1 - The Scent Of Murder
New series. Check Website For Details.
Doyle, a retired police detective and master chef, and his Bloodhound (Copper) face a life filled with luxury and murder.
A cozy mystery for all ages.

www.duanewurst.com ~ duane0w@gmail.com

Share your opinion and do a review on Amazon.com

Made in the USA
Columbia, SC
22 August 2018